Tony Burnett's novel, *Watermelon Tattoo*, is one wild ride. This Texas hill country bildungsroman features Jacqui Benderman, a feral, beautiful, and musically talented eighteen-year-old on her journey from daddy Sarge's watermelon farm to international stardom. journey from daddy Sarge's watermelon farm to international stardom. Fast-paced, lusty, and chocked full of wry and insightful commentary on self-discovery, the music industry, and religion, this is one great read by a seasoned author."
—Gary V. Powell, author of *Lucky Bastard, Beyond Redemption,* and *Super Blood Wolf Moon*

Jaqui's a tough heroine, tougher than the meth-fueled menace, gritty music business, corruption, and betrayal that close in on her. Hair-raising, unafraid, and ever-unpredictable, Tony Burnett's Watermelon Tattoo is part psycho thriller, part love story, told with the heart-stopping speed of a runaway train..
—Lesley Bannatyne, author of Unaccustomed to Grace, Runner-up for the Acacia Fiction Prize

In his debut novel *Watermelon Tattoo,* Tony Burnett serves up the fecundity of Texas in temperatures hovering *just above triple digits.* **P**art high octane thriller, part love story, the reader moves fluidly between rural earthiness and Austin's scintillating music scene. We follow Burnett's protagonist Jaqui, a gorgeous 18-year-old with an Ella Fitzgerald voice from a tractor seat to the open mic stage and beyond. Her meth-fueled antagonist is never far behind. The author has an eye for detail, an ear for dialogue, but what's so extraordinary is the novel's ease at blending pacing, plotting, and supple syntax. *Spinning cones of dust briefly appeared and disintegrated. This season had ended, for melons, for rain, for redemption.* Burnett's characters

all seem set on a kind of liberation, a release from or a rescue of the self. His body-on-body scenes—and be forewarned Burnett writes of coupling in myriad forms—are breathtaking, some down and dirty, others beautifully transcendent. A thriller that Don Winslow would not be ashamed to claim, the pages turn by themselves.

—Stephanie Dickinson, author of Razor Wire Wilderness

Watermelon Tattoo

ISBN:979-8-985598-21-6

This is a work of Fiction. Although landmarks and locations are valid, any similarities to events or individuals are coincidental and have been created from the author's imagination.

Watertower Press
709 Stoneleigh Road
Baltimore, MD 21212

Watermelon Tattoo

Tony Burnett

Acknowledgments

So many folks say writing is a solitary occupation and I suppose when you speak of putting words on the page there's a certain truth in that. The creation of a novel, however, would not be possible without a crew of talented and tenacious folk supporting, encouraging, and yes, at times taunting you. Although the cover bears my name, it would have been impossible for this story to reach fruition without these generous souls. My thanks to the editors - in - chief of the dozens of literary magazines and journals who accepted my stories for publication. The ones who said sweet things about my efforts and especially those who said, "You know, I would love to print this if only you'd ..." I'd like to thank Marc Hess, Rodney Sprott, Beth Ann Sample, Gina Shirley-Springer and the other board members of the Writers' League of Texas, especially Becka Oliver who clued me in as to how this all works. Thanks to Russell Ashworth, Gogi Hale, Mary Day Long, Joseph Borden, Tate Lewis-Carroll, Andrea Barbosa, and the editorial staff Matt, Robin, Libby, William, Korey, Ramona, Greta, and Carson, who I consider friends at Kallisto Gaia Press. A very special thanks to Charlotte Gullick who read an early version of this manuscript and told me I had something worthwhile if I'd only .... A load of respect to my daughter, Jerica Glover, who after reading an early draft, said "Eeww, Dad, NO, this is NOT Young Adult!". She's now in acquisitions for the local city library and she was unquestionably correct. A huge **Thank You** to Chris Kosmides of Water Tower Press who found this in a rather hefty slush pile and literally saved it from extinction. This book would never have happened without the unwavering support of my lovely trophy bride, Robin E. Burnett, who has never, ever, not even once, failed to support me in any artistic endeavor I attempted. She was there for the entire eleven years it took for this novel to grow from seed and another 19 years prior when I envisioned being the world's most mature debut rock star. "Everything I Have Is Yours".

Playlist

for **ROBIN**

Tattoos & Scars

- Carter Falco

The acrid scent of asphalt and auto exhaust intensified as the stagnant air approached 100°. Jaqui didn't mind. Being new to city life she had no frame of reference. The excitement of being completely independent put a keen edge to her quest, an edge that was dulled somewhat by its apparent futility. The crazies were beginning to get aggressive as the 5 o'clock rush hour approached. The little coupe's air conditioner failed to keep up with the extreme heat, not having been designed to cool both the passenger compartment and the cargo area, since the back seat no longer isolated the resonating trunk space. At least she didn't have to smell the iron bite of all that blood.

She pulled into the only empty spot in the parking lot, cutting off a tall dreadlocked blonde guy in a Mazda several years newer than hers. She'd learned to accept the competition in Austin traffic. In front of her was the third "parlor" she'd visited, in addition to five "studios", two "shops" and an "express" that turned out to be a front for God knows what. No artists were in residence there. As she extricated her long body from the little car, she gave the dreadlocked boy her sweetest Friday Night cheerleader smile.

Peering in the frosted glass of the blue wooden door, her hand on the knob, she hesitated, instinctively polishing the silver inlaid toes of her dogging boots on the calves of her Levi's. She exhaled and entered Sly Dog Tattoo Parlor where an eccentric array of characters were draped over various pieces of odd shaped furniture.

"I want a Black Diamond as close to actual size as will fit on my ass," she stated. Conversation stopped. She had that effect on people. The fact that she was on the brink of disintegration intensified her magnetism.

The only guy in the room not ogling her turned from an intricate drawing he was shading. The ink pen still in hand he tossed a pencil thin gray braid off his shoulder, "We've got any size or color of diamond you can imagine. Come on over here and check out our files"

"You don't understand. You're not going to have what I want in your files. I've been looking at files all day. That's why I need an artist. I've got cash. Do you want to work with me or not?"

"Wait, I think I know what she wants, Ronnie. Give me a minute." The skinny redheaded kid with spiked hair put down his video game. He adjusted the black iron nail in his eyebrow and ambled over to a drawing table. Five minutes later he handed a sketch to Jaqui. "It's just a rough drawing but is this close?"

Jaqui studied the drawing. "You're my man!" She grabbed the boy and kissed him square on the mouth. "Can we do it tonight?"

"Whoa, hold on there. He don't even have his license yet. He can do the art. Somebody else

will need to do the procedure." Old Ronnie was getting his drawers in a wad. "What you got there?"

Jaqui stuffed the drawing into her hip pocket. "I've got $500 says he can do it just fine. Ain't that right, uh, what was your name?"

"J-Jason," the boy stuttered, still reeling from the kiss. "Dad, you know I can."

"I don't care about the rules," Jaqui said. "Jason does it or no one does. It's my money. It's his art."

Ronnie bowed up to his son. "It ain't going to happen. You hear me!" Turning to Jaqui he said, "Sorry Miss" and stomped off to the back room.

Frustrated to have been so close to finally getting what she been searching for, she turned to leave, realizing she'd let her mouth screw up her plans again. The other customers gawked at her, and although Jaqui had been receiving such stares her whole life, this time it pissed her off. "What the fuck are y'all staring at!" She shouted to no one in particular.

She slammed the door behind her, refusing to let the tears welling in her eyes fall. As she walked to the car, out of nowhere, someone grabbed her arm. Scared and angry, she twirled toward her attacker but came to a halt as she recognized the spiky red hair as Jason.

"Come back around 10 tonight. I'll have the artwork ready."

Hundreds of wasps were attacking Jaqui when she awoke from her nightmare. The cheap hotel alarm clock beeped 9:30. She wasted no time primping, just pulled on a sweatshirt, sweat-pants, and a ragged pair of sneakers. By the time she arrived at Sly Dog Tattoo studio it was after ten. The hall was dark behind the locked door. She knocked lightly on the glass and waited. After a few seconds she knocked harder, still no answer.

"Damn it!' she said, beating on the door and kicking the door jamb. A pale blue light came on in the hall. She exhaled.

"Take it easy, Ma'am. Come on in." Jason opened the door. She stepped in. He locked it behind her. He led her to the back of the shop where he handed her a large drawing. "If you like it, I can make it any size you want."

3

"Can you make it big enough to cover my butt cheeks?" It was perfect, the exact image of a prize-winning watermelon, with the darker blue-green broken stripes that were the signature of the Black Diamond strain.

"You know the image will be split by your butt crack," Jason said.

"Oh no! Really?" She put her fingers to her face in an overdone gesture of mock surprise. "See, that's the point. Every time I take a dump I want to shit through it."

Jason shrugged it off. "Do you have any other tattoos?"

"Nope."

"Okay, here's some stuff you need to read and sign. Your butt's going to be sore for a few days. I wouldn't plan any road trips."

"Are you really that concerned about my creamy white ass?" Jaqui asked.

Jason snorted, almost doubling over. "Don't worry. I've seen a few."

"Well I hear they're all different."

Jaqui tensed at the hum of the needle then relaxed when the warm ink spread across her skin. The first prick felt like an anemic honeybee. It was just physical pain, a minor inconvenience compared to what she'd recently experienced.

Farther Along

- Ellen McIlwaine

Mama **loved the cowboys.** Daddy was a farmer. Daddy had a commitment to the land, to his family, even to his wife. Mama was a free spirit. She couldn't even get a good solid handle on monogamy. Somehow, though, they found a love strong enough to bring little Jacquelyn into the world and raise her to be a gangly eleven-year-old with a mean fastpitch, a quick wit, and more charisma than the law should allow. One day the rodeo came to town. When it left, it took Mama. If Daddy noticed, it was only that he had more responsibility for raising Jacquelyn. Daddy, in addition to being a farmer, had come from a long line of horse traders and bootstrap philosophers.

Growing up, Jacquelyn had no shortage of free advice. "It's worth every penny," Sarge's standard line. Her dad had never been a sergeant, but an officer in the Marines. He just liked the sound of Sarge. He was a junior, named after his father, and who wants to be a junior anything. So, here's Sarge, left with a gangly smart-assed daughter just about to hit puberty and he's a lost ball in the high weeds.

Sarge knew he had little influence on Jaqui's success through her teenage years. The fact is, some kids grow like weeds; left alone, they make it, but don't amount to much. Some kids grow like orchids; beautiful and talented, but require a lot of care and maintenance. Then there's the wild roses, the ones that grow up beautiful, fragrant, and hardy, pretty much on their own. Jaqui was a wild rose. She worked the fields alongside Sarge and knew more about farming than most of the men in her county. Still, she had to get away. The melon farm was fine for her dad but she needed to see the world, to be somebody. It wasn't that she didn't like farming; the paperwork, the planning, all the little details of getting the plants to produce melons, those were fine. It was the endless hours on the back of the old Case tractor, the incessant boredom. Eight feet. That was the width of a melon row. Eight feet; over and over and over, times 200 acres. Drudgery. The only thing that saved her was the Blues.

At age nine, when she first started plowing, it was a Walkman. Now, with Y2K looming in the immediate future, she put 1000 songs on a device the size of a matchbox. Technology is wonderful. She had all her old favorite 1940s blues artists. She had the new pop culture singers with attitude. But most of all she liked the old jazz songs of love and longing and commitment, unlike the booty call anthems of today. She would sing at the top of her lungs to nobody, to the earth, and the sky. Now that they had a tractor with an air-conditioned cab, she put on headphones. She practiced singing harmony to the melody, working odd voices into existing harmonies. Jaqui loved to sing.

By her junior year she was editor of the high school paper. Journalism was another possible escape plan. Dating held no interest but she loved hanging out with her many friends. She dreamed of attending a university and studying journalism. She devoted most of her free time to singing and reading, honing her skills at both.

Benderman Farm did pretty well most years but Mother Nature is a fickle mistress. The last couple of years were rough. The drought left wilted vines and the high irrigation bills ate away all but the most meager sustenance. Only a scholarship could save Jaqui's dream.

Her best friend, Langley, had the answer. He circulated a petition nominating her for Watermelon Queen. The local festival brought people from all over the U.S. The scholarship fund would pay for at least two years at a major university.

She knew little about beauty contests but she had the beauty. She also had brains and that amazing charisma that drew people to her like bees to a melon blossom. The only thing she needed was an act, something visible. It's not like she could circulate an article about using earthworm casings as fertilizer. She needed to come up with a performance to blow the judges away and guarantee a win in the competition.

April Fool's Day of her senior year, Sunday, Jaqui usually slept in. Today, she was in the shower at 6:30. She dressed, ate breakfast, then drove to pick up Langley, who came up with the idea of free singing lessons. He'd suggested that she find a local church choir. As soon as she began asking around, she felt like an *objet d'art*, on the auction block, available to the highest bidder.

"You don't understand, I just need to sing." Her cohorts assumed she had been touched by Jesus. As it turned out, the Presbyterians had a contemporary second service, with a decent rock band and a congregation so desperate to save Jaqui they found a place for her in the ensemble. As the group's bass player, Langley pulled a few strings.

Her debut duet, a top ten hit on Christian radio, was new to her. *God, I hope I can remember the words,* she thought. Then a chill hit her. *Had she really asked God?* She felt the spotlight like ice on her skin. She had to push the sound from her throat but once it broke free it was just like in rehearsal. She relaxed. By the end of the song the congregation was hooked, certain that the Lord

God himself was speaking through this child. She felt the joy of working in harmony with these talented souls, and was pretty sure Jesus or his dad had nothing to do with it.

Jaqui paced the large open living area, occasionally stepping out on the porch to gaze down the long gravel driveway. Darkness had since fallen and Sarge had yet to return home. He often spent time at Julio's on the weekend and today he celebrated the sale of a combine. Still, she needed to talk to him and only one hour remained on Saturday. She was turning off some of the lights when the dogs started raising a ruckus. Headlights weaved up the lane. She stood on the porch with her hand on her hip as Sarge poured himself out of his truck, obviously inebriated. She was about to stomp back into the living room when Sarge tripped on his stupor and landed face first in the yard.

She ran to him. "Dad! Are you alright?"

"Yeah, damn dogs just tripped me up. I'm okay." The hound was licking his face. "Get on out of here, Blue. Shit...dogs!" Jaqui helped him to his feet. Shrugging her off, he stumbled into the house.

"What are you doing still up? I thought you had to go play with your little church buddies tomorrow."

"I was just waiting up for you. I need to ask you a favor."

"Anything, sweetie."

"I want you to come to church tomorrow."

"Okay, anything but that."

"But, Dad, I'm singing a solo and I want you to hear me."

"Babydoll, you know how I feel about that. I'm not going to anyone's house who would ask somebody to kill their own kid. That's just fucked up!"

"It's not about that. It's my first solo ever."

"We'll see. Right now I need a shower and you need your beauty rest."

Why even bother? The sun's first rays flooded Jaqui's bedroom. She showered and dressed and pulled her hair up in a high bun. *He can't understand. I shouldn't care. It's not about me,* she rationalized. In the kitchen she prepared enough sausage, pancakes, grits and eggs to feed three grown men.

She beat on his door. "Dad, I made breakfast."

"Give me a minute." Shortly Sarge emerged dressed in slacks, polished boots, a white shirt and bolo tie. "Thanks for breakfast. I'll drive you to the church if you want."

"Cool, Dad. Thanks. You know this isn't about religion, right?"

"I don't know what it's about but if it's important to you, I'm there."

"You know you shouldn't drive when you get messed up. If you got stopped it could cost us a bundle."

"I was okay when I left the bar. I guess the night got to me."

"Just call me if you need a ride, okay? I don't mind picking you up." Jaqui said.

"I got here, didn't I? You just worry about you."

"I'm just saying, if you need me, well, you know...."

The preacher spoke about salvation, big surprise, as he stared at Sarge, defiant and upright in the back row. Sarge glared back into the preacher's eyes. After a long prayer begging for divine intervention, Jaqui took the podium. The lights went down. A single spotlight illuminated her like a halo. She began acapella with the old standard "Farther Along". The bass and organ joined in. By the end, the song was full tilt rocking, drums flailing and the backup singers belting out the chorus. Jaqui gyrated to the music, her long blue skirt waving at the standing congregation. Sarge had a lump in his throat. He knew his daughter was talented but this was beyond anything he'd imagined. Sarge waited in the truck after the service while Jaqui made her way through the crowd of parishioners. She was torn between receiving her accolades and joining Sarge. She turned down several invitations with the excuse it was family day. What lay in store was a long afternoon on the tractor planting cantaloupe.

Langley felt like the campaign manager for an uncontested candidate. Still on the campaign trail, he assured several high-ranking members of the congregation that the quality of her performance could only be divinely inspired. Everyone assumed that Jaqui would be the next Watermelon Queen even though she was competing against Lilah Snipes, the mayor's daughter and last fall's homecoming queen. Lilah had been humiliated by a nasty break-up with the star wide receiver over her infidelities.

Langley initially considered trying to dig up some dirt on Jaqui's competitors, but he wasn't like most campaign managers. He decided to put his energies directly into promoting Jaqui as the underdog, single parent family, working the farm and late bloomer. He also suggested she sing hymns at the local nursing home where his mom played piano and serve meals at the county homeless shelter.

Now when Sarge went to town he wasn't recognized as just a melon farmer or used farm equipment dealer. He was Jaqui's dad. He reveled in it. He even made a couple more appearances at the Presbyterian Church until someone invited him to a Bible study group.

Jaqui was in the top ten percent of the Luling High School graduating class. Her gown sported a shimmering silver stole provided by the National Honor Society. Texas law guaranteed her entrance into any state university, if she could afford it. She walked on air across the stage. Langley, who also made the top ten percent, had no intention of attending a four-year university. He planned to work in law enforcement as a detective and had decided on a quicker and much less expensive route. Jaqui's goals included working as a foreign correspondent for Time magazine or CNN, complete with travel allowance. Look out world!

As soon as the ceremony ended and the mortarboards went airborne, Jaqui shucked her gown and stuffed it in her gym bag. When she turned around, she ran smack dab into a wall of male complete with a cologne overdose.

"Shit, Randy! You scared me."

"Sorry, but wouldn't startled be more appropriate. You're the English major," Randy was the wide receiver Lilah had spurned. "Yeah, startled and possibly pissed if you don't back off." Jaqui raised a fist in a mock threat. She shared several classes with Randy. He stepped back and leaned his hulking body against the bleachers.

"So where are you running off to next year."

"Oxford of course, haven't you heard? I won the lottery," she said. "No seriously, I've been accepted at UT, Sam Houston State and UNT. I'm leaning toward UT, good journalism school and close to home. I'd like to be able to check on Sarge once in a while."

"Cool, I was hoping you wouldn't run off too far."

"Really, why?"

"I'd like to hang out with you some this summer, see if we hit it off."

"I bet Lilah would love that."

"Screw Lilah. That's over. She can kiss my ass."

"Wow! Taking it hard, huh?" Jaqui jousted with him to cover the feeling of goldfish in her stomach as she processed this information.

"You hungry? Want to go get a burger at Dean-O's? My treat."

"Sure. Half the class will probably be there. It may take a

11

while," Jaqui said. "Let me ditch all this stuff in my car and change into my boots. Want to ride with me?"

"Dad got me a new truck for graduation. Let's take it. It's got a kick-ass stereo."

"Cool, I'll meet you in the parking lot."

When they arrived at Dean-O's more than half the class was there. Lilah was holding court at a corner table with a delegation of the cheerleading squad. Jaqui waved at the group since she'd been a cheerleader during football season. Lilah began to return her greeting then noticed that Randy was her escort. Her gesture froze. The squad turned as one. Randy slid his arm around Jaqui's waist. She stiffened momentarily then, realizing what was happening, leaned into Randy and put her cheek against his bicep. *Kid games*, she thought. They ambled over to the table where the cheerleaders sat.

"What's up? Y'all scoot over." Jaqui said.

"There's really no room," Lilah stated. The other girls began scooting around to make a spot but Lilah's quick glance froze them in their places

"Don't worry, Jaqui. We can go outside and eat in my new truck. I have an iPod dock so we can listen to whatever you like," Randy bragged. "See you ladies on the flip side." He bowed deeply and took Jaqui's hand leading her outside.

"That was beyond strange," Jaqui said.

"That was Lilah."

"I don't know about this. It's a little weird. Maybe we should do it another time. I think I need to get back to my car and head home.

"Is it okay if I call you, though?"

"Sure. I'd love to hang out some this summer. It'd be fun. You can holler at me tomorrow."

After the ceremony Langley retrieved his mortarboard and removed his gown, carefully folding it and placing it behind the

seat of his truck. He stood alone in the parking lot. There was no hurry. Let the crowd thin out. Maybe he could squeeze a little more juice out of the lemon. There had never been quite enough to make lemonade. An older Buick sedan eased past him as he lowered the tailgate to sit. The driver pulled out of the queue, circled around and parked. He didn't recognize the car as belonging to anyone he knew. When the door opened the first thing he saw was a woman's long shapely legs encased in sheer pantyhose. He didn't realize anyone but his mother still wore those. Still, the legs looked fine. When the woman stepped into full view he saw it was Amy, or a version of her. She was in his speech class during that final semester but he'd never really noticed her. He certainly would have noticed if she had come to school looking like this. The oily brown strands of tangled hair were washed and curled, she wore a tasteful amount of makeup and the baggy gray t-shirt and jeans were traded for a sleek sleeveless dress that clung to her thin body like a second skin. The transformation would have been amazing had she posed without moving. As soon as she stepped toward him the gangly gait set the makeover on its end.

"Damn, Amy, you clean up plum sweet!" He piled all the twang he could muster on his Texas accent.

"Why thanks, Langley. Right back at you," she sat beside him, crossing her legs at the ankles." I guess it's the end of an era."

"I reckon. None too soon if you ask me."

"I hear you want to work for the DPS." Isn't that kind of dangerous?"

"No more than clerking at a convenience store and the pay's better, besides I want to be a detective. That's safer than patrol."

"Well it should be interesting at least."

"I hope so. Thanks to the dual credits I've been taking I only have two more semesters of college; then the academy is like military boot camp. I should be making the streets safer by the end of the year. What about you?"

"I have a pretty good shot at getting on at the bank. My aunt works there. My math scores are okay and I can type. No way can I afford college, plus my mom is in pretty bad shape so I need to take care of her. She gave me her car though, even paid a guy to detail it out for me. I thought that was a real nice graduation present."

"Don't say 'nice'. Ms. Kramer might be hiding in the bushes."

"Well my nice diploma is sitting on the seat of my nice car so she can take her butt back to her nice house and get over it in the same nice khaki pants that she wore to school every day."

"I liked speech class," Langley said." It was an easy A. Ms. Kramer was a little quirky, though."

"It was fun because of the oddball group of students, but if I have to listen to one more recording of some unknown poet whining about his gay lover I'm going to toss my cookies."

"I guess that probably won't happen too much at the bank."

"No and I don't have to worry about it at home either. If my dad thought we even discussed homosexuality in speech, he would have yanked me out of that class so fast it would have made my head spin."

"Tough parents?'

"They're okay, just old-fashioned."

"Nothing wrong with that. It seems like the world is getting weirder every day."

"And here we are getting shoved out into it," she said. Amy turned toward Langley and picked up his hand. "This might sound even weirder but I'm really going to miss you. You really lit up that class. Every day I came to school just waiting for last period so I could see you." Amy's voice began to quiver. "I'm sorry. I must sound silly to you. I was afraid I might not see you again. I had to say it."

"No I ... I didn't have any idea," Langley said, then with no warning Amy's lips were on his. He didn't even have time to kiss her back. All he could think of was how her kiss tasted like Juicy Fruit gum.

"Call me if you get a chance," she said over her shoulder as she stumbled back to her car. The parking lot was almost empty. She pulled away as Langley sat slack jawed trying to figure out what had just happened.

"Hey Langley! You look either stoned or lost. Knowing you I'm guessing it's neither. So what's up?" Jaqui hollered from inside her car.

"What? Oh, the strangest thing just happened," Langley said.

"Must be the night for it. Something in the water I guess." As a sliver of moon rose from the east they sat on the tailgate of Langley's pickup and compared notes.

"I don't know if he was serious or just trying to make Lilah jealous," Jaqui said. "If he was bullshitting me he was good at it. I think the boy might really want to spend some time with me. He's got to make it quick. I'm bailing out of here in a few months. So what's got you all googly eyed?"

"You know Amy?"

"Which one?"

"Phillips, brown hair, lives down by the river."

"I know who you mean. What about her?"

"She kissed me, right on the mouth!"

"Oooh, Studly! Break it down for me."

"She just said she was going to miss me and laid one on me, then took off." Langley's experience about matters of the heart was minimal.

The conversation came back around to the Watermelon Queen contest. Jaqui confirmed that Langley had posters of Jaqui in formal attire placed in every store and business in the county, often next to Lilah in her swimsuit. Lilah was one of Jaqui's serious competitors. She held the coveted head lifeguard position at the city pool.

Randy also worked at the pool most summers doing maintenance but the manager had elected to contract it out to a fledgling pool service company started by one of the city councilman's nephews. It's typical small-town politics. It also kept Randy and Lilah apart. He used it as a chance to ask Sarge if he needed summer help on the farm. Unfortunately, Sarge wasn't in a position to hire full time help but he did offer Randy weekend work hauling trailer loads of melons to the broker in San Antonio. Randy took the job so he would be able to spend some of his summer near Jaqui. She even accompanied him on a few trips to help unload. After the market one evening Randy took her to the River Walk and spent his whole day's pay treating her to dinner. He finally asked her out on a real date.

"Sure, can we go to Austin and see a band?" She asked. We could stay overnight so you don't have to drive back so late. I can help out with the funds if you like. I know Sarge isn't paying you much."

Randy was reeling. "I can cover it," he said. "Who do you want to see?"

"We'll find somebody we both like. We have to go during the week so you don't miss work." Jaqui liked hanging out with Randy. He was no rocket scientist but he was easy going with an endearing silly side.

When they got back to the farm it was approaching midnight with Sarge well into a belligerent buzz. He stood on the porch as they came up the driveway, fist firmly planted on hip, boot bouncing on the planks. Before Randy even parked, Sarge charged toward the truck. Jaqui jumped out on an interception path.

"Where the hell have ya'll been? It's midnight! This is bullshit!" Sarge bellowed.

"Easy, Dad. Randy just took me out to eat. No harm. I

didn't call; I didn't want to wake you up. Don't you think you're overreacting?"

"You go unhook the trailer and put the truck away. I need to have a talk with Randy."

"Go easy. I'm the one who was hungry."

"You just do what I said, little girl! We'll talk later."

Jaqui spun on her boot heel. She let the "little girl" comment go, for now. Sarge stumbled into Randy's personal space. Randy didn't look away.

"Let me explain something to you, son," Sarge said. "That little girl of mine has big plans. She's getting out of this God-forsaken hell hole and I'll be damned if some town kid is going to stand in her way. Do you understand that?"

"Yes, sir, I do. With all due respect, Jaqui's old enough to make her own choices. I know what her plans are and I won't interfere. We're friends. I just want to hang out with her while she's still here, if that's okay."

"We'll see." Sarge was still wavering in Randy's face. "How'd we do at the market?"

"Here's the check. It seems like everybody wants the Benderman melons."

"Good. Help Jaqui with the trailer. She has church in the morning. I'll see you next Saturday." Sarge turned and stumbled back toward the house. By the time Randy made it to the barn, Jaqui had the trailer put away and was standing by the truck.

"Need help?" Randy asked.

"I've got it," Jaqui replied. "I was just waiting for you. Dad surprised me this time."

"You can't blame him. You're all he has."

"That's crap! He has this farm. He has lots of friends. I wish he'd get a girlfriend. Lord knows there're plenty of women around here who would jump at the chance. Even with the drinking, he's still a good catch. Most days he's funny as shit and easy to get along with."

"He was pretty definite about me not being a part of your life," Randy said.

"That's not up to him." Jaqui slipped her arm around Randy's neck and pulled herself close to him. Randy wrapped his arms around her and their lips met in a series of passionate kisses. Before his desire passed the point of questionable return, Jaqui slipped out of his grasp. "Let's save something for our date." She brushed his cheek with her fingers.

"Yeah, you have church in the morning," Randy said.

"You should come."

"I'm in a Baptist family. They wouldn't understand."

"Your loss." Jaqui grabbed his butt cheek, giving it a squeeze. "See ya' later." She jogged toward the house. Randy floated over to his truck and picked out a CD of country love songs to accompany his slow ride home.

Jaqui saw Sarge sitting at the kitchen table staring at a bottle of Evan Williams Kentucky Bourbon. The quart bottle was half empty, or half full depending on your perspective. Tears washed a trail in the dust on his weathered face. He didn't notice Jaqui. She walked behind him and wrapped her arms around his neck.

"I love you, Daddy."

He burst into a low wail. "I'm sorry," he cried. "I didn't mean to embarrass you." He put his face in his hands.

Jaqui went into the kitchen and fixed herself a three-quarter full glass of cola. At the table, she took the bottle of bourbon and topped off the glass. "We should talk," she said, and took a sip from the glass. The sweet warmth of the whiskey was surprisingly agreeable.

This whole scene took Sarge by surprise. "Okay," he said. "Shoot."

"First, Dad, you know I had a birthday in April. I'm an

adult. I've been helping you run this farm for seven years. I do the books. I file the papers. I work the fields. I want to go to college and do something for me. What you probably don't know is that I'm still a virgin, only because I'm too busy. This summer before I leave, I'm going to have some adult fun. This isn't to rebel or piss you off. I just need to catch up with my life, okay?"

Sarge stared, dumbfounded, trying to process this. "Ever since your mom … left, I've tried to take care of you. I was never sure if I was doing it right. I just love you so much." The tears were starting again. "I'm really proud of you. You've become more than I ever dreamed. I just don't want you to throw that away."

"Life goes on, Dad. Mine. Yours. Maybe it's time for you to think about yourself. I've got my situation pretty well sewn up, but what are you going to do after I leave? Why don't you get a girlfriend or remarry? There's Jeanine Buckholtz or Miriam Rogers, either of them would jump at the chance to hang out here. Brenda Bartlett might drag you to church on Sunday but you've got to admit, she's a hottie. All these women have a little sparkle in their eyes when they see you. I've seen it. Maybe it's time for you to have some fun."

"Yeah, I have such good luck with women."

"Hey, not every woman is a traveler. These ladies I'm talking about have been here their whole lives. They're not going anywhere."

"I don't know, I'm getting a little old for that shit."

"You ain't pushing up the little daisies, you ain't too old." Jaqui smiled and Sarge busted into a deep belly laugh. How did his little girl get to be so smart?

Jaqui topped off her soda with another half ounce of bourbon.

"Better watch that," Sarge said. "The better you feel tonight, the worse you feel in the morning."

"You coming to church with me?"

"I doubt it. They want me to join a study group. I just don't see the point. You know how I feel about that."

"Maybe you should think of it as a social club without the jukebox. Brenda will be there. There's a potluck after. It would be pretty damn easy to toss a Black Diamond in the truck."

"Holler at me when you get up. We'll see." Sarge stood up, stretched the age out of his back and wandered off to bed. Jaqui turned off the lights and sat back down. The bourbon's warmth traveled to her extremities bringing with it a quiet tranquility. All was well with the world, at least for now.

Someone To Watch Over Me

- Ella Fitzgerald

J aqui stood behind a grain truck. She knew the driver couldn't see her because she couldn't see his mirrors. The backup alarm started beeping. She needed to step out of the way but her legs wouldn't move. She looked down and realized that her feet were buried almost to the knees in thick black mud. The truck was almost on top of her, red taillights glowing. She opened her eyes. The glowing red light said it was 6:30. She reached over and turned off the alarm. Her sheets were damp and a moist fog hovered in the room. She peeled her tongue from the roof of her mouth and considered rolling over and going back to sleep. The thought of finding herself back behind the truck encouraged her to get out of bed. *Is this a hangover?* It felt more like the flu.

The warm water sliding down her body washed away the fog. Black coffee lubricated her tongue and restored her balance. All that remained was an annoying thickness between her eyes. She focused. Church. Choir. Today it felt like a job.

"Dad," she hollered.

"I'm up." A light came on through the transom above his door.

"What do you want for breakfast?" She asked.

"I don't care, something light."

Jaqui started oatmeal and scrambled some eggs. Meat just didn't sound good right now.

Langley arrived at the church not long after sunrise. His dad was an elder or some kind of elected honcho. For Langley it meant that Sunday was not the proverbial day of rest. He attended the traditional early service then, while everyone else did an hour of Bible study, Langley set up the sanctuary stage for the contemporary service. He considered this to be a reprieve from all the Bible stories. He lived a moral life, but not because a supreme being told him to. Today, in addition to the sanctuary, he'd been asked to help get the dining area ready for a potluck dinner. He was about to assist some of the church ladies when Jaqui and Sarge showed up. They had a watermelon that, sliced in half, could have been hollowed out into matching canoes.

"Hey, Langley, how've you been?"

"Great, Mr. Benderman. Glad to be done with high school, already started college at SACC though. I should be gainfully employed by the first of the year."

"Need help?" Jaqui asked.

"You can make the tea and fill the jugs."

"Where can I cut up this melon?" Sarge asked.

Brenda Bartlett peeked out from the kitchen. "If you can bring that in here by the sink I'll slice it for you," she said.

With the large melon on his broad shoulders Sarge had to turn sideways to get through the door.

"Oh my, you have a big one," Brenda said, eagerly wiping her hands on her crisp apron.

Jaqui smiled when Langley rolled his eyes.

"Do you think she knows she does that?" Langley asked.

"Does what?!" Jaqui's eyes expanded in mock surprise.

"You know what I mean," Langley said.

"Yeah, I know, and she does too. Dad, I figure, is probably clueless."

"You think he'll ever catch on?"

"Maybe. I gave him a little hint yesterday."

"Those two would be a hoot together," Langley said.

"If they can get past the religion thing."

"That's not important. People can get past that."

"Some can. Most don't from what I've seen."

Back in the kitchen, Brenda drew a long blade through the melon.

"I would have chilled it but my refrigerator isn't big enough," Sarge said.

"That's okay. I like 'em hot." Brenda shot Sarge a sideways glance. "Better flavor."

"I don't see anything but desserts and veggies. Is this some kind of vegan cult?" Sarge joked.

"No, silly, I'm keeping the meat hot in the oven. We have a meatloaf, a huge ham, four dozen tamales and a couple of barbecued chickens in here." Brenda checked the oven. Bent at the waist with her posterior toward Sarge, she'd finally gotten his attention. As she stood back up he noticed her sky-blue eyes and the faint dusting of freckles across the bridge of her nose. She allowed him to study her until his eyes shifted down to her ample breasts. She put a hand in front of them and waved two fingers. "Help me set this out, okay? The service starts in 20 minutes. We can at least get the plates and utensils out, fill up some glasses with ice and put them in the freezer."

"Maybe we could go out sometime?" Sarge blurted out.

"My, aren't you the smooth talker," Brenda said. "Why don't you come up with a plan and ask me? You never know."

"Okay, How about..."

"How about you call me," Brenda said. "Here's my

number." She scribbled it on the back of last week's church bulletin and handed it to him. "Let's finish setting up."

As the congregation began filing in for the contemporary service, Jaqui and Langley had already taken their places on stage. Sarge and Brenda entered the sanctuary together. When Sarge turned toward his regular seat in the rear pew, Brenda caught him by the fingers and motioned him to join her. After a brief hesitation Sarge ended up in the third row, right in front of the band. The musicians were already into a medley of contemporary Christian hits. Jaqui saw her dad on the third row beside Brenda and shot him a wink. Sarge thought how ironic it was to be having fun in church.

The dust billowed behind the truck as Sarge maneuvered down the caliche county roads. Jaqui reclined in the passenger seat. Their bellies were full and their hangovers were history.

"What's on the agenda for this afternoon?" Jaqui asked.

"Nothing critical. We can stop on the way home and switch the irrigation valve to the southwest field. If everything's good there I was thinking that a nap might be in order. I should probably spot check for cucumber beetles but that can wait 'til tomorrow," Sarge said.

"Wait 'til tomorrow and I'll help. Right now a nap sounds really good. I'm so full I can barely walk," Jaqui said. "So, what's up with you and Brenda? Did I note some interest there?"

"I don't know. I tried to ask her out but she put me off."

"Did she say no?"

"No, but she didn't say yes. She did give me her number and me sitting with her, that was her idea."

"Don't worry, Dad, you're in. She just wants you to play the game."

"The game?"

"Yeah, like cat and mouse. She wants to be pursued but she was dropping hints like anvils."

"Really? I'm out of the loop here. What should I do next?"

"Wait a few days before you call her, maybe mid-week. That will give you time to decide how serious you want to get, too. If you really want to impress her take her to the city and wine and dine her."

"I don't know her well enough to know how serious I want to get."

"Well then, take her to a local event or something casual. She has that antique shop downtown. Maybe take her to an auction, offer to bring your trailer. She would at least know you thought it out. You might find something you like and you would get a feel for her tastes. Take her out to dinner afterwards. That way you have a chance to talk. Don't overdo the first date. Leave something to the imagination but clean up pretty."

Sarge contemplated for a short time. "This sounds like fun. I never really dated. Your mom and I grew up together and the few encounters I've had since she left were brief."

"Well, remember, if you're getting back into circulation, she's not the only one available. If she doesn't work out there are other women who would love to hang out with you. You are a pretty good catch but make sure there's something mutual happening."

"This is a weird conversation to be having with my daughter."

"I'm just trying to give a woman's point of view but, honestly, I don't have much hands on experience if you'll forgive the pun."

"That's good, from a father's point of view."

Sarge pulled to the side of the road and walked down the creek bank to the irrigation pump. He switched the valve, started the pump and set the timer. By the time he got back to the truck Jaqui was snoring.

Monday was brutal with temperatures in the triple digits. Unseasonable heat dominated the next week with little chance of rain. Melon farming became an around the clock job, fighting pests by day, irrigating by night. Jaqui's butt became one with the tractor's seat. She took a brief break on Tuesday afternoon to rehearse her Watermelon Queen act at Langley's house. She was working on three songs with Langley on bass and his mom on piano. Langley tried to explain the concept of jazz piano to his mom. She was a gospel pianist with a forceful melodic style. Langley suggested she only fill riffs with chord fragments on the offbeat. She didn't understand the concept so they opted to pick out some recordings for her to study and try again later. They went over a couple of hymns for the folks at the retirement center. "I'm sorry. I'm beat," Jaqui said. It's our busy season on the farm and I've been working day and night. I need to get home and take a nap. It's my night to deal with the irrigation schedule."

"Be careful," Langley's mom said. "You look worn out." Langley walked her to the car and gave her a goodbye hug.

"What an incredible young lady," his mom remarked when he returned.

"Yeah, she's something else," Langley said, letting the screen door slam behind him. "Especially considering what she's been through." Langley's mom cocked her head. "It's just her and her dad and they run a huge farm."

"I've noticed her in church lately. Are you two, uh, dating?"

"Come on, Mom, are you okay? Jaqui and I've been hanging out since grade school. She's been here over a dozen times. It's been a while but she hasn't changed that much."

"Y'all just make a pretty couple," his mom said.

"We're not a couple. She's like a sister to me." Langley observed his mother closely. She seemed to be forgetting a lot of little details lately.

Jaqui was navigating her coupe down Main when a pickup pulled up beside her, blasting out a country ballad.

"Want to get a burger?" Randy hollered out.

Jaqui considered. She was tired but hungry. "Sure. Dean O's?"

Follow me," Randy said, punching the throttle and making the pickup squeal the tires.

"Boys!" Jaqui thought. She tried to squeal the tires on her coupe. It didn't happen.

They ordered their burgers and slid into a corner booth. Jaqui laid her head on the table. Her golden hair fanned out across the Formica. "I'm exhausted," she sighed. Randy put his hands on her shoulders and firmly massaged her muscles, working down her back and pressing his thumbs into the tight ridges of muscle along the edges of her backbone.

"That feels heavenly," Jaqui moaned. "Where'd you learn to do that?"

"A class I took last summer. I'm glad you like it. Check out what else I've got." He pulled a rolled-up copy of the *Austin Chronicle* from his back pocket. "Every entertainment option in central Texas is listed; music, movies, stuff you couldn't imagine, from opera to nude Jell-O wrestling."

"Okay maybe something in between," Jaqui chuckled, "a band, maybe something we can dance to. Do you dance?"

"I can pull off country. I don't know about the mosh pit. I might break somebody."

"Yeah and I don't want it to be me!" Jaqui's eyes were sparkling. The exhaustion had left her body.

"Check this out," Randy said. "This place called Midnight Cowboy has some big-name country acts and they let in people under 21. Their lineup looks pretty good. Almost every night they have somebody I've heard of."

"I'm okay with country but you probably know more about

it. We have to go on a Wednesday or Thursday if we're going to stay overnight. You pick something and let me know the date. I'll get us a room."

"I can cover it," Randy said.

"No, I want to do this. I'm going to pick someplace special. It will be my first time." She hadn't planned to give Randy that much information. It slipped out. Randy turned ghostly pale.

"I had no idea. Are you sure you want to do this?" His eyes were locked on hers.

She squeezed his hand. "Yeah, I'm sure."

The food came. Jaqui wolfed her burger and fries. Randy nibbled at his burger. Jaqui ate his fries too. "I'd love to hang out," she said, "but I'm going to be up all night. I've got to get some sleep. I'll see you Saturday." She leaned over, gave him a quick kiss and walked out the door. It was all she could do to keep her eyes open as she drove home.

Saturday morning hadn't been on the clock long enough to push the sun past the horizon. The golden glow beginning to the east barely silhouetted the sprawling mesquite tree outside the kitchen window. Jaqui made breakfast. Sarge would be back from the irrigation rounds any minute. The barking dogs drew her to the window where she saw Sarge's truck closely followed by Randy. She put on two more sausage patties and broke three more eggs.

"Look what I drug up," Sarge bellowed as he kicked off his mud boots.

Jaqui smiled and kissed Randy's cheek. "Hungry?"

"Always."

"Good. I saw you coming and butchered another pig. What brings you out so early? I didn't expect you 'til at least after daylight."

"I figured I'd take one more shot at talking you into joining me on the delivery."

"I've got to rehearse my act today. The pageant is in two weeks and Langley's mom is having a hard time with the music."

"So you'll be hanging out with Langley all day then?" Jaqui cut him a glance with just enough sting in it that he knew he'd crossed the line.

"Don't go there, Randy. You know what this means to me. Besides, he's like my brother."

"Lucky brother!" Randy said.

"We'll see. He may not think so after today. It's like pulling teeth getting his mom to ease up on the melody."

"Jaqui, I need you to pick up some two-inch hose gaskets while you're in town," Sarge broke in. "The main line in the north field is pissin' like a racehorse."

"See, Randy, another reason I can't go. It's a never-ending catastrophe around here. As much as I'd love to toss 40-pound watermelons around all afternoon, I just can't work it into my schedule."

"I got these." Randy handed an envelope to Jaqui. She opened it and found tickets for next Wednesday's show at the Midnight Cowboy.

"Okay, Dad," Jaqui started, "I'm... we're...Randy and I are going to Austin on Wednesday and won't be back until Thursday afternoon."

Sarge just grunted.

"I'll come Tuesday and Friday to help with the harvest," Randy offered.

Sarge considered, slowly. "Just Friday will do but you'll need to be here about sunup."

"No charge," Randy offered.

"Bullshit! I'll pay you."

"Your call."

"Let's eat," Jaqui said, placing a steaming platter of sausage, eggs and homemade biscuits on the table.

As soon as breakfast was over Sarge went back to work. The thirty acres he had planted in early cantaloupes were finished producing. He needed to get it turned under and seeded with a cover crop since rain was predicted for mid-week. If he could get an early set of buckwheat and clover he might be able to harvest some hay and get enough re-growth to improve the soil. Sarge wasn't an organic farmer but he had to admit some of the techniques he gleaned from organic agriculture continued to improve his crops and keep his overhead low.

Jaqui helped Randy transfer his lunch and CD collection to the farm truck he was driving to San Antonio. The box van and an accompanying trailer were brimming with melons. Once loaded he gave her a cheek kiss and started to climb into the cab. *Cosmopolitan* warned against leaving arguments unsettled before a trip.

"Oh hell no, buddy! You're not getting off that easy," she said. She grabbed his arm and pulled him out of the truck, backing him against the bed. She pressed her body against his. Her fingers grasp the back of his neck and she kissed him firmly with parted lips, inviting his tongue to explore hers. Her other hand, thumb in his rear belt loop, pulled his pelvis toward hers. She could feel the excitement rising in his loins. "I'm really looking forward to this trip," she whispered in his ear after their lips broke free. She allowed his thigh to slide between her legs as his arms engulfed her. She told herself the twisting in her stomach was excitement instead of foreboding.

"Me too," he breathed. "I can't wait."

"Afraid you'll have to, but be sure and think about me while you're handling those melons today." She took his hand and placed it on her breast. He could feel the absence of a bra through her t-shirt. "I'll be imagining your sweaty body handling them," she whispered. "Be gentle. You should probably go before I drag you in the house and make you late." She turned and trotted back toward the house. On the porch she turned and blew him a kiss just like the magazines had suggested.

Just after lunch, Jaqui arrived at Langley's house. She'd spent the morning downloading some sparse jazz renditions of the songs she was considering for the competition and burning them to a disc. Langley met her outside the door. "Mom's been in bed all day with a headache. I don't think she can rehearse today. Now she's saying her vision is blurry. I called Dad. He said to give her some aspirin. I did, an hour ago. It didn't help." Langley was pale.

"She needs to go to the doctor," Jaqui said.

"She called his answering service. She's waiting on him to get back to her. She only mentioned the headache though."

"You need to call an ambulance or we need to take her now. This could be serious."

"I'll call Dad."

"Tell him to meet us at the emergency room. I'll go with you." While Langley called his dad, Jaqui knocked on his mom's bedroom door. "Mrs. Scott, you need to get dressed. Langley and I are going to take you to the emergency room."

"I'll be fine. Langley gave me some medicine."

"Is your headache gone?"

"No. I don't think I can rehearse today. My fingers aren't working right."

"That's not good. You need to see a doctor."

"You kids are worry-warts."

Langley found Jaqui in the hall. "Dad said he could be at the hospital in 30 minutes." He opened the bedroom door. His mom was sitting on the bed staring at the floor. Tears were streaming down her cheeks.

31

"I can't do this," she cried. "It hurts so bad and nothing works."

"What do you mean?" Langley asked.

"My fingers, I can't see right. I stood up and got so dizzy I ...." She fell sideways on the bed.

"I'll call an ambulance," Jaqui said. "You get her comfortable, keep an eye on her." The ambulance took less than ten minutes to arrive. Jaqui and Langley followed in her car.

Mr. Scott arrived at the hospital a few minutes behind his wife. He wheeled the Lincoln into the emergency drop off area, jumped out and hit the alarm button on his keychain. Jogging through the automatic doors, he searched the waiting room for his family. Jaqui saw him.

"Mr. Scott, they're doing an MRI. Marjorie has a bad headache, blurry vision and her left hand is numb."

"Thanks for coming, Jaqui. Where's Langley?"

"He went back with her. I have to wait here for now since I'm not related."

"You might as well be," Mr. Scott said.

The intercom crackled, *"Would the owner of a blue Lincoln Town Car please move it from the emergency drive. It's blocking ambulance access."*

"That's me," Mr. Scott said. "Would you please be a sweetie and park it for me?" He dangled a cluttered key chain in front of Jaqui.

"Sure. Go check on Marjorie."

As she slipped behind the wheel of the Lincoln, Jaqui couldn't help but notice the contrast between the plush leather interior and the Spartan decor of the Scott's home. Could be Marjorie. she thought. In a way it made sense. Maybe he needs the car to impress his clients. He did own the most successful insurance agency in the county. She parked the car in the far lot, isolated beyond the tangle of lesser vehicles, and returned to the waiting area. She waited. She read a *US News and World Report* from cover to cover. It was dated seven weeks earlier. She noticed how the articles were concise and how any bias was well camouflaged in rhetoric and nuance, masterful reporting with a moderately conservative slant.

Eventually Langley appeared, a scared and confused child. Jaqui wrapped him in her arms and felt the first tremors of a sob shudder through him.

"She had a stroke," he said, "a small one. Thank you for insisting we come. It may have saved her life."

"So she's going to be okay?" Jaqui asked.

"We're waiting on the neurologist's report but her doctor is optimistic. It's going to take time though. She won't be able to play for the pageant."

"It's no big deal. Let me worry about that, as long as your mom is okay."

"You should probably go home. It's going to be a long night. I'm going to stay here with her and ride home with Dad later."

"I'll call you tomorrow. If there's anything I can do, just call. I mean it, anything."

"I will. I'll let you know of any changes. Thanks so much. I don't know what I would do without you."

Jaqui gave him one more hug and left. She drove the last quarter mile home at 15 miles per hour in a cloud of dust kicked up by Sarge's tractor tires. He didn't notice her until he parked and she pulled up beside him.

"Look at this shit!" She hollered. "You owe me a car wash."

"Right, well let me just go grab the hose," he joked. "How was rehearsal?"

"It wasn't. Marjorie had a stroke. I've been at the hospital all afternoon."

"Oh my God! Is she okay?"

"She will be, they think. It's too soon to say for sure."

"Why didn't you call me?"

"And what, Dad! What could you do?"

"I don't know, just, never mind."

"I'm sorry, Dad. I'm just a little testy. It's been a strange day.

I'm going inside." She left Sarge tending to the equipment. Jaqui went to the kitchen and made a sandwich, mostly for something to do. Her stomach was dancing from the day's disappointments. The guilt got to her. It wasn't fair that her performance was going to have to be completely reworked. In the grand scheme of things it was a minor detail, but still. She pulled down a glass and filled it with ice. She grabbed a can of cola from the cabinet. That's when she noticed Sarge's bottle of bourbon on the shelf. Remembering the feeling of warmth and contentment it had previously provided, she filled the glass one third full of the golden liquid and placed it back on the shelf exactly as it had been. She heard Sarge's boots on the porch. She closed the cabinet and topped off her glass with cola.

"Hungry?" She asked as Sarge entered. "Can I fix you something?"

"I'm good," he replied.

Jaqui bagged the sandwich and put it in the refrigerator. She took her drink out to the porch and sat sipping as she stared out at the endless field. It only took the whiskey minutes to work its magic on an empty stomach. Her body became lighter. The fields grew greener. She decided that nothing was worth getting worked up over.

She emptied the glass, now she was hungry. She went inside but didn't see Sarge. She checked his office. He had his computer on and was hunched over a column of numbers, his reading glasses hanging from the end of his nose.

"What'cha doin'?" She asked, leaning against the door jamb.

"Catching up on paperwork." He looked at her over the top of his glasses. "Feeling better?"

"Oh, yeah. I'm fine. I just needed to chill for a bit."

Sarge resumed his computations. Jaqui ate her sandwich, fixed another drink and returned to her outpost on the porch. The sun began to bathe the western sky in orange marmalade. Just to the north of the sunset, thunderheads were building, reflecting the flashes of lightning beyond the horizon. The air was still and damp.

∾

She startled awake to the hound dog baying beside her. Rain fell heavily on the porch roof. Headlights were coming up the drive. By the sound of the diesel engine and the empty trailer rattling she knew it was Randy coming back from market. She stumbled from the porch not noticing that her feet weren't functioning properly. A few paces into her jog she stumbled and dropped front first into a puddle. Her arms barely kept her face from the mud. Jumping up, she realized she was covered in sticky black soup. At the edge of the house she showered in the torrent of cold water cascading from the roof. *Oh shit! I'm drunk!* she thought. She tried to regroup but total clarity failed her. She spent a few more moments letting the water pour over her. She turned toward the barn. Randy. She needed Randy to hold her, make it all better. Long, sure steps, no running. She threw her head back and, bringing herself to her full height, walked briskly to meet him.

"Need help?" She asked.

"I've got it. How was your date with Langley?" He was bent over fumbling with the hitch. Jaqui barely suppressed the urge to punt his butt.

"Jealousy, Randy. Really?! Will you just get over it! You don't look good in green!" She turned back toward the house. In less than two steps his hand was on her shoulder. She jerked loose and spun to face him. "Don't fucking touch me! You have no idea what I've been through today! I really don't need this shit right now!" A sane part of her was outside her body watching as she blew everything to hell.

"Whoa, easy, Baby. I'm sorry. You're right. I'm out of line. It's .., It's just .., I missed you today. You are all I thought about." Suddenly her arms were around his neck. She was hanging on him like a loose sweater, shivering from the sudden chill. Sobs racked her body. Randy wrapped his arms around the soggy girl and cradled her against him. He wondered if all women were crazy. Even so, he realized he liked this one a lot.

"So what happened, Baby? Are you okay?"

Jaqui snuggled deeper into his chest. "Marjorie had a stroke."

"Marjorie?"

"Langley's mom. She was going to play piano for my performance."

"Oh no! Is she okay?"

"She's alive. She'll probably recover. I've been at the hospital most of the day. She was so scared."

"How's Langley holding up?"

"I'm sure it's hard on him but he's not one to show it much."

"Let's get inside. You're soaking wet," he said. Jaqui raised her head from his chest. He kissed her then recoiled slightly. "Have you been drinking?"

"I had some bourbon to relax."

"I didn't know you drank."

"I don't, usually. Don't tell Dad, okay?"

"No, it's none of my business." He loosened his hold on her. "You've had a rough day. Tomorrow will be better. You should get cleaned up. Look, you're bleeding."

Jaqui checked a spot near her elbow. Blood was oozing from a scrape and mixing with the rainwater. She'd left a pink smudge on Randy's shirt. "I'm sorry. I messed up your shirt."

"Let's go inside."

Jaqui went to her room. Randy went to Sarge's office. "Some storm." Randy handed Sarge a check.

"We need the rain," Sarge said, examining the document.

"Hit it in Seguin. The drive home was slow. I had to stop a couple of times and wait out the heaviest."

"How was market?"

"M&H brought four semi loads up from the valley. They were low-balling."

"It's been a good crop this year. We can expect some of that. Looks like we did okay."

"I held out for premium. You've still got 'em beat in size and quality."

"That's okay this time. If it gets too tough, though, I'd rather sell 'em cheap than bring 'em back. Good call this week." Sarge reached in the bottom drawer and pulled out some cash. "Here's your pay. Thanks." He handed Randy two hundred dollars.

"You gave me too much." Randy held out some bills.

"Nope. It's a bonus. You're getting pretty good at this. You're worth it."

"Thanks." Randy was beaming, unaccustomed to compliments.

Jaqui came in wearing a clean t-shirt and cutoffs. "You guys hungry? I could whip something up."

"I'm okay. I stopped on the way back." Randy said. "I should be getting home, church tomorrow."

"I'll make a sandwich later. I'm going to finish up here," Sarge said.

"Well then, I already ate so I guess we'll leave it at that."

"Walk me out?" Randy asked.

"Sure, the rain has stopped. Let me slip on my sandals."

"Are you sure you're okay?" Randy asked, once outside.

"I'm good. Like you say, tomorrow will be better."

"If you need anything, just call."

"Can you accompany me on piano?" Jaqui joked.

"Not unless you know the words to 'Chopsticks'." Randy took her hand. "You know you should probably leave the liquor alone."

"It's not like it's a regular thing."

"Just saying."

"I know. Don't worry about me. Just be here Wednesday to haul my ass to Austin. I'm excited."

"Me too. It's going to be fun. I'll see you Wednesday." A brief kiss, a parting hug and gone.

The Presbyterian Church was a solemn place to be on Sunday. The music was hollow without Langley on bass and Marjorie on piano. Harold Scott was there to be the center of prayer groups focusing on Marjorie. Sarge even joined one of the prayer groups, the one Brenda participated in. He'd asked her to an antique auction the following week. He'd been waiting to see if she could get someone to run her shop while she went. She could. Sarge was much happier than the somber surroundings called for, making it more difficult for him to fit in than usual.

After church, Jaqui went to the hospital to check on Marjorie and Langley. She was surprised that Mr. Scott didn't show up but neither Langley nor Marjorie seemed to notice. Except for the numbness in her hand, Marjorie was almost back to normal. Langley was obviously exhausted. Marjorie was drowsy from the medication, slurring her words.

"Come on. Let's get some lunch, let your mom take a nap," Jaqui said. She knew he hadn't left her side in 24 hours. He was still wearing the same clothes.

"Yeah, I should eat," he admitted.

"It's a beautiful day. Let's go get some chicken and eat in the park."

"Sure, whatever."

"Langley, are you okay? This has to be rough on you."

"I'm fine. Have you seen Dad? Was he in church this morning?"

"Yeah. Everyone was praying for Marjorie. He led several prayer groups."

"Did he say he was coming to the hospital?"

"He didn't say, not to me anyway. I think he was going to the pastor's house. They'll both probably stop by later." They ate quickly. Langley was in a hurry to get back to the hospital.

"I can take you by your house to clean up and change if you want," Jaqui offered.

"No, I'll catch up with Dad later. I'll ride home with him and pick up my truck."

"Okay, I'll drop you back at the hospital. I need to get home. There's a lot to do around the farm this time of year."

Teen Lovers

The Virgins

Six outfits, not counting the sleepwear, were packed neatly in a large leather suitcase. She didn't own a "nightie" so she picked a long pink t-shirt with "Cowgirl" emblazoned across the breast in flowery script and some lacey pink bikini underwear. She planned on shucking them promptly anyway. Three more choice outfits were arranged on her bed. Picking up the dress, not really her style, she held it to her freshly scrubbed and scented body then placed it back beside the others, unable to decide. She'd shelled out a serious chunk of change booking a room on the upper floors of the Four Seasons Hotel. It featured a panoramic view of the Austin skyline. The shower set a personal record for the use of hot water. She'd shaved away every renegade hair on her body that was appropriate without seeming strange. The rest were clipped short. She had studied, perusing numerous issues of *Cosmopolitan* magazine for tips on what to expect and how to deal with it. None of the articles dealt with deflowering virgins. She went online and Googled "deflowering virgins", immediately finding that it was not going to contain the information she was looking for. She made ham and eggs with homemade biscuits. She wanted to treat Sarge to a special breakfast. Other than school sponsored trips, this was the first night she'd spent away from home since middle school. Although he hadn't mentioned it, she figured he was a bit apprehensive about her journey. Just as the biscuits came out of the oven, Sarge surged through the door.

"What's up?" Jaqui asked.

"Starter's shot on the river pump."

"Sure it's not the battery? It's pretty old."

"No, I tried jumping it. Nearly got the truck stuck getting back in there."

"So what's the plan?"

"It's a Continental engine. One of these little tractors in the equipment yard might have a starter that will interchange."

"Why not just buy one. We're in pretty good shape financially. A starter isn't going to kill us."

"It's not the money. It's the time. That pump feeds the entire system. The south and west ponds are too low to pump from. If I don't get them refilled today I'll lose a day, maybe two, of irrigation."

"You'll handle it. You always do. Right now stop for breakfast. You have to eat and thirty minutes won't make a difference one way or the other. Two eggs over medium?"

"Sure, thanks." She placed the plate of warm biscuits on the table.

"So what's the occasion?" He continued.

Jaqui gave him a sly smile. "I'm not going to be here to cook for you in the morning."

"Maybe I'll go out to breakfast. I can cook for myself, you know."

"I know. I've eaten it. You should go out. Give Brenda a call. I bet she would jump at the chance to join you."

"Yeah and then I don't get anything done for the rest of the day."

"You're not that lucky. She has to open her shop at ten."

"Wishful thinking on my part."

41

"Wow! That almost sounds like you have some feelings for her. That's cool. I hope it works out."

"Too soon to tell. What about you and Randy?"

"Today's the big day, for me anyway. I'm not planning anything long term. He's sweet but he doesn't really fit my plan."

"So he's your boy toy?"

"Dad! No! It's not like that. We're just having fun. There's no promises either way."

"Be careful. I get the feeling he doesn't see it quite the same. I know I should have told you about the birds and bees and all that. I guess I figured you'd pick it up through osmosis. One thing, though, men aren't like birds or bees. They're more like puppies, you feed 'em once and they're yours for life."

"Randy's not like that, Dad. He has his own plan."

"Really? What is it?"

"I don't know but I'm sure he has one."

"Maybe you should ask him before y'all's legs get all tangled up."

"Dad!"

"Just sayin'. I'd hate for either one of you to get hurt. He seems like a decent kid."

"Just eat, Dad. Quit while you're behind."

The dress didn't make the cut. A short denim skirt did. So did a gauzy white sleeveless top that barely allowed her baby blue bra to show through. She polished her black cowboy boots, the ones with sterling silver inlays and high dogging heels. After spending a frustrating hour and a half trying to get her makeup just right, she scrubbed her face clean and put on a light tan eyeliner with some clear lip gloss. A couple of freckles showed, enhanced by exposure to the sun. Oh well, country is as country does. Once dressed, she studied her reflection in the full-length mirror.

"Luscious candy" were the two words that came to mind. She plopped down on the bed and pulled out her collection of *Cosmopolitan*. She scanned the sex articles to review as much as she could. It felt like trying to learn about skydiving without ever being in an airplane. She knew Randy had relations with Lilah a few times but she doubted he had much experience other than that. She figured if she at least paid attention to what he liked she could be a satisfying lover, experience or not.

Dogs barked. She hoped it was Randy arriving. She wanted to leave before Sarge saw her dressed so provocatively. It was her lucky day. Advancing very slowly up the driveway Randy's freshly detailed new truck gleamed in the sun. She stood on the porch waiting; wanting him to come to her, *Cosmo*'s idea. When he stepped out of the truck she saw he had taken as much care as she had. His new jeans were ironed with perfect creases. His ice white pearl snap Western shirt was accented with a turquoise inlaid silver bolo tie, a perfect complement to her boots. He even had a fresh haircut.

He joined her on the porch and wrapped his muscular arms around her waist. "You clean up real nice," he said.

She rolled her eyes and put two fingers to his lips. "You were perfect until you opened your mouth." She reached down and squeezed his butt cheek, one of her favorite moves. "Can you get my suitcase? I want to get out of here before Dad gets back."

"What happened to you? When did you become so dependent?"

"It's the lip gloss, Baby. It completely incapacitates me. Besides, It's heavy!" She reached up and stroked his bicep. She was feeling a couple of degrees warmer already.

Randy put the suitcase in the truck bed. Jaqui got in the cab and shifted to the center of the bench seat. Randy slid behind the wheel. "I love trucks," he said. "You can't get a car with a bench seat."

"Actually, I drove Mr. Scott's Town Car the other day. It has a bench seat that feels like a leather sofa."

"You drove his Lincoln?"

"Just to park it for him. Talk about loaded, I think it comes with maid service."

"I hear he has his own maid service."

"What do you mean?"

"Him and Jeanine Buckholtz, she does more than answer phones in his office."

"No, I don't see that. She's been his receptionist for years. Harold's a family man, big shot in the church. He wouldn't do that."

"Just what I heard."

"You shouldn't spread that around. I'm pretty sure it's not true."

"So, where are we headed?"

"The Four Seasons"

"Holy shit, Miss Moneybags! You went all out!"

"I hate cockroaches," she joked. "We can check in anytime after three. If we stop somewhere for lunch we'll get there about three-thirty or four."

"Dean-O's?"

"Oh hell no! Let's get the fuck outta Dodge! There's a place in Austin just north of UT called Trudy's. We ate there when I toured the campus. I think I can find it. Food was great, Tex-Mex basically, and not too pricey."

"Sounds good. I've got a little extra spending money. Sarge gave me a bonus."

"Really? Cool! He likes you. You've made this season a lot easier on us. We've never had help before and he says you're a natural at the marketing."

"I like it okay, mostly the physical part though. I don't want to make a career out of it."

"So what do you want to make a career out of? Football?"

"Not likely."

"Hey, you were the star player. You made half the points the team scored this season."

"Yeah but we didn't make the playoffs so I didn't get scouted by any Big 12 or SEC guys. Dad was devastated. He was a hotshot at Texas Tech back in the day."

"Everybody knows that. It must be tough following in his footsteps."

"He really wanted to keep the legend alive."

"So what are you going to do?"

"I got offered a full ride by Texas State in San Marcos. Also UMHB and Sam Houston gave good offers, tuition, books and work study. I want an MBA so I can help Dad expand his business. He wants to break into Austin and San Antonio. The housing market is so unstable. It can be hard some years, kind of like farming, I guess. I was leaning toward Sam Houston but now with us together like this Texas State is starting to look a lot better, It's right down the highway from UT."

"You shouldn't let that influence your decision," Jaqui said.

"Why not? I really like spending time with you. We could do a lot of that if we were only thirty miles apart."

"We're just getting to know each other. Who knows what will happen with us. I'm just saying it's too big of a decision to let this be a factor. If we decide we can't live without each other we'll figure something out. Hell, Sam Houston was on my short list. I've been accepted there. I'm also looking at UNT which isn't close to any of them. Just make the decision based on the college, nothing else."

"What about you?" Randy asked. You told me you were considering UT because it was close to home and you could check on Sarge."

"That's different."

"How so?"

"He's family. He needs me."

Randy was quiet. Jaqui slid her hand down the inside of his upper thigh. "Let's just concentrate on having fun this trip," she said, moving closer to him and touching her cheek to his shoulder. Her dad was right. Randy thought of them as a couple. It made Jaqui uneasy. She really liked Randy but the thought of a relationship with all the attached responsibility made her uncomfortable. She flashed briefly on her mother and wondered if there might be some genetics working here.

Even at mid-afternoon the restaurant was busy. They had to wait fifteen minutes for a table. Noise in the dining room seemed to have a sharp edge. The acoustics were strange in that, though one could plainly understand the words of a conversation three tables away, it was almost impossible to discern what your partner across from you said. The couple soon gave up on conversation and watched each other chewing and smiling. The food was outstanding. Anticipation was building and a certain nervousness was beginning to interfere with communication. Words dwindled and glances and gentle touches became the preferred modes of discourse. They both kept an eye on the time.

Randy carried their bags although he relinquished his key to the valet parking attendant. They checked in under Jaqui's name. She handed the key card to Randy. On the elevator they didn't speak though they were alone. When the elevator stopped on the fourteenth floor they sighed in unison and exited the compartment. The room was spacious and modern with an understated elegance. Jaqui opened the curtains and stepped out onto the balcony. The city was alive with the energy of a thriving center of business and government. Randy stood behind her and wrapped her in his arms. She leaned into him. "It's like another world, a completely different civilization.," she said.

"Get used to it. You'll be going to school only a few blocks from here."

"I know. It's exciting, really, but kind of a culture shock." She turned and kissed him. Their tongues danced a playful game of tag. The summer heat radiating from the concrete walls met the primal warmth emanating from within. Hearts beat faster and moisture formed on their lips, hands and darker places. Jaqui slipped her hand into his and led him back inside. He closed the door behind them and pulled the drapes. The room grew dark.

Jaqui retrieved a hanger from the closet. "Take off your shirt," she said. Randy obliged. As she placed the shirt on the hanger he slipped out of his boots. She picked up her suitcase. "Get out of the pants and get comfortable. I'll be right back." After closing the bathroom door behind her she disrobed and put on the pink outfit. On a whim she pulled her boots back on.

When she reentered the room Randy was lying on the bed, the covers up to his waist, his fingers laced behind his head. She walked toward him just beyond arm's length, put her hands on her hips, and twisted at the waist.

"My God," Randy said, "I knew you were beautiful but... I don't even have words for this."

She knew she looked good and was reveling in his reaction. She went to him. As he reached for her she grabbed his wrists and firmly placed them back above his head. She straddled him as if he were a green-broke colt, one boot on each side of his knees. She leaned down and kissed him aggressively. When his tongue slipped past her lips she gently bit down on it. She felt an expansion under the covers just in front of her pelvis.

"Don't move," she said, releasing the grip on his wrists. Rising up on her knees, she crossed her arms and yanked the pink top off over her head. Her honey blond hair floated back down around her shoulders. She grabbed his wrists again and leaned over to kiss him. She didn't lie on him but instead let her taut nipples brush against his smooth chest. He moaned low and

47

long. She slid down and pulled back the covers. His erection was straining against his jockey briefs.

"I was right," she said. I had you figured for a whitey-tighty guy." She slipped her fingers under the elastic band. "These have got to go." As she was about to pull his underwear off it occurred to her that she had never seen an erection. She trembled. She decided to be honest with him. She dismounted and pulled back the covers. She stroked the inside of his thigh and brought her hand up to touch his underwear between his legs. His legs parted.

"I've never seen one," she said, "pictures, but not erect. Can you take them off? I don't want to hurt you." Her voice cracked. A dampness was saturating her own panties. In one quick motion he raised his hips and yanked off the underwear, tossing them on the floor. She put a hand on his chest and pushed him back down on the pillow. She couldn't take her eyes off the erection. "Can I touch it?"

"Please do," Randy panted in a disembodied voice. He reached up and grazed his knuckles against her nipple. Her breath caught in her throat. She took his hand and placed the palm firmly on her breast and left it there. Her breathing was becoming shallow. She reached out to touch the shaft. It was firmer than she expected but the skin was soft and loose. She wrapped her fingers around it and squeezed. It didn't give. "That doesn't hurt does it?" She asked.

"No. It feels really good."

She felt down where the balls were in a tight package. As she touched them the shaft twitched. She bent over and kissed its little head. She ran her tongue along the base of the shaft, Cosmo's suggestion. "Does that feel good?" she asked.

Randy grunted. He could no longer form words. She licked it a couple of times. It didn't seem to have any particular taste but the soft skin was pleasant on her tongue. She took it in her mouth and pretended it was a popsicle. She could feel Randy's pulse in it. His heart was pounding. She must be doing something right. He put his hand on the back of her head and pushed it into her throat. She jumped back, afraid she would gag. It startled her. She wrapped her fist around it before putting it back in her mouth so it couldn't go in so far. She kissed the head some more and licked around the edges but she couldn't bring herself to put the whole thing in her mouth again. Her nipple was getting sore from Randy pinching it too hard. She took his hand and placed it on the other breast.

"Would you like to put it in me now?" she asked.

"Are you ready?"

"I think so. I'm really wet." She pulled down her panties and drew one boot out. She straddled him again. Her inner thighs were slick almost to her knees. She placed the tip of the shaft against her opening. She tried to take it in but it didn't fit. She pressed down harder. Suddenly the little head popped in and she felt a twinge of pain shoot through her groin. One spot near the entrance felt really good, the same spot that felt good when she masturbated. She rubbed her fingers across that spot. As she held the spot between her fingers she pushed down hard. She yelped as something inside her gave way. For a split-second pain made her nauseous then the magic spot slammed against Randy's pelvis.

"Damn!" She screamed and slammed into him again. Part of her felt she was being ripped apart. Another part wanted to pound against Randy repeatedly. That part won out. She pounded against him. She had handfuls of Randy's shoulders gripped tightly and was throwing her hair around, slinging her head back and forth. Her eyes were out of focus. Saliva was leaking from her mouth. All she could think about was slamming that spot. It was swelling. So was the shaft inside her. She pulled her knees up and fell over on Randy's chest, her sweaty breasts sliding against his muscles while he began thrusting into her. She took him in as deep as she could, scrubbing the spot against his coarse pubic hair.

She realized she was screaming, or yelping, or crying. It was a primal animal sound. She began trembling. The shaft was bursting. Somehow she scrubbed harder. She felt the heat, the liquid filling her insides as the waves started. Trembling waves were emanating from the spot and flowing outward to her extremities, wave after wave. She couldn't breathe. She was leaking, sweating, trembling. Her insides were melting. The waves began to subside. She draped over Randy like a wet towel. A puddle of her drool was running down his neck. She tried to reach her hand to her mouth to stop it but the effort was just too much. Randy wrapped his arms around her. She felt his shaft softening, shrinking. Hot liquid flowed out of her. There was no further motion. Her senses were acute, the warm wet skin tingling, the primal animal smell, the sound of Randy's breath in her ear. Every synapse in her nervous system was humming. The intensity faded as the feeling of contentment washed over her. She wondered if her definition of normal might have changed forever.

Eventually she gathered enough energy to roll off of him. They were together, damp and warm. Randy's bicep was a substantial pillow for her head as they slipped away into a daze of fantastic relaxation; sleep without dreams, the ultimate perfect sleep. Time passed in slow breaths and subdued sighs until Randy moved out of bed. He looked down at Jaqui, naked except for her black boots, one of which sported tangled pink panties.

"You are without a doubt the most beautiful woman I have ever known." He closed the bathroom door behind him. She buried her head in the pillow to inhale the aboriginal aroma and slid back into nothingness. Outside the rain began falling.

∾

They sparkled that evening as they left for the dance hall. Jaqui had spent most of an hour showering and restoring herself to her previous state of innocence. The warm ache in her abdomen drove her desire to return to where the day had begun. She sensed that what she had experienced could never be repeated. She didn't want to do it again. She wanted to do it the first time again. Just maybe, if she returned to innocence, just maybe.

When they stepped out into the light rain the city was in heat. The last glow of natural light glistened on the wet pavement as streetlight and neon turned every angle into a prism. Dampness engulfed them and the wet still air smelled of people; people in languid repose, sloshing their bodies together, running on vibrant lust. The city pulled at Jaqui from somewhere low and dark. Animals lived here, in packs, for prey and protection, to devour or offer up graciously, their muscle, bone, and tendons for the common good.

"It's raining." Randy said. "We should have brought umbrellas."

"I'm good," Jaqui stated. "It's just rain."

Jaqui rode in the passenger seat, leaning against the door. She was alone. stuck in this container with the magnificent city trying to reach her, the asphalt tendrils unable to penetrate the steel. The throbbing heartbeat of downtown urging a tarantella dance while her feet were encased in the suffocating cab.

"Are you okay?" Randy asked. You're quiet."

"I'm good, just checking out the city. It's so beautiful in the rain."

"I guess. I'm kind of partial to the country, myself."

"I know. That's okay."

At the dance hall a veil of colored cellophane encased the building. It was a weeknight so for a mere eight dollars per couple they unwrapped the prize and stepped inside. It was movie-set perfect. Rock musicians in sparkly clothes pretended to play country music. Government workers and wrecker drivers in pearl snap shirts and fringed skirts pretended to be cowboys and cowgirls. Temporary couples pretended to be in love.

Jaqui danced every dance with Randy until he faded, then

others until the band took a break. Jaqui knew they had neither the instrumentation nor inclination to play a tarantella. She was pretending to dance. She laid her distracted head against Randy's shoulder. "This isn't what I hoped it would be. Can we go somewhere quieter?"

"Do you want to go back to the hotel?"

"I don't know. I'm hungry for something. Can we eat?"

"Sure, I could use a meal too. It's been quite a day."

Jaqui smiled with her mouth. Randy saw her eyes and knew he was losing her. if he ever had her. Maybe it would pass, this restlessness. They made a couple of passes down the major highways and only found chain restaurants open.

"The hotel restaurant is highly rated," Randy suggested. "Let's check it out."

"Sure." Anything to get out of the truck. She wanted to participate, not observe.

The restaurant was closed but the bar was serving light fare. As they entered, Jaqui imagined herself stepping back a half century in time. The environment was black and white, dark wood, hanging crystal, white towels and carefully choreographed white light dancing around the perimeters of darkness. Near one end of the bar a small very white man in a black turtleneck played a black baby grand piano. He artfully manipulated the black and white keys into haunting renditions of jazz standards and lounge versions of more contemporary melodies. They sat at a table closer to the piano than the other half dozen patrons. A pencil thin waitress in semi formal attire approached their table.

"What can I get you to drink?" She asked.

"Bourbon and Coke, Evan Williams if you have it," Jaqui said.

Randy looked at the table in front of him and hesitated. "Bud light," he sighed.

"I'll need to see your ID," the waitress said. Randy knew this was coming. He tried a trick he learned from his friends. He wrapped his license in a fifty-dollar bill and handed it to the waitress. She stepped to the other side of his chair with her back to the bartender. She slipped the bill into her breast pocket and studied his license. "Are you staying with us, Mr. Carson?"

"Yes, fourteenth floor, room 1423."

"Nice view."

"It sure is."

"I'll have those drinks right out."

"We'd like something from the kitchen too."

"I'll bring menus."

As the waitress left, Jaqui took Randy's hand. "Pretty damn smooth for a hillbilly. You probably could've got the same results by blowing her a kiss."

"Not with you sitting here outclassing her a hundred to one," Randy smiled. Jaqui was back, for now.

They spent the next hour nibbling at an appetizer tray and running up a pretty hefty bar bill. They drank and flirted and touched under the table. Heat was rising again. Jaqui was riding the warm wave of the bourbon. She hummed along with her favorite jazz standards and began forming an idea.

She rose and glided gracefully toward the piano, timing her arrival to coincide with the end of a popular up-tempo medley of Memphis style blues. She placed a five-dollar bill on top of the piano and leaned low over the keyboard suspending her cleavage within inches of the piano player's eyes.

"Do you happen to know a song from the forties or fifties called 'Someone to Watch Over Me'?" She asked in the most conspiratorial voice she could muster.

"Sure, I can play that," the gentleman replied, pulling his gaze up to meet hers.

"I would like it if you accompany me while I sing it."

"Well, okay, I don't have a mic."

"That's fine. It's a small room."

"What key?"

"I do it in A"

"Eight bar intro?"

"Sure"

He began the ballad. Jaqui leaned against the piano. When she began singing all motion in the bar stopped. Even the bartender put down his cloth and turned toward the piano. It took only seconds for the pianist to realize what was happening. He let Jaqui carry the melody. He added the occasional flourish and kept the meter steady in the bass line. When the song was over a unanimous round of applause awakened in the cozy room. Even the bartender and the piano player clapped. Randy stared in awe, unable to move or speak. Jaqui blew the patrons a kiss then turned and leaned over to the piano player again.

"Could you stop by my table when you take a break?"

"Ten minutes," the musician said.

Randy stood when Jaqui approached the table. She took his hand and gave him a peck on the cheek.

"Damn," he said. "I had no idea! That was incredible. I just wanted to take you in my arms and hold you forever. Girl, you can sing!"

"Thanks, Honey. That's the song I'm planning to sing for the talent part of the Watermelon Queen Pageant."

"You've got that locked up then."

"We'll see. There's some tough competition. Lilah is one girl that will be hard to beat."

"She's got nothing on you. Trust me, I know."

"Not everyone has the first-hand knowledge that you have." She gave Randy her most seductive glance.

The waitress brought another round of drinks to the table. "These are on the house," she said.

"See, paying off already," Randy stated.

"Quite a voice you have there, young lady. Bruce Lane." The piano player extended a hand. He was about as tall standing up as Jaqui was sitting down.

Jaqui Benderman," Jaqui offered her hand. "This is my friend, Randy Carson."

Randy stood and shook his hand. "You're quite a musician yourself, Bruce. Pleased to meet you. Can I get you a drink?"

"Thanks, but mine are free. So, Jaqui, what's up?"

"I have a business proposition. I'm entered in a pageant about 70 miles south of here and I want to hire you to accompany me on that song and maybe a couple of others. It's the Saturday after next in the afternoon. I have a bass player. We'd like to rehearse at least once but our schedule is flexible. If you are interested I need to know what you'd charge."

"We can probably work something out. First, though, can I make a suggestion?"

"Sure, anything."

"You should try the song in G. Your low range has a torch like quality that would come through in a slightly lower key."

"I could do that."

"I can give you a price but I'd like you to consider a barter deal. I'm playing a wedding reception the second week in July. If we could put a dozen songs together you could help me out, I could help you out. Maybe bring your bass player too. I could pay him a little and make sure he gets fed."

"Sounds like fun. I'll ask him."

"Would you like to sing a couple more."

"I know 'Somewhere Over the Rainbow' and a few Chicago blues standards. My favorites are the early twentieth century torch songs."

"Good stuff. Working here, I get to play a lot of that but they don't always work well as instrumentals."

Over the course of the next set Jaqui did three more songs and sang "Someone to Watch Over Me" in G. The couple didn't have to purchase any more drinks. Jaqui was feeling lightheaded when they shuffled back to their room. The elevator was almost too much.

Jaqui came to bed in shorts and a t-shirt. Randy was simultaneously disappointed and relieved, being unsure of his ability. He wasn't used to drinking, at least to that extent.

The drapes at the Four Seasons were designed to keep the room in total darkness, 24 hours a day if needed. Completely out of sync from their late night at the bar, Jaqui and Randy barely had time to shower and dress before checkout. Had they chosen to shower together, as they briefly discussed, it would have undoubtedly cost them additionally to extend their stay. They dropped the key card at the desk, at ten minutes before eleven. The brightness pierced their retinas when they stepped outside. Their brains jelled in the heat.

"Go eat?" Randy mustered. The two-word question being an enormous effort.

"Sure, whatever." Jaqui's brief reply, equally torturous. The humid city air clung to them like used shrink wrap from a back-street meat market. They found a busy taqueria nearby where they stood in line to order migas floating in melted orange queso. Randy bought a side order of menudo, a traditional hangover cure, but inedible after one bite. The food worked its magic, however, and by the time they reached their hometown they were holding hands and singing along with the radio.

They were only minutes away from Jaqui's house when Randy had to pull the truck to the edge of the narrow lane. A small pickup approached at an alarming rate of speed for a dirt road. The driver was wearing a maniacal grin and waved vigorously as she sped past. Jaqui waved back and laughed.

"Who was that?" Randy asked.

"Brenda Bartlett. She's about four hours late opening her shop and I think I know why."

"Isn't Sarge seeing her?"

"I'm guessing he saw pretty much all of her just recently."

"Oooh! Sarge is so bad!"

"As late as she was running he must actually be pretty good." Jaqui slid over next to Randy and leaned into his shoulder. "I'm glad he's happy," she said.

St. James Infirmary

Rickie Lee Jones

F riday morning's first light shone on an alien invasion of melons. From all directions, various sizes and colors of orbs peeked from beneath the broadleaf foliage. To the west a small field bore the final harvest of tan cantaloupes the size of volleyballs. To the south, light green elongated Ali Baba watermelons dotted several acres. It was an endangered strain Sarge had rescued from the agricultural devastation of Iraq. The huge, round, forest green Stone Mountain watermelons pimpled the landscape of the eastern plot. The north field of over 50 acres contained a dense population of the dramatically striped, Black Diamond strain that made Benderman Farm regionally famous. Two 24-foot enclosed trailers and a long flatbed were hitched to trucks and a tractor lined up alongside the road in front of the farmhouse. With the harvest at its peak, Sarge, Jaqui, Randy, Langley, three future varsity football players and a young couple scraping together date money had finished off a large platter of breakfast tacos. Each tow vehicle was equipped with a 5-gallon cooler of ice water. As the first sliver of solar orb snuck above the horizon, the crew pulled on their work gloves and sheathed their knives. A long day of back-shattering work lay ahead and yet the mood was boisterous. Sarge, Jaqui and

Randy each headed a three-person crew. Jaqui ended up with the starry-eyed couple. Randy picked two of the ballplayers that he hung out with on a regular basis. That left Sarge with Langley and the other football player. They didn't care for each other but Sarge wasn't putting up with any bullshit and made it clear.

"It's a job, it's not supposed to be fun. Grunts get a dime a melon and a nickel per cantaloupe, paid by the load. If you bust your ass you can make a hundred bucks or more each today - cash. Let's get these melons in. We'll break for lunch around two, otherwise figure on working 'til dark. It ain't easy money."

Jaqui drove the tractor. Randy and Sarge each had a truck. Jaqui had the flatbed trailer so was assigned the cantaloupe field. They had to be packed in crates. On the job training took two minutes. "Half inch of stem, except cantaloupes. Place the melons gently - no tossing, no dropping, no money for broken melons."

As always, with such a youthful group, an unspoken competition existed between the crews. Of course, the football players assumed their superiority. They didn't know Jaqui hoped to outpace Randy's team. She understood the motivation of her love-struck couple. Everything was in place for a record harvest. Poor Sarge didn't have a chance of winning the secret competition, or did he. Maybe he could foster some internal competition in his crew. In the agricultural community of Texas, work ethic is akin to a religion.

By lunch time the temperature hovering above the black clay was just above the triple digits. Sarge had shut down the irrigation a few days earlier to sweeten the melons. Beautiful broadleaf foliage wilted to limp sheets draped over the wandering vines like furniture in a long-abandoned plantation house. The flaccid foliage failed to protect the cracked soil from the searing sun. Heat radiated from the fractured earth. The only moisture came from the humid Texas air and the sweat that refused to evaporate from the skin of the picking crew. Rivulets of salty perspiration cut tiny channels in the layered dirt stuck to their faces. These were no longer pretty people. Their feisty demeanor had deteriorated to a grumbling acceptance of their fate. Income was being calculated on a melon-by-melon basis to distract from the growing discomfort. When lunch time came, no one ran, jumped or skipped. Their bodies converged like the walking dead on Sarge's truck where roast beef sandwiches, sweet tea and ice-cold watermelon awaited. The air seemed ten degrees cooler under the spreading oak. A light breeze rustled the leaves of the ancient tree.

Lunch eaten, the rejuvenated athletes decided to climb through the branches of the oak showing off their superior dexterity. The other workers used the brief respite to lie back in the grass and nap. The break seemed short. Sunburned fields awaited.

Jaqui and her efficient team had almost cleared the field of cantaloupes. Once done, she was to hook up another trailer and help out in the field of Black Diamonds. Sarge had used his break to slip into the house and retrieve his bottle of bourbon. After growing tired of the posturing between Langley and his crew mate, he decided to turn up the radio, sip the bourbon and let his charges do the heavy lifting. His efforts to pacify the young men had been futile so the new plan was to ignore them when possible.

As the trailers slunk through the wilted fields, time seemed to slow. Conversation degenerated to an occasional rude grunt. Even Jaqui's adolescent couple bickered about minor details; who would pick, who would crate, who was too slow. Fortunately the pickers were too exhausted for any physical confrontation.

Langley assumed it was exhaustion when Sarge dropped the second melon. It burst open. Sarge nearly tripped over the debris. "Shit!" Sarge said.

"Why don't you just drive the truck? The kid and I will finish picking this field," Langley suggested. He drew a cup of water from the cooler and offered it to the older man. Sarge gulped it down.

"Probably be better for the bottom line. My fingers seem to be a little slippery," Sarge agreed. As Langley took the cup back from Sarge, he smelled the sweetness of the bourbon on his boss' breath. Nothing was said. Langley guided Sarge to the door of the truck.

"Take it easy. We've got this, just drive," Langley assured. He went back to picking. Sarge reached under the seat for his bourbon. The sweet amber liquid washed the grit from his tongue. Through the windshield, the dusty images shimmered in the heat waves making his eyes water.

Acres of devastation stretched to the edge of sight as the day dimmed. The only melons left in the field were the unfortunate victims of exuberant adolescents. Thousands of honeybees were taking advantage of these human foibles. Even as the sun was slipping away the radiant heat was relentless.

A sixty-foot enclosed trailer stood next to the barn. Sarge's truck driver buddy was scheduled to pick it up prior to the next dawn. Like most rental containers, the floor was dock height. A conveyor lifted the melons from ground level. Four workers and a pallet jack were making quick work of crating and stacking while the remainder of the crew loaded the conveyor belt. Almost completely exhausted, they were taking 20-minute breaks between unloading each trailer. The end was in sight. As Sarge was prepared to back the last load up to the conveyor, the sun was history but the mercury vapor light attached to the front of the barn shone a ghostly light over the crew. A light breeze carried their stink but did little to cool their skin.

Jaqui stood at the base of the conveyor, one hand on her hip, watching Randy direct Sarge as he backed the final trailer load of melons into position. Something in the authoritative way

Randy handled the job connected with a hormonal trip wire somewhere in her southern hemisphere. Her free hand had no recourse but to reach out and give the sweat-sheened denim covering his gluteus maximus a firm squeeze. He spun, but upon seeing Jaqui broke into a red-faced grin. Suddenly his expression turned to confusion as he seemed to lunge, open armed, toward her. She jumped back as he fell to the ground. Screams came from the workers in the container as the brake lights from the trailer turned the scene blood red, illuminating only the upper half of Randy's twisting body. The corner of the trailer had ripped through his jeans and buried deeply into the exact muscle Jaqui had fondled moments earlier.

"Get it off me!" Randy screamed. Jaqui knelt beside him as the crew yelled at Sarge to pull forward.

Jaqui cupped her hands around Randy's face. "I'm sorry," she cried as Randy was jerked from her. The angle iron frame of the loaded trailer had attached to the torn jeans, dragging the screaming boy through a pool of blood-soaked dirt, finally releasing him 10 feet away. A fresh pool of blood formed around him. His boot heel rested between his shoulder blades.

"Get some towels," Langley ordered, taking charge. Everyone tossed sweat soaked bandanas and hand towels toward Randy's twisted frame. "No time for an ambulance. He's bleeding bad! Get your car!" He was staring at Jaqui. "Now! Hurry!"

It took Jaqui a second to respond. She was trying to wake up from the nightmare but in a moment she was running. As Jaqui pulled up in the car the crew slid a tarp under Randy. He had stopped screaming.

"Get him in the back! Jaqui, you, too. I'll drive. Somebody call the ER and let them know we're coming." Randy's legs had been straightened out and were across Jaqui's lap. Langley shouted instructions. "Keep pressure on the bleeding. Keep him awake."

Langley's eyes never left the road as he burned through the

darkness at speeds in excess of 90 miles per hour. In the back seat the lovers pledged their undying devotion. Jaqui whispered holy plea bargains. By the time they reached the hospital Randy's bleeding had stopped, so had his breathing. His parents were waiting at the hospital when they pulled his body from the car and pronounced him dead on arrival.

Jaqui heard the voices but never spoke, or cried, or moved as the warm blood coagulated into a goo. Eventually, Langley drove her back home. The darkness was turning gray when they made the final turn back to the farm. Through the cloud of dust ahead, red taillights burned. The truck was bobtailing in to pick up the load of melons. When the dust got in Jaqui's throat she coughed once and the flood burst loose. Langley just drove.

Empty Bed Blues

- Bessie Smith

C louds are unusual during the last weekend in June. Texas summers are notoriously hot and dry. This morning, however, they're boiling on the western horizon, a suggestion of a future storm if not a promise. The normally laconic town is electric with tourists; decorations and other trappings of the festival; including a parade and carnival.

Jaqui was still devastated from Randy's death and the town was looking for someone to blame for the untimely death of their celebrated football star. Her feeling that the town held her responsible was not unfounded, though Sarge was the true untouchable here. Jaqui blamed him too. Like most folks, she couldn't accept the official version that it was merely an unfortunate accident.

Jaqui had missed rehearsing with Bruce and Langley, due to the funeral, until last night when they spent a few distracted minutes going over three songs. It was a desperate but uninspired rendering, almost causing Jaqui to bail on the whole idea. Still, life goes on.

Langley offered to pick up Bruce and bring him out from Austin. He took his mother along to get her out of the house.

His dad was spending a lot of time working since her release from the hospital. She'd been slipping into a state of depression from being at home and unable to perform as a homemaker. Her motor skills hadn't returned to normal. Even her speech was difficult to understand to the point she rarely spoke. Langley hoped spending some time on the road with her would encourage her to put in some effort.

As Jaqui entered the pageant headquarters it didn't surprise her that everyone stopped to stare without acknowledging her. This had become the norm. She was surprised that Lilah immediately left her entourage to come over and share a hug. Her tension became a glow of gratitude as Lilah's petite frame leaned into her.

"Oh, Jaqui, wasn't Randy's funeral service just beautiful? What a memorial! The whole town is going to miss him but nowhere near as much as we will," Lilah said. Jaqui tried to return the gesture but the confusion was causing a tornado in her brain.

"He died right in my lap. I tried. I just… I couldn't… I thought he would make it." Jaqui felt tears burning her cheeks. Lilah gripped her tighter, digging fingertips into Jaqui's back.

"C'mon, let's get you cleaned up. I'll show you where they set up the dressing rooms. It's like a couple of closets. I brought a lighted mirror you can use. It'll be okay."

Jaqui followed Lilah to what only hours earlier had been maintenance closets. A single dim light bulb hung from a rack of overhead pipes. A couple of folding tables and various folding chairs were scattered about. Maintenance supplies were pushed to the corner and covered with dinghy sheets.

"Well, this is it. Pretty lame, right?" Lilah said. She pulled a suitcase from the corner. "The mirror's in here."

Jaqui hung her garment bag over a wire dangling from one of the overhead pipe racks while Lilah pulled the mirror from the luggage and plugged it into a power strip. She took out a flask and offered it to Jaqui.

"This helps with the butterflies. I'll share. I know it's been a rough week for you." Jaqui didn't hesitate. When the bourbon hit her tongue it reminded her of her first night with Randy. The tears welled up again and she took a long drag on the bottle as if the flavor could carry her back to that night.

"Hey, easy!" Lilah said. "It's a long evening. I mean, you can have as much as you want, but, just saying…"

Jaqui stared at her face in the mirror. She saw how drawn and tired she looked. The whiskey warmed her core but on the outside she looked lost. "I'm sorry," she said, a phrase that had become her mantra. The woman in the mirror spoke words unfamiliar to Jaqui "I'm not sure I can do this."

"Oh bull, we're going to get you fixed up real pretty. Take another sip if you need to," Lilah said, and pulled out an elaborate makeup kit.

Jaqui relaxed. She remembered back to the fall semester of their senior year when she and Lilah were part of a tight knit group of cheerleaders following the football bus in their sponsors' Suburban; talking about high school crushes and designer clothes, how she always felt slightly out of sync. She felt that way again. This time, though, Lilah seemed to want her to be a part of it.

There was a knock on the door. Lilah slipped the flask back in her suitcase. "Come in," she said.

Langley entered, followed by Bruce, making the space crowded. "Hey guys," Jaqui said. "This is my band," she told Lilah. "You know Langley. This other handsome devil is Bruce Lane, possibly the best pianist in Austin. Bruce, this pretty lady is Lilah, my best girlfriend from school and my fiercest competition."

"Yeah, very fierce, Grrrr," Lilah growled.

Jaqui almost smiled then noticed the strange look on Langley's face as he studied her.

"How's your mom?" she asked.

"About the same. It was good to get her out of the house," Langley replied.

"She here?"

"No, I took her home. She really liked Bruce though." Langley still had an intense focus on Jaqui. "Are you okay?" He asked.

"Never better. We're going to rock this, right guys?"

"Yup," Bruce said.

"Where should we stash our gear?" Langley asked.

"I'll show you. Jaqui's still getting ready." Lilah said. "Girl, use whatever you need of mine. I'll be right back."

Jaqui was alone in the dank utility closet. She stared at her reflection, laid out her makeup kit and dug the flask out of Lila's bag. After taking a long pull she put it back. "Whatever I need," she said to the scared little girl in the mirror.

There were two public events in the Watermelon Queen pageant, the formal attire portion, after which the contestants each had a private Q&A with a panel of out-of-town judges, and the talent program. In previous years the competition was opened by a swimsuit contest. It drew a huge crowd. The local Council of Churches negotiated this crowd pleaser out of existence. Now the Intergalactic Seed Spitting contest and the Saturday Night Boot Scootin' dance were the festival's biggest draws. The pageant still had the big prize money, however, partly due to some savvy negotiating by the former pageant director in charge during the ruckus with the Council of Churches.

Jaqui and Lilah had differing opinions on how Jaqui should wear her hair. No big surprise there. Jaqui always liked having her hair flowing loose but she finally agreed to let Lilah put it up for the formal competition. There was plenty of time to brush it out before the talent contest. This negotiation dwarfed many Senate budget hearings. All nine contestants appeared onstage simultaneously in their formals after which the Q&A was done in alphabetical order. The talent was then performed in reverse alphabetical order giving Jaqui plenty of time to change and set up for her performance.

The judges seemed pleased with her plans to study journalism but less than thrilled that all her religious training happened in the last few months. Jaqui had enough insight to at least feign a dramatic conversion. The mint gum she swallowed just before going onstage masked the whiskey. The whiskey masked her jitters. She'd made a reasonably good impression in the interview.

Lilah was second in line at the talent show. She followed a lackluster dramatic reading by a high school sophomore. Lilah's energetic dance routine to a medley of military marches managed to work in a red, white and blue one-piece dance outfit that came dangerously close to thumbing a nose at the swimsuit ban. Who would complain? After all, it was patriotic. Jaqui missed most of the other acts. Reportedly the acts included twirlers, tap dancers, a poetry reading and a girl who sang country karaoke. Before catching up with Langley and Bruce she had another conversation with Lilah's flask as she brushed out her hair and changed into her diaphanous baby doll dress and stiletto heels. The heels brought her height to over 6 feet, most of which appeared to be leg. The liquor made her feel the breeze in an enclosed room. She felt sexy, and looked it.

Bruce played the opening bars to "Summertime" as Jaqui strutted onto the stage, her flouncy blue dress swinging with the motion of her hips. She gave the judges a tiny parade wave, took the mike off the stand and hit the first note perfectly on cue. She worked the front of the stage as if she were playing Vegas. The audience was mesmerized. For the judges benefit her second song was an old gospel number that she belted out with her voice and her body, Mavis Staples style, causing strands of sun-bleached hair to stick to her cheeks, a good look for her. By the end of the song the audience was on their feet and she was reveling in the moment. When Bruce and Langley began "Someone to Watch Over Me " for her final number, she held a finger up to the audience indicating a pause. She leaned over and whispered in Bruce's ear then stepped over and hung her elbow on Langley's shoulder, whispered in his ear and gave him a little kiss on the cheek. She took her place in front of the duo, spread her feet apart and set the tempo by snapping her fingers. The boys launched into a raucous blues progression while Jaqui kept time with her hips. Twelve bars in she began growling Bessie Smith's "Empty Bed Blues". Men and boys in the crowd were whistling and yelling. You could smell the testosterone in the air. After holding a powerful final note she set the mic back in the stand, blew the audience a kiss and turned to leave. Even the judges were on their feet.

On her second step away from center stage, as she was still smiling and waving at the audience, she felt the microphone cord snake around her ankle. She looked down in time to see the floor coming toward her. The hand she used to break her fall gave with a pop and her forehead hit the floor. Just before losing consciousness she saw Langley lean down over her.

When she woke up in the ambulance a paramedic and Langley were beside her, along with a deputy sheriff.

"How are you feeling?" Langley asked.

She stared back and groaned. "What ... happened?" She whispered.

"You tripped and hit your head."

"My hand hurts." She tried to raise her right wrist but the shooting pain almost made her puke.

"We're going to get you to the hospital," the EMT said. "How much have you had to drink?"

"What?" Jaqui moaned.

"Someone reported that you had been drinking. We need to know before we can treat you."

"Just a couple of sips, much earlier."

"The Breathalyzer put you at 0.15, almost twice the legal limit."

Langley shook his head. "This is all bullshit. She's been with me. She needs to go to the hospital. We can work this out later."

"Sure," the deputy said. "I'll follow."

Sarge sat in the truck staring through the dusty windshield. Of the two other vehicles in the parking lot one of them belonged to Julio. He eased out of the cab and kicked an empty beer can toward the building. The can made it about halfway. Deciding he didn't want to put any more effort into the project, he crushed it with the heel of a cracked leather work boot and let it lie. As he entered the door he could only see the usual neon beer signs until his eyes adjusted, then, Julio behind the bar, staring with a confused look on his face.

"Hey, Sarge," Julio said, " didn't think I'd see you in here today, what with Jaqui's big show." He poured a double shot of Jim Beam into tall glass and sat it in front of Sarge.

"Better put some water and ice in there. I may be here a while," Sarge said.

"Everything okay?"

"Shit, Julio, nothing's been okay for a week. Jaqui barely talks to me, or anyone for that matter. She did talk long enough to ask me to stay away from the pageant."

"Oh, damn!"

And Brenda, all she's done since the thing with Randy is try to get me baptized."

"Well?"

"I told her I preferred showers but I swear if I have to live without her loving much longer I might just let 'em hold me under. It's one thing to not have it, it's another to have it and get it taken away."

"So are y'all still seeing each other?"

"Some, when I'm not here or working but all she talks about these days is 'the redeeming power of our Lord and Savior'. This is the only place in town I can go without folks looking at me like some kind of monster. Hell, I didn't murder the kid. It was an accident. He wasn't paying attention." Sarge picked up the glass, swirled the ice cubes around in the brown liquid and sat it back down. Two young guys in the corner motioned to Julio. He went to serve them.

Sarge looked at his reflection in the bar glass. He was haggard and a little dustier than usual. Realizing that some body maintenance might improve his disposition, he downed his drink and set the empty glass on a $10.00 bill.

"I'm out of here," he hollered to Julio. "I've got to get cleaned up. I've got a show to see."

He was right, a good shower and shave was restorative. He even trimmed his mustache and fingernails. When he arrived at the civic center he had to wait on the street while an ambulance with police escort pulled out of the parking lot. He assumed someone had fallen off a carnival ride or choked on a water-melon seed. It didn't take long to find out the facts. Something had happened to Jaqui. Either she tripped and broke her nose, or her arm, or passed out drunk, but everyone agreed she had put on one hell of a show. He ran back to the truck and gunned it toward the hospital.

It was almost 24 hours later when Sarge and Jaqui headed toward home from the county courthouse. During the 6 hours she spent in the emergency room Sarge and Langley never left her side, neither did the deputy. Once released from the hospital she was taken into custody. Langley went home. Sarge, of course, tried to work out her release. As late as it was, there was no way she wouldn't have to spend the night in jail. Fortunately, her wrist was only sprained. With a charge of drinking in public as a minor hanging over her head she failed to see the positive side of intact bones.

Sarge drove slowly, occasionally glancing over at Jaqui who stared directly ahead. She was still wearing the blue baby doll dress but it no longer maintained any of its bounce. They were on the last dirt road of the journey before either of them spoke.

"I hate this town," Jaqui muttered.

"I don't think you can blame the town for this," Sarge replied. Jaqui shot him a look that should have seared his flesh.

"Take me to pick up my car."

"You need to get some rest. We'll get it tomorrow."

"No, I need it now!" She was emphatic. "I've got some things I need to take care of. Take me!"

Sarge turned the truck around. Silence resumed.

Jaqui wasn't sure exactly what she wanted to do but some of her things were at the civic center and she wished to leave no trace. When she got to the dressing room her things had been ransacked. She threw them in her car and went to find the pageant coordinator. She located him at the civic center office. All motion stopped when she stepped in.

"Jaqui? Are you okay?" He asked.

"I'll live. It's only a sprain. How did I place?"

"Can you step in here?" Jaqui was led into the copier room and the door shut behind her. "That was one of the most amazing performances I have ever seen but... we had to disqualify you."

"What! Why?"

"Come on, Jaqui. You were drunk. The police found the bourbon in your luggage and the Vicodin."

"Bullshit, I don't take pills and the bourbon wasn't mine. You saw me perform. A drunk couldn't do that."

"I also saw you collapse."

"I tripped. Stiletto heels aren't exactly natural footwear for me."

"Your breath test puts you at twice the limit. You have

incredible talent. You might want to consider getting some help."

"This is bullshit! That test was so bogus! Fuck you and fuck this bullshit contest! Y'all can kiss my ass!" She ran out of the building before anyone could see the tears start flowing.

Jaqui sat in her car and let the anger burn off her tears. Once she could breathe she drove straight to Lilah's house. She parked in the driveway and leaned on the horn. Mrs. Snipes came out. Jaqui rolled down the window.

"Get Lilah, I need to talk to her."

"She's not here."

"Bullshit. That's her car right there!"

"She's with friends."

"I pity them. Tell that cheating cunt to keep her back to the wall. I'll be looking for her."

"You need to leave before I call the police."

"Fuck you, call 'em. I don't give a fuck!" she pulled out and chirped the tires as she left, wishing she had a more powerful vehicle. Once again, the clouds were rolling on the western horizon as she turned off the paved road, likely another broken promise of rain. Closer to home the melon fields were tangles of brown dry vines. Crows scattered through the litter noisily sparring for the last vestiges of rotted melon. Dry leaves lifted lazily on the building breezes as spinning cones of dust briefly appeared and disintegrated. This season had ended, for melons, for rain, for redemption.

As the car bumped down the last mile, the echo rumbling from the bloody rear seat having been removed, Jaqui had calmed enough to consider her situation. She had enough money saved for maybe a semester and a half of tuition. Her arrest would likely nullify her acceptances to the universities but maybe she could attend community college, not what she wanted. Then there was the town, she had no intention of living like a pariah. She'd burned those bridges anyway.

By the time she made it home she was exhausted. She

needed sleep. She needed a hug. She needed her daddy. When she pulled in, though, the house was empty. Sarge hadn't made it back. She went to the cabinet and got the bottle of Evan Williams. She sat at the table with a shot glass and got busy. Yeah, I've heard the whispers. *What happened to the Bendermans? All the Bendermans are drunks. See what happens when there's no mama, no woman of the house.* She dialed Brenda Bartlett. "Brenda, have you seen my daddy?"

"No, sweetie, not for a couple of days. Y'all let me know if there's anything I can do."

"Thanks, I'm okay. If you see him, please tell him to call home?"

"I will, Honey. See you Sunday?"

"Sure." Jaqui hung up and poured another shot.

The wind picked up as the sky darkened. The old house began to creak and moan. Shadows disappeared but she didn't need to see well to cram her clothes and the basic essentials into backpacks and pillowcases. She went out and backed her car up to the front porch. Without a backseat she had a lot of cargo space. She tossed what was left of her life into the vehicle and slammed the trunk. Back inside, she took the bottle by the neck and turned it up. When she couldn't take the burn anymore she slammed it down on the table leaving the cap off. She tore the cover off the front of one of Sarge's Louis L'amour novels and wrote a note:

Dad,
I'm done.
-Jaqui.

She'd only driven a few hundred yards when the first fat raindrops began popping on the windshield, leaving pockmarks in the dust. When she hit the wipers her view was obliterated by streaks of mud. She forged ahead. When the windshield began to clear she saw the headlights weaving toward her. She knew it was Sarge. He pulled to the side of the lane and put his hand out the window. She focused her eyes straight ahead and passed without slowing. Once past, she allowed herself a glance in the rearview mirror. The brake lights on the truck stayed on for quite some time. Then the truck wobbled back onto the road toward the house. It was 70 miles to the city. She knew if she had any tears left they would be falling. They weren't.

A Change Is Gonna Come
Otis Redding

Jaqui woke up in the Motel 6. She felt a numbness that neither the interstate traffic nor the couple arguing upstairs could penetrate. She went out to the car and grabbed a couple of random bags. After a hot shower she walked across the parking lot to the Waffle House, picked up a free newspaper and ordered breakfast. *Time to regroup. Where to start. I've got to put this behind me.* An ad on the back page caught her eye. She snickered under her breath. Behind me...right, too fucking perfect. She tore out ads for local tattoo parlors.

"She left," Sarge said. He'd been awakened by Langley's call. When he looked at the wall clock it said 6:30. With melon season essentially over it was early for him to be awake. He thought maybe the clock stopped. Then he noticed the plastic tail of the cat was swinging back and forth and the eyes shifted side to side as if they were searching for the next tragic event.

"She was gone when I got home last night, and from her note, I reckon she'll be gone a while, maybe for good."

"What about her wrist?" Langley asked.

"She's tough, she'll manage. It's just a sprain."

"Any idea where she went?"

"Austin, probably. She loves it there."

"I should go see her. I don't guess you know where she'd hang out?"

"Not a clue, but I'll holler if I hear from her."

"Cool. How are you holding up?"

"I'm okay for now." Sarge took a deep breath. "I just hope she doesn't do anything stupid. She's pretty pissed off."

"Yeah, well, maybe she has a right to be. Just checking. I've got to get to school. Stay in touch."

Sarge looked around at the empty house. Everything seemed older and more worn than it had been. He crawled back into bed and stared out the window.

Summertime

Janis Joplin

H e sat alone in the student center trying to look like he belonged there, which was strange, because he did. He'd hoped college would be different from high school. After six weeks as a full-time student at SACC, he decided it was more of a continuation. The classes weren't difficult. Langley was smart. School wasn't the problem, it was the isolation. His intelligence, coupled with a steadfast moral compass, put a lot of people off. It didn't help that he had the chiseled features of a Norse god. The few people that got past this visage ran into a shyness making him seem aloof. His handful of friends found an endearing wit and quirky sense of humor. Those friends, it seemed, were fluttering away to the corners of the globe.

Plan and execute had been his mantra. It had always worked for him. But the older he got, the more shades of gray he noticed. "It sucks to be smart," he'd recently told his dad. "Most people just do what's expected of them or what the TV or government tells them to. They make it through just fine."

"You'll be fine as long as you keep God on your side," his dad replied. Langley didn't know what that meant. God had never got around to mentioning whether He was on his side or not. In fact, God had never said anything to Langley.

"It's just not fair!" Langley said.

Dad chuckled. "Show me the contract."

"What contract?"

"The one you were born with saying life would be fair. I didn't get to sign that contract, did you?"

Still it seemed there should be some reward for being smart. He missed his best friend. They'd known each other since grade school. When she was eleven and her mama wandered off one day, they became very close. She saw through his shyness and he nudged her through her grief with his sardonic wit, two independent souls who meshed well. He couldn't really blame her for her meltdown. Life had thrown her a curve. Still, he figured, that's what friends are for. Now he didn't even know where she was.

"Your name's Langley, right?" The girl asked.

"Yeah."

"I'm Sara. I sit behind you in Criminal Justice?"

"Right. Sara." Langley was afraid the skinny little girl was going to pee her pants. She looked terrified.

"I had car trouble on Monday and I missed class. I wondered if I could look at your notes. I mean, were there any notes? What went on?" Sara was shifting her weight from one foot to the other.

"We worked through chapter four. I made some notes. Have a seat and I'll dig them out. Seems like the teacher stayed pretty close to the book but let's see what I've got."

A wave of relief washed over Sara and she plopped down beside him, her big brown eyes sparkling. "You don't know how much this means to me. I was freaking out. I figure we're due a pop quiz in that class any day."

"Yeah, but that class is pretty easy. This stuff is mostly common knowledge."

"I don't know," Sara said. "I have trouble with the history and all those laws."

"I'm like that with English Lit. I can do the math and

78

science and stuff you can prove but you start in with that emotional and spiritual stuff and I have trouble getting my head around it." That was more than Langley had told anyone about himself in weeks. He'd startled himself. "Not that it matters to you," he said.

"I can usually bullshit my way through that stuff. Maybe we should team up on some of this."

Langley was trying to figure out if this waif was serious or just friendly or what. He could use the company. "Sure, who do you have for English Lit?"

"Markham, just like you. Same class, two rows over. You probably haven't noticed me."

It was true. He hadn't. "Yeah, now I remember. You have that pink backpack."

"This one?" She picked it up from the floor. "Don't worry. It happens all the time." She almost smiled then looked away as she dropped the backpack.

Langley found something about the little woman intriguing. Her ability to overcome her shyness seemed contagious.

Several patrons sat idly on the porch in quiet conversations. Others were absorbed in their notebooks and iPads. They were all sweating in the thick air and none seemed to mind. Jaqui stood on the porch taking in the building. Except for the doors, it resembled a barn. An acrid aroma of roasting coffee permeated the atmosphere. The double doors before her were ornately carved slabs of some exotic dark wood with long ribbons of blond grain running through the entire nine-foot height, beautiful but foreboding in their massiveness. Her stomach churned. She grabbed the handle. As she pushed the door open her body was awash in cool air. Numerous mechanical noises mingled with an agricultural smell. Behind the bar, to the left, baristas prepared exquisite caffeinated beverages for a throng of mostly pierced and tattooed customers. Near the back of the building, a tall forest green machine hissed as the stainless-steel arms spun through freshly roasted coffee beans,

Jaqui turned toward the far end of the building. Gathered around a low stage was a group of people as diverse as one might find at the Department of Motor Vehicles. Most of them had guitars. There was an old upright piano at one side of the stage. Several other instruments were being simultaneously tuned and tinkered with, including a banjo, a mandolin, an accordion and what looked like a long tube made from large diameter bamboo. This was the group Jaqui was looking for. As she approached, a grizzled man with a thin black ponytail looked up. He was clutching a scarred and faded mandolin.

"Is this where I sign up for the open mic?" she asked. The man pointed toward a bespectacled boy not much older than Jaqui. "See Anton. He's the dude," the mandolin player said and returned to caressing his instrument.

Jaqui made her way through the small crowd surrounding Anton. "Can I sign up?"

"I've got a couple of spots left, 8:15 and 10:30. You're new here, right?" Anton asked.

"Yes, sir," Jaqui answered, drawing a subdued chuckle from the crowd.

"Just Anton is fine," Anton said. "This ain't the UK. You get fifteen minutes or three songs whichever is shorter. What's your instrument?"

"I sing," Jaqui replied.

"No, I mean what do you accompany yourself on?"

"I'll sing acapella tonight."

"Great," Anton sighed. A slight sneer wafted across his lips. "Which time do you want?"

"I'm not in a hurry. Give me the 10:30 spot."

"Name?"

"Jaqui Benderman, J-A-Q-U-I."

"I'm Anton, A-N-T-O-N." The group snickered again.

"Tough crowd," Jaqui said and found an empty table near the back of the area. She perched her raw butt cheeks on the edge of the only metal chair around. The coolness soothed the burn of the fresh tattoo. Almost immediately a heavy-set woman ambled over to Jaqui's table. Her long brown hair was beginning to show streaks of gray. Her smile lit up her face. Without hesitation she pulled out a chair, flipped it around and straddled it backward.

"Don't mind Anton. The little shit is full of himself," the woman said. "He had a record deal a couple of years ago but the label went belly up. If he was half as good as he thinks he is, he'd own Nashville."

"No, he doesn't bother me. I'm just new at this. I don't know what to expect," Jaqui said.

"Don't worry, most of us are pretty easy going. It's a weekly deal for a lot of us, then you get your local heroes that stop by to try out new material. Sometimes a road act sneaks in incognito. Hell, once we had Eddie Vedder come in and perform under an assumed name. Most of us knew who he was. Funny, though, Anton didn't. When Eddie asked if he could do an extra song Anton ran him off the stage. A reviewer from The Chronicle was here. Anton nearly got fired. It was hilarious! I'm Penny, by the way, Penny Huckster. It's a stage name but it's what I use here."

Jaqui was settling into a pleasant conversation with Penny when the door slammed. A little girl who looked to be about twelve years old ran toward Anton, dragging a guitar case almost as big as she was.

"Anton, honey, you save a spot for me, please? I am so sorry for being late." The girl was yelling from across the room. "I've got 8:15 left," Anton replied.

"Too early. What else you have?" The girl was obviously flustered.

"8:15 is it."

The girl looked around at the others. When no one spoke

her eyes began to smolder. "Shit! I guess I am stuck with it." She stomped over and sat down at the table with the mandolin player who looked up briefly before turning his attention back to his instrument. The girl set her face in a pout.

"That's Katrine Boneta," Penny said. "She's from Europe somewhere. She came here to be a big star, like most of us. She's really good. She might even make it someday. She just hasn't figured out how it works yet."

"How does it work?" Jaqui asked.

Penny laughed. "Hell, if I knew, I wouldn't be sitting here right now. Far as I can tell, some make it, some don't. It doesn't necessarily have much to do with talent. More like luck, looks and who you know."

"She seems upset," Jaqui observed, motioning toward Katrine.

"Her shit don't stink, if you know what I mean, a bit of a prima donna."

"Weird attitude for a little kid."

"Little yeah, kid, well, she's probably older than you are," Penny said.

"Seriously? She looks about twelve."

"I know she's at least drinking age. In fact, she usually has a pretty good buzz on by the end of the night."

"When does the show start?" Jaqui asked.

"Seven-thirty, about five minutes from now. We should get a better seat."

"Where's the audience?"

"They don't start showing up 'til around nine. That's why nobody wants the early spots." Penny stood and started toward the table where Katrine and the mandolin player were sitting. "C'mon," she said. Jaqui followed.

"Connor, this is Jaqui," Penny said to the mandolin player.

"What?" Conner replied.

"I said, 'This is Jaqui'. Jaqui, Connor Forest, we play together sometimes. Connor sits in with folks a lot."

The mandolin player watched Penny as she spoke then turned to Jaqui. "Sorry. I'm deaf on this side, too many years of rock and roll. Jaqui is it? You'll have to talk into my good ear. Pleased to meet you." Conner extended a thin well-manicured hand that didn't fit with the rest of his unkempt look.

Jaqui closed both hands around his diminutive appendage. "Good to meet you, too, Conner," she said.

"What?" Conner replied, "Oh, yeah, sure. Have a seat."

"Katrine, this is Jaqui. She's new at this. We're going to show her the ropes, right?" Penny said.

"Sure." Katrine focused on Jaqui. "You write?"

"What do you mean?" Jaqui asked, puzzled.

"Your material, you are a songwriter?"

"Oh, -- no I, well, I've written a couple but they pretty much suck. I like to sing jazz standards," Jaqui explained. Conner glanced up from his instrument. a smile came to his lips.

"Conner and I put out a CD of 20s and 30s songs, stuff that originally came out on 78s," Penny said, "about 2 years ago, I guess. We sold a couple thousand copies, got some airplay on public radio. It worked pretty well for us, got some paying gigs out of the deal."

"Cool!" Jaqui's eyes brightened. "I've only sang in front of people a few times outside of church."

"Where's your guitar?" Katrine asked.

"I don't have one," Jaqui replied.

"You can use mine," Katrine offered. Penny's eyebrows elevated.

"Thanks, Katrine," Jaqui said, "but it wouldn't do any good. I don't know how to play one."

Feedback from the PA halted the conversation, followed by a thumping on the microphone. "I'd like to welcome everyone to the Wednesday night Open Mike here at the Ruta Maya Coffee House. I'm your host, Anton Decker. I'm going to open with a short set and then we'll have a diverse array of live music for your listening pleasure all the way 'til midnight."

Without further adieu Anton played. His songs were well crafted country tearjerkers performed with a nasal twang, backed by acoustic guitar work that was precise but uninspired.

Various acts followed. One notable performer was a college-age kid who flat picked Delta blues on an old Martin guitar. The kid, who billed himself as The Kid, rocked back and forth in another dimension as his fingers danced across the fretboard. He didn't sing. He didn't need to. The guitar knew the language. Conner joined him for his last song. It was obvious they had played together. Jaqui was transfixed, as were most of the patrons of the coffeehouse. When The Kid finished his set the applause lasted for over a minute. Jaqui looked around and noticed Katrine was nowhere to be seen.

"What happened to Katrine?" Jaqui asked. "Isn't she up in a few minutes?"

"Probably went outside to tune," Penny said.

Jaqui took leave and stepped into the swampy outside air. It was still light; though the sunset was being blocked by tall, angry thunderheads, intermittently illuminated by blinding arcs of intense white lightning. She walked around the building until she saw Katrine sitting on a wooden box. Katrine appeared to be lost in meditation, her eyes closed, her head tilted back. She was leaning against the building. She exhaled smoke.

"Katrine?" Jaqui spoke.

"Hey," Katrine said, opening one eye. She offered the joint to Jaqui.

"No, I'm good," Jaqui said. Why'd you leave? The Kid was awesome."

"He is Adam Wolf, not Kid!" Katrine said. "He is fucking asshole!"

"Oh, y'all have a history?"

"No. He would not be with me. I am devil to him." Katrine took a silver flask from between her legs, unscrewed the cap and took a deep swallow. She held the flask out to Jaqui."

"What have we here?" asked Jaqui, taking the flask from Katrine's tiny hand.

"El Presidente, it is brandy, I think from Mexico. Very tasty." Jaqui took a sip. "Yummy!"

"Have more if you want. I have whole bottle in guitar case." Katrine took a deep drag from the joint. "Tuning up," she laughed, "me, not guitar."

Jaqui smiled. "I know what you mean. I always like a little bourbon to loosen the vocal cords." She sat down beside Katrine. "Looks like we're going to get some weather."

"Good. Might be cooler. When I come to Texas I did not know it was in Hell."

"Well, if you are the Devil, you should fit right in."

"I am only Devil to fool who lives in Bible land. I do not live by Bible."

"Yeah, I went to church for a while but mainly to sing, and all my friends went."

"Silly friends," Katrine said. Jaqui had to giggle at Katrine's point of view. Katrine put out the joint and reached in her purse. She pulled out a tiny bottle of perfume and spritzed herself. "Want some?" she asked Jaqui. "It is time for me to play, almost."

"No, but thanks," Jaqui said. They stood up and Jaqui dwarfed the little woman. She wanted to take Katrine's hand and guide her back inside as if she were a child. The distant thunder was finally cutting through the traffic noise from South Congress Avenue as if the flashes of lightning were disturbing some long dormant beast.

Katrine took the stage. She sat on a wooden chair with the flat top guitar hiding most of her body. Only her head and shoulders were visible above the instrument. Her hands tickled the strings producing an intricate melody over a structured counterpoint, a masterful combination of folk and classical fingerpicking. She finally began singing a Celtic murder ballad from centuries past, her voice all breath and sorrow. Her second

song was a humorous, quick paced ditty with political under-
tones, a contemporary original that pleased the small audience
of mostly musicians. After the applause she spoke. "My last song
for this night I will sing in my native language. I am Romany,
you call 'Gypsy'. It is likely you do not know of Romany so I will
tell you story. Song is about father who is raising daughter alone.
They argue over daughter's choice of lover. Daughter leaves in
anger into the night. A storm comes. The song is of father out
in storm looking for lost daughter." She began playing a rhythmic, dark progression. When her voice came in it was a
mournful wail. Though few could decipher the exact meaning,
everyone stopped what they were doing, mesmerized by the
dramatic melody and the piercing, haunting voice. Jaqui felt a
stray tear roll down her cheek. She wasn't the only listener so
affected. At the close of the song, Katrine's face was ghostly
pale. She couldn't smile for the standing ovation but she bowed
deeply before walking off stage toward Jaqui. Once Katrine had
put away her instrument, several of the other musicians came
over to congratulate her. Jaqui noticed that Adam was staring at
Katrine from across the room, a look on his face as though his
gaze were a weapon. Katrine failed to acknowledge him.

As the evening progressed, the crowd began to arrive in spite
of the weather. The coffee shop end of the building filled up.
Many patrons purchased their treats and went straight to the
performance area. Soon the staff was putting out additional
tables.

"Is it always like this?" Jaqui asked.

"The Chronicle did a story on this open mic last month and
mentioned that West Coast stars and touring acts occasionally
stop by," Penny said. "Since then we've had real good turnout,
mostly folks looking for somebody famous. I'm not famous but
I'll give them the best show I can.

Jaqui grew even more apprehensive. Flashes of lightning
were framed in the windows and thunder rolled over the long
building. Night had fallen behind the curtain of thunderheads.

With only one more act before Jaqui was to take the stage, Anton got up to make the introduction. "The next set will be performed by Dan and Liam Anders. For those of you who aren't familiar with the instrument, Liam is performing on the diggery-do, an instrument native to Australia and New Zealand." Anton stepped away from the mic as Dan positioned it in front of his guitar. "Do you need a mike?" Anton asked Liam.

"Not for this. They'll hear it at the capitol," Liam replied. As Anton stepped from the stage, the power went out. The room was plunged into darkness, only the lightning and headlights from passing cars illuminated the windows. The gasp from the audience was more like a collective sigh, then silence, as the coffee machines, cash registers and even the giant roaster in the rear of the building fell silent. The baristas began handing out candles on saucers and in glasses. Within minutes the hushed room was aglow in warm candlelight. Most of the patrons remained as the staff provided free refills of brewed coffee.

Dan began picking his guitar. When Liam joined him on the diggery-do, the eerie sound summoned ancient spirits from the depth of the evening, hypnotizing the crowd. Everyone was ghostly quiet as the music washed over them. Even Jaqui, who'd been plagued with stage fright, felt the tension flow from the core of her body and dissipate through her extremities. Katrine passed the flask of brandy to Jaqui after taking a sip. Jaqui drank from the silver container, reflecting candlelight across the table, then passed it back. Katrine drew her chair close and lay her head on Jaqui's shoulder. A gentle spirituality overtook the two as they watched Dan and Liam improvise on a repetitive drone. It had the mesmerizing effect of staring into a campfire. For possibly the first time in recorded history, Anton allowed an act to continue beyond the 15-minute limit. He was captured by the spell cast by the duo and the candlelight, as was everyone in the building. When the Anders brothers finished, you could hear the crowd collectively inhale before applauding. Anton took to the stage briefly, saying only, "Jaqui Benderman, acapella vocals."

Jaqui found that she was totally relaxed. Not wanting to break the mood, she began slowly in a strong but subdued voice, "*Summertime, and the livin' is easy* ..." She followed with Farther Along, then closed with an old Bessie Smith standard that brought forth a flirtatiousness in her demeanor. The audience remained fixated, the spell unbroken. She returned to her table just as the lights came on.

"That was beautiful," Katrine told her and kissed Jaqui lightly on the cheek. Jaqui felt a warm wave roll across her abdomen. The kiss felt so innocent coming from the little girl that Jaqui attributed it to the magic in the room. Although the noise came back in the environment, it didn't penetrate Jaqui's thoughts. She felt peaceful and privileged as she enjoyed the rest of the show. By midnight, the crowd had dwindled.

"Where do you live?" Katrine asked Jaqui as they were standing up to leave.

"I'm in a fleabag weekly rental over on the east side for now. It's cheaper than the Motel 6 I was staying in. Safer too, I think. It's just until I get a job and find a place."

"My roommate moved out a month ago. She is married now. I am needing a replacement," Katrine offered. "It's in Clarksville, a good place to be. Downtown is close, so good for finding job."

"I don't have much money right now," Jaqui explained.

"Is not expensive," Katrine said. "Maybe we learn songs together. Give me ride home. I show you.'

"Where's your car?" Jaqui asked.

"I came on bus. I only have scooter," Katrine laughed. "Guitar and scooter not good plan with little bitty girl."

"I'll give you a ride home, no problem. I don't know about the roommate thing but we'll see." Jaqui felt maybe her luck was changing.

The rain subsided to a slimy mist by the time she dropped

off Katrine. She navigated her coupe through the deserted downtown streets. The girl's offer seemed to fall in the "too good to be true" category Jaqui had recently become suspicious of. How did Katrine benefit? Well, Jaqui owned a car. Cool, no problem, She would be glad to help with rides. Drinking buddies? Buddies of any kind, okay with Jaqui. Even the musical collaboration seemed like something that could be mutually beneficial. Katrine was undoubtedly overflowing with talent and passion. Still, Jaqui felt something more, something inexplicable, almost desperate in Katrine's offer. Maybe, Jaqui thought, it was her own paranoia.

Jaqui pulled her car between the two dilapidated fourplexes to the alley parking area. The rain had all but stopped and a sliver of a moon hung behind a thin fog directly above. Jaqui turned off her ignition and sat for a moment staring at the entrance to her ground floor apartment. Something was off kilter. The tiny blond hairs on her forearm stood at attention. Her keys, instead of finding her palm, spread between the fingers of her right hand, a rudimentary weapon. Her dad's lessons in self-defense spun through her brain as her pulse increased. Why? What is it? Then she realized she had left her porch light on knowing it would be dark when she arrived home. It probably just burned out, she figured, but her body wouldn't buy it. She scanned the parking lot and jogged to the door. When she inserted her key into the deadbolt she found it unlocked. She always locked it. The doorknob, though, was locked. She had to use her key to open it. Taking a deep breath and crouching, she flung the door open hard against the wall. The tiny apartment was only a living area, a small kitchen partitioned off by a breakfast bar and a single bedroom that you had to go through to get to the bathroom. The only light on was in the bedroom, not how she left it. She felt electricity coursing through every cell. She left the door opened back against the wall.

"Who's here," she hollered. Anyone here? Come out!" The rooms were silent. She turned on the living room light and crossed to the kitchen. Reaching over the bar, she retrieved a dirty carving knife from the sink and held it against her waist as she approached the bedroom. The door was partially open. She kicked it wide. No one. She checked the bathroom, pulled back the shower curtain. All clear. She went back, closed the front door and secured the deadbolt.

Still holding the knife, she began to investigate. Someone had been here. The closet door was open as was the medicine cabinet. The doorknob had been locked. She checked the windows, both locked. Someone had a key. She looked for clues. The kitchen appeared undisturbed. On the coffee table in the living room the magazines were neatly stacked, not her doing. The bed was still unmade but she wasn't sure exactly how she'd left it. The closet, however, was a different story. The hanging clothes were pushed to one end, boxes were scattered. Her prize pair of exotic royal python boots had been removed from their box. A pair of her nylon lace panties, that she was fairly certain had been left on the bathroom floor, was stuffed into the top of one boot. When she pulled them out she found them soaked in a snot-like liquid. She realized it wasn't snot and it was still warm. She dropped them in the toilet and flushed. As they swirled away she fell back against the door as bile began to erupt from her stomach.

She thought about calling Katrine. Instead, she wedged a chair under the front doorknob and sat down at the kitchen table. Her hands were trembling as she poured herself a triple shot of bourbon. She downed it, placed the carving knife under her pillow, crawled under the sheets and cried herself into a fitful sleep.

∽

Langley had spent more than a few evenings with Sara working on various academic projects, yet, though both of their grades had improved, they still hadn't made an official date. Oh, they had fun together, especially when their cultural observations brought their quirky wit into play. There seemed to be a sexual tension when they parted that Langley hoped to explore. He was pondering what restaurant to treat her to when he hit on the idea of a romantic sunset picnic, a handmade banquet in a basket. When he finally worked up the courage to suggest a Saturday evening rendezvous, her disappointment caught him by surprise.

"I can't," she said. "In fact, Saturdays aren't good for me at all. Maybe Sunday?"

"I have church on Sunday. I play bass with the worship team. Can't really miss," he replied. He considered asking her to join him but that didn't strike him as a very romantic move.

"We could go out on a weeknight," Sara suggested, "or maybe on semester break I'd be up for a road trip, camping maybe?'

Langley was flabbergasted, almost speechless, but he managed to utter, "Cool, sure."

When they said goodbye that evening, not only did Sara initiate their first kiss but she pressed her skinny little body firmly against Langley's gangly frame. He made it all the way home and was crawling into bed before he even thought to wonder what event took up every one of Sara's Saturday nights. If he had known the answer to that question the story of Langley and Sara might have ended right here.

Jaqui woke up early, still a little jittery from the previous night. She checked the locks again. Both doors and all three windows were secure. When she peeked out from the blinds her car seemed to be untouched. She moved the kitchen chair back to the table and started coffee. A little fog had settled in her head but the coffee made quick work of that.

She contemplated who could have gotten into her apartment. No one from back home knew where she was. She'd made certain of that, only dropping Sarge a postcard saying she was in the city, not to worry, and that she had transferred her money. She didn't even mention what city but he probably knew. She had no intention of ever setting foot in that county again, even for her bogus court case. She even got a post office box in an upscale part of town near the arts district. It seemed logical. That's where she planned on ending up, but even the postmaster didn't have her physical address, not this one. She doubted that the apartment owner, a geriatric widow, had anything to do with the break in. The maintenance department obviously didn't exist. The owner had just instructed her to "call if you need anything". The only people she had contact with within the 10 days she had been in town were the tattoo artists and the folks from the coffeehouse. She had the tattoo before she moved here. So, if it wasn't random, which it could have been, it had to be somebody from the coffee house. She'd done some networking last night, mentioning to several folks she was interested in working up an act. It was definitely a male, eliminating Penny and Katrine, besides she'd been with Katrine the whole time. Anton didn't ask for her address. Dan and Liam had invited her to a jam session barbecue but didn't ask where she lived, not specifically. She'd mentioned the name of her apartment complex to a few people but not where it was located. It had to have been random, but why? Nothing was missing. Whoever did it had to have spent some time here. Maybe it was time to move. She gave Katrine a call.

Rainy Night in Georgia

- Brook Benton

"There is nice room back here, not as big as master suite but with many windows. You will have your bathroom, nice big shower, all new, but sorry no tub. Door to back porch. Sometimes, if I have date you must come in this way. Very pretty backyard with private fence for tanning whole body. Little herb garden there. You cook?" Katrine asked. She was giving Jaqui the grand tour.

"I cook some," Jaqui replied. "I was raised by my dad. He didn't require anything fancy and we grew most of it."

"My father, too, raised me until they took him when I was 14. He is how I learned guitar."

"Took him?"

"In Romania you must go along. No 'rocking of boat' like here, or you are taken."

"Taken where?"

"Away, to work. I was raised in home run by Romania until I married out. Long story for another time. So, you like house?"

"It's beautiful. You're very good with decor but I'm pretty sure it's out of my price range."

"I pay fourteen hundred for house a month but since I have biggest room I only charge you six hundred and half electric.

All new appliances and windows are making bills very cheap. Less than two hundred total at most."

"I'd pay almost that much to stay in the dump I'm in now. You're sure you don't want more?"

"No. I can pay all if I need but I don't like to live alone."

"Yeah, I'm not crazy about that either after last night."

"So, it is good?" Katrine asked.

"Sure, when can I move in?"

"Now, tomorrow, whenever."

"Don't you want a background check, a deposit?"

"I know you. Can you pay first month?"

"Sure." Jaqui was ecstatic, the house was beautiful and she really hit it off with Katrine. "This will give me an incentive to get off my ass and find a job."

"I might know of job for you. It is for singing but you might have to travel some. Only some though, mostly here in town."

"What do you mean, a singing gig?"

"Yes, it is backup for R&B band with horns, maybe 10 or 12 people. You know of Keegan Stone?"

"Wasn't he the singer for Frostfire back in the eighties? He must be in his forties now."

"Almost 50, but has new band here. Many gigs and some touring."

"Why don't you take the gig?"

"Not my style. He already say no. My voice too 'sweet' he say. You have voice with meat, might work. I will show him you but first we move you."

"Yes, thank you! This has turned out to be a great day." Jaqui felt like giving the little woman a hug, so she did.

"Can I get my stuff and move in today? I really hate that hell hole I'm in."

"Sure, you want help?"

After stopping at a liquor store and picking up some empty boxes they embarked on their adventure. As they became acquainted, they kept the conversation light, talking about bands and movies they liked, pretty people in the news, and how to get famous.

"Why no backseat?" Katrine asked.

Jaqui looked where the seat used to be and Katrine saw her cloud over. It looked like she might cry. "It got ruined. I had to take it out."

"We can probably find another one." Katrine suggested.

"No. I'm leaving it like that." They rode to Jaqui's fourplex in silence. This time Jaqui was relieved to find the door properly locked. She switched on the AC. "I'll start in the kitchen if you want to grab a box and pack what's in the bathroom," Jaqui said, motioning back through the bedroom. "Please don't judge me. I'm not usually such a slob." Jaqui began pulling cups from the cabinets.

"Jaqui, come please?" Something in Katrine's voice made Jaqui sprint into the bathroom. Katrine was ghostly pale. Jaqui looked in the mirror and fell back against the towel rack. Someone had used her beige lip gloss to write "You are Dancing with the Devil. Repent or Be Damned!" One of her Cosmopolitan magazines had been ripped up and placed in the bathtub. All of her underwear, dirty and clean, had been piled on top and someone had tried to light it. Fortunately, the fire had gone out but nothing was salvageable. Katrine took Jaqui's hand as they stared at each other through that disturbing message.

"See what I mean. I've got to get away from this place?" Jaqui said.

"Yes I do, and now."

Jaqui's coupe was straining with the steepness on some of the ranch roads west of town. The summer heat made the road oil ooze from the pavement causing the tires to hiss like snakes as they negotiated the hairpin curves. Katrine was fidgeting in the passenger seat. Other than driving directions, she had said very little. Even with the AC blowing full blast, heat was radiating from the dash causing sweat to bead on Jaqui's temples.

"If you don't want this, is okay," Katrine said. "I have known Keegan long time. He is not a nice man, but he has money and he needs singer."

"Not a problem. I've dealt with my share of jerks. I know it's hard to get into this business. Beats flipping burgers."

Katrine guided her down a tree lined road to a gate with a keypad. She rattled off the number from memory, raising Jaqui's eyebrows. They continued over 1/4 mile until they reached a sprawling house of wood, stone, and glass. Parking out front they had to cross a trickle of creek to reach the entry. Keegan looked nothing like the anemic, big hair rocker Jaqui remembered from the eighties. His head was shaved, he had a large diamond stud in one ear and he looked like he lived at the gym, when he wasn't at the tanning salon. Jaqui started to think of this gig in a whole new way. The guy didn't look anywhere near 50. He was solid.

"So you're Jaqui?" he said, extending his hand. "Kat wasn't lying. You are drop-dead gorgeous. I hope you sing as good as you look."

"Give me a try," Jaqui said. She refused to be intimidated.

"Oh, I plan to, but first, can you give us a minute." Keegan led Katrine down a hall. They left Jaqui just standing in what seemed to be the main room. The back wall was glass. Outside a cedar deck with a swimming pool extended out over a jagged valley. Jaqui wandered about. The decor was minimal, no books, no art other than some exotic musical instruments and a few animal heads hanging from the wall, nothing native to Texas. The furniture was nondescript black leather, more like office furniture. Over in the corner a baby grand piano appeared to be on display. Jaqui had time to examine the room in detail before Katrine and Keegan finally returned. Katrine looked the same but Keegan had changed into a bathing suit and had a towel thrown around his neck.

"Let's see what you've got," he said to Jaqui as he slid onto the piano bench. "What do you want to sing? How about some Motown? Do you know "Heat Wave," by Martha and the Van Dellas?"

"Didn't Linda Ronstadt have a hit with that?" Jaqui asked.

"Yeah, but she sucked. Do it Van Dellas style." Keegan jumped right into the intro while Jaqui struggled to remember the words. It was a fiasco. Jaqui didn't know the whole song and Keegan's piano playing was rudimentary.

"Stop!" Jaqui said. "This isn't working. How about I sing something I know and you just listen."

Keegan threw up his hands and backed away from the piano. Jaqui began to moan "Rainy Night in Georgia" a cappella. The raw cedar walls made great acoustics for her voice.

"That's what I think of when I think Motown," Jaqui said, after Keegan caught his breath.

"I think we may have something here," Keegan said. "We'll give it a try. We rehearse in Austin Tuesday and Thursday nights, union scale. Here's some charts and a CD for you. You'll be singing alto. There're two other backup girls. You'll need to call them and schedule a couple of extra sessions. Another one of them is new too. Their contact info and the studio address is in there." He handed her a manila envelope and began walking toward the door. It was obvious the audition was over. Jaqui looked at Katrine but Katrine didn't move.

Keegan smiled when he noticed. "I'll drop her off later. She's going to hang out."

Jaqui shrugged and turned to go just as Katrine's smile faded into something desperate. Jaqui stopped.

"Go on, I'll catch up with you later," Katrine said.

Crazy

- Willie Nelson

The oaks dripped Spanish moss. The sprawling limbs intertwined above the wandering blacktop. Langley steered the large sedan through the enclosed lane. Since his mom's stroke it had been a rare day when the car left the garage, her recovery having been slow and incomplete. So incomplete, Langley feared, that his mother may never drive again. Her piano was what she missed most, a passion Langley could only sympathize with. He could, however, take her car out for an occasional spin to keep the battery up and the engine saturated with oil. His dad could have just as well handled it if he were ever home. Since Mom's stroke Dad had been spending more and more time at the office, working well into the night most evenings. Today was Saturday so Langley figured his dad would stay home, but after lunch he left without even saying where he was going.

Saturday. It had become the weirdest day of the week; the day they practiced pretending to still be a family so they could pull it off the next day at church. From the looks they received from fellow parishioners it was clearly an inadequate effort. Saturday was also the day that Sara dropped out of his life for several hours. For a while he didn't even notice, then, as they grew closer, he chose to ignore it.

"It's my private time," she'd say, "like your Sunday."

"Are you Jewish or Mormon?" he asked.

She laughed. "Not hardly."

He didn't really care about her religion. Hell, if it weren't for the chance to play music he wouldn't even care about his own. Still, that last half of Saturday remained hers and she didn't share, at least not with him. Though she had declined, he had invited her to join him for church. The fact that she never saw him the last half of Saturday was beginning to sandpaper his nerves. He considered demanding an explanation but he didn't want to throw a monkey wrench into the one relationship he still felt confident in. Maybe he really didn't want to know.

The shadows of the trees broke across the polished hood like ocean waves. He decided he did want to know but he didn't want to confront her. An idea formed as he wandered the rural roads; one that would give him the answer without confrontation but made him queasy about his own desire.

He felt a bond with Sara. They dated, laughed together, played, acted silly. They had panted through several long make-out sessions and even attempted a clumsy, groping sexual encounter in the back seat of her Honda Civic with less than satisfying results. They even joked about that later. That's how close they were. It made Langley uncomfortable when he realized what he knew he was going to do. He headed toward her house.

The sun was about to connect with the horizon when he parked the car on a side street down the block from Sara's parents' house. Her Civic was parked at the curb. He waited, but not long, until she came out carrying a gym bag and a hook shaped walking stick that was longer than she was tall. She wore a long-sleeved gray dress that came down past her knees. Strikingly beautiful, he thought. Then he realized she never dressed up for him and a pang of jealousy broadsided him. She loaded her gear and left. He started the sedan and drove around the block falling in at a distance behind as she left the subdivision. He kept back a ways even though he knew the sedan was unfamiliar to her. His conscience urged him to turn away at several intersections but his curiosity prevailed and he followed her into the parking lot of the Branch Creek shopping center.

Instead of parking near the conglomeration of upscale boutiques, Sara pulled her Civic around to the back edge of the parking lot where a few other cars were parked. The terrain behind the lot dropped off steeply to Branch Creek. Occasionally hikers would use this to access the hiking trail along the creek, but not in the dark and Sara was certainly not dressed for hiking. Langley pulled into a spot near the building where employees parked and watched as Sara got out and waited. Another car pulled up and two older women and a young man got out and joined her. These women were also in dresses. The man appeared to be wearing pajamas. They waited together for a few minutes then checked their watches, unloaded a few bags and utensils, then walked over the edge of the parking lot and down toward the creek.

Langley started his car and put it into gear, then put it back in park, killed the engine and sat. It would have been a good time to leave. He didn't. Instead he got out and walked toward the back edge of the parking lot, looked down the path and rejected his last opportunity to turn back.

It was a good quarter mile to the creek. The mercury vapor light from the parking lot illuminated the sky making it easy to see the trail, at least for the first few hundred yards. He progressed slowly so as not to catch up. The sounds of nature began to blend with the hum of traffic when he noticed a side trail. He'd passed a couple of these already but this one had a silver ribbon tied to a tree limb near the entrance, a ribbon that reflected the night light but wouldn't have been noticed by day. He chose the side trail. Soon the sounds of nature mixed with the murmuring of humans. He slowed and left the trail, inching silently through the trees and brush toward the voices. He soon spotted a clearing through the trees. It couldn't have been more than 30 feet in diameter. A circle of football sized stones had been assembled to enclose a space roughly the size of a small car. Twelve people wandered around the clearing hugging and chatting, eight women and four men. The men were young but with the exception of Sara and one other girl the women were on the far side of middle aged. The oldest woman had long silver hair that hung halfway to the ground. When she took a carton of salt from her bag and began sprinkling it on the rocks, the other people formed a circle. They seemed to have preappointed places. Langley began to get an inkling of what he was seeing. His girlfriend was a witch. Being a Christian, he had heard horror stories about black magic and human sacrifice but being a well-read 21st century adult he knew most of these stories were bullshit. He had always wondered what all the fuss was about and now he was going to find out. He only wished that Sara wasn't part of it. "Hide and watch" had never meant this much to him. He squatted behind a tree and peered through the brush.

Four Sheppard's hooks were plunged into the soil at opposing points of the circle. It was obvious that a small fire had once burned in the center of the circle but no fire was started tonight. Lit candles in closed containers were suspended from each hook. Sara was in the circle with her back to Langley. The old woman was directly opposite her. The twelve held hands long enough to space themselves equidistantly. The old woman spoke a few words in a foreign tongue and everyone stepped out of their garments and held their hands toward the sky. With the exception of a few necklaces and bracelets they were completely naked.

"What the hell," Langley thought, or did he say it? When the entire coven turned to face his direction he knew he must have said it.

"Shit!" He knew he said that. He ran. He couldn't find the

trail at first. Then he thought he saw a clear spot ahead. Just before he reached it he tripped and fell hard. Something ripped through his shirt and gashed his shoulder. He jumped up and found the trail, or a trail. He followed it in the direction of the light. It came out in the parking lot but not where he started. It took him a moment to orient himself. He looked back but didn't see anyone. For some reason he looked into the trees, no one there either. What had he expected? He remembered when they all looked at him, when Sara looked at him, the disappointment in her eyes. There was no way she could have seen that it was him, but she knew it was and Langley knew she knew. He put his hands on his knees. Tears mixed with the blood dripping from his fingertips.

Riding Shotgun Down the Avalanche

- Shawn Colvin

"**W**hat is that thing you say** about baskets of eggs?"
Katrine asked. She was trying to decide between two
pairs of shoes, sandals and sneakers. "You know, keep choices."

"Yeah, don't put all your eggs in one basket, why?" Jaqui
was barely paying attention.

"It's open mic night, you should come. I know Keegan offer
you job, but I've known him a long time, very flaky. Could be
good, maybe not. Besides, is fun, open mic. Come on, drive me,
sing songs." Katrine urged.

"Sure, why not." Jaqui thought maybe it would get her mind
off Langley. She missed him, not all the drama back home, but
him. She wanted him to know she was okay and tell him about
Katrine. She put on her dress boots and brushed out her hair.

It was early when they reached the Ruta Maya coffee house.
A handful of patrons sat inside with their tablets and laptops in
various poses of creative contemplation. The girls were the first
musicians to arrive. Even Anton wasn't there yet.

"Let's get coffee," Jaqui said. "It's a little early to hit the
bottle." Katrine opted for hibiscus tea. They took a seat by the
stage.

"We should work on songs together," Katrine said. "Can

you make harmony?"

"We could give it a shot. Your voice is higher but I could do alto to your soprano if you carry the melody."

"You know that song ' Riding Shotgun Down the Avalanche'? Is done by local girl."

"Sure, I'll bet our voices would work on some of those Indigo Girls songs, too?" Jaqui added.

"I don't know all the words to those girl's songs, but we can learn for maybe next time. We try 'Avalanche' tonight, though, okay?"

"Break out your guitar. Let's get busy."

Katrine gave Jaqui a hug around the neck. She was grinning and very animated as if she had just received a present. "Oh, thank you. This is being so much fun." They found a couple of chairs in the corner by the stage and began working out harmonies. In less than 15 minutes they had nailed it.

"Hey, Jaqui, I'm glad you made it back," Anton had slipped in unnoticed. "I'm sorry I gave you a hard time last week. You have no idea how many karaoke queens show up expecting to sing with a taped background. We don't do that. But your voice, well, you don't really need backup. It's so pure and strong."

"Thanks, Anton." Jaqui felt herself blushing. Since she'd last seen Langley she hadn't had anyone be so straightforward with her.

"Would you consider maybe doing a duet or singing harmony on one of my songs?"

"I don't know any of your stuff but we can do a cover if you want. My dad's a big fan of country. I know a lot of the older stuff; Jones and Wynette, stuff like that." Jaqui glanced over to see that Katrine was almost in a pout. "Sign us up for some good later spots, okay? Then we'll go over something."

"How about 10:30 and 11?" He asked. Jaqui looked to Katrine. "You pick."

"Ten and 11:00, I'll be 10."

"You got it."

"I'll get up with you in a bit. Katrine and I are still working on something."

"Sweet! I bet y'all's voices really work well together." Anton left to sign up the gathering musicians.

"I think you are star of show tonight," Katrine said. She wasn't smiling.

"Hey, easy. We're here to have fun, remember? Let's go through this all again, at least the chorus."

"I'm sorry. I'm silly. Let's sing." Katrine picked up her guitar. By the time 7:30 rolled around most of the regulars had gathered around Jaqui and Katrine's table. Penny and Conner were there. Dan and Liam were too but instead of the diggery-do, Liam brought an autoharp. The kid, Adam, sat a couple of tables away. He had set out several harmonicas and was arranging them in various configurations like loose dominoes. Occasionally Jaqui would look up and catch him staring at her. He'd shift his gaze back to the harmonicas. Once, when she caught his eye, she motioned for him to join the group. He pretended not to notice and continued sorting harmonicas.

As always, Anton opened the show. Tonight, instead of doing only original material, he invited Jaqui and Conner up to join him on 'Crazy', an old Willie Nelson composition made famous by Patsy Cline. The harmonies were tricky for Jaqui. It was passable but not her best effort. The small crowd loved it. Jaqui was glad the crowd was still small. About 9:30 Jaqui and Katrine stepped outside to "tune". The sticky August night was still brutally hot so they didn't have to hide behind the building to pass the flask. The porch was deserted. Katrine elected to save her joint for later. It was the first time she'd worked with another singer. They sang the song a couple more times, playing with some unusual harmonies, until they came up with something a little unconventional. When they sang they could predict the others' phrasing and inflection like they sang together every day. Jaqui felt like she was singing with a sister. They went back in and performed the song and blew the crowd away, including the fickle group of musicians. When the applause died down Anton introduced "The Kid". Once again Adam lost himself in his performance, his fingers dancing across the strings like a man possessed. For his final song he strapped on a harmonica holder. Jaqui suspected she was the only one that noticed he finished with the exact same Bessie Smith song she had ended her set with the previous week. The harmonica eerily reprised the melody she sang, to the note. Everyone applauded when he was done. He didn't seem to hear it, he was staring at Jaqui, his smile containing a trace of sneer, she thought. This time Jaqui looked away.

Jaqui went for a coffee refill. She planned to doctor it with a shot of Katrine's EL Presidente to calm the jitters she hoped were just a touch of stage fright. As she approached the counter, she felt a hand on her arm and startled like a colt in a lightning storm.

"Easy," Katrine said. "I not mean to scare you. Just going to restroom, letting you know." There was concern in Katrine's eyes.

"I'm just jumpy, stage fright I guess, weird mood. I'm okay."
"Hold my purse," Katrine said. "Little silver friend in there will help." When Jaqui got her coffee she added a large dose of brandy. Back at the table she took a deep breath and closed her eyes.

"So, what did you think?" It was a deep voice, almost a radio voice. It took Jaqui a second to realize it was directed at her. She opened her eyes. Adams face was inches from hers. His ice blue eyes were fixed on her. Loose strands of dark brown hair dangled over his forehead. He smiled. Her stomach did a little flip.

"Was that on purpose, that song, the one I did last week?" She asked.

"Yeah," He broke into a sheepish grin. "I just wanted you to know that I noticed. Maybe I could back you up on a song or two."

"I didn't think you'd did that."

"I don't… usually, but you're good, and you like the good stuff. You sing any Etta James?"

"Some," Jaqui replied. "I know 'Sunday Kind of Love', a couple of others."

"Maybe I could play back up?"

"I guess, we could give it a try." She noticed his eyes still hadn't left hers. It was making her uncomfortably warm.

"Let's go outside and see what we can come up with." He got up to leave. Not sure why, she followed.

"What key?" he asked, perched on the porch railing. "I… don't know."

"It's okay. Start singing. I'll figure it out."

She began. Her voice cracked. She started over. He began picking the rhythm.

"You're in A," he said. "Relax, let's try it in G, a little slower." He started playing again. She tried to relax and the music began to flow out of her. Adam closed his eyes, leaned back, and let his fingers do the talking. By the end of the song they had it.

"Big finish," Adam said and slowed his playing. Jaqui laid into the final notes. "See, that wasn't so bad. Can we play it for the folks inside?" he asked.

"Sure."

Katrine was back at the table. When they walked in, a look of cold horror came over her face. "Where you go?" She hissed.

"Working on a song with Adam."

"No! No, that bad idea!"

"What, it's just a song. I'm not fucking him." The thought had crossed her mind.

"Be careful. He has evil in him."

"Oh, bullshit, anyway we're just doing a song."

"I tell you, just be careful."

"Sure, okay." Jaqui thought Katrine was overreacting, but those earlier feelings of discomfort returned. Katrine was pale and very quiet. Jaqui was up next. She did a couple of Motown numbers acappella. They went over well. She invited Adam up and sang it in G. It dripped with sensuality. She took the mic in her hand and strutted the stage. Adam rocked with the beat, eyes half mast, fingers flying.

While the crowd was on their feet, Jaqui blew a kiss and took a bow. Adam sneaked off the right side of the stage, his guitar in front of him like a shield and trotted for the restroom.

"See, that worked," Jaqui told Katrine.

"Yeah, he is good. Just be careful." Katrine said.

"What the hell happened with you two, anyway?" Jaqui asked. "We can talk later." Katrine motioned toward the others.

Adam was coming back. He was all smiles.

"That was beautiful," he said. "We should work up some more stuff, maybe an act."

"Maybe someday. I've got a couple of projects I'm working on right now."

"I could stop by sometime when you're not busy," he suggested. "Do you still live in that fourplex on the east side?"

"No," Jaqui felt her abdomen tighten. "I've got to work tomorrow. We need to go." She grabbed Katrine by the hand and almost jerked her out of the seat.

"Later then," Anton called after. Jaqui didn't look back. "You're right. I should've listened." She said when she was back in the car with Katrine. "It was him, in my apartment. I mentioned I lived on the east side but I didn't say anything about a four-plex. He didn't just break in. I didn't tell you, but he did some creepy shit while he was there."

"I'm not surprised."

"So what happened with you two?"

"It was just a ... strangeness, more feeling. He wanted more than singing. I didn't. Hard to say."

"It's cool. I get it. I'm sorry I didn't listen."

"Is okay." Katrine took Jaqui's hand and held it in tight desperation.

Hard Times

- Ryan Bingham

Sunday morning worship found Langley just going
through the motions. The band didn't seem to have the
same energy without his mom's pounding piano melodies, and
without Jaqui's voice the harmonies were hollow. It had been
over a month since she left without a word. The painful lacera-
tion on his shoulder lay directly beneath the strap his bass hung
from. Not unbearable, just annoying enough to remind him how
it got there. He hadn't talked to Sara about last night. The only
things about the morning that gave him hope were his mother
sitting in the pew beside his dad and old Sarge Benderman
sidled up next to Brenda Bartlett in the third row. He could see
his mom's better hand keeping time with the beat. It made it
worthwhile to be up there. Langley's family went out to lunch
after church, courtesy of Dad.

When they went home he spent the rest of the day planning
to give Sara a call. He never quite got around to it.

Monday began the week before the second summer session
finals at SACC. Langley arrived early to try talking to Sara. She
was already there waiting beside her Civic near where they
parked at the end of the lot.

"Are you okay?" she asked as he got out. "Yeah, sure, why?"

"Well, let's see, I haven't heard from you all weekend, and then there is the blood."

"Blood?"

Sara shook her head. " Let's don't do this. You know what I'm talking about. I was worried."

"I'm okay. How about you?"

"Not really."

"I'm sorry. I didn't... "

"Are you?" She interrupted. "Are you sorry? Do you know what you saw, what you did?"

"Kind of."

"What do you think you saw?"

"You're a witch?"

"Jeez, Langley, I don't know if I should slap you, kick you in your nuts or just walk away. Hey! I know! Why don't I turn you into some kind of fucking animal? What kind of animal would you like to be, Langley? How about an ass!" Sara stomped around in a circle stopping occasionally to glare at him. "Do you know what you did?"

"I'm sorry," Langley said again.

"Yeah, yeah, so I hear. Get in the car we need to talk, not out here."

"More room in the truck."

She narrowed her eyes. "Car, now!" When they were in the car she pulled to a secluded section of the lot. She left the AC on and the windows up.

"First off," she said, "it's Wiccan although 'witch' isn't exactly wrong and, as much as I'd like to right now, I can't turn you into an ass. You don't need any help with that anyway."

"Look, Sara, I don't give a damn about your religion, one way or the other."

"Really? So why the stalking shit?"

"I just wondered what you did on Saturday."

"If you really wanted to know I would have told you."

"I did ask."

"No, you suggested. We don't broadcast who we are. Thousands of my religion have died at the hands of yours."

"Maybe way back. There's no persecution anymore."

"Are you high? This is the fucking buckle of the Bible belt!

"Still, it's not like you're a Muslim or something."

Sarah slammed her forehead into the steering wheel and growled. "I'm not taking these courses so I can go out and bust folks. I actually want to help people you know, social work. I think I may have mentioned that like a couple hundred times."

"Yeah, so?"

"What chance do you think I would have of getting a job in this holy roller state if they figured out I was Wiccan."

"It shouldn't matter."

"No shit, Sherlock, but guess what? It does. Big time! Here's the problem, that coven, they're my sisters and brothers.

"Big family!" Langley quipped.

"Shut up! First, it's not easy to find a private place with all the right elements. It took us over a year to find and anoint that one. Now we have to move."

"Why?"

"You scared the shit out of the coven and desecrated our space."

"I won't tell anyone."

"Assuming I believed you, they still wouldn't. It doesn't work that way."

"Damn, I'm really sorry."

"I know. I'm sorry for you. You really fucked shit up."

"How about us? Are we okay? I mean…"

"I know what you mean. I hope so. I guess we'll see. I'm not changing this. It's who I am."

"I'm cool with it." "Yeah, we'll see."

"One question, why does everyone have to get naked."

"Oh my god! See, this is what I mean. You know what? We need to get to class. Let's get together later and talk. I'll try to teach Wiccan 101 when I'm not so pissed off."

Jaqui arrived early for rehearsal so she could meet some of the band members. Since she had no formal training, she'd needed Katrine to help her pick out the alto lines in the backup harmonies. The CD only had five songs. Surely there was more to it. As soon as she met the other two backup singers she realized that her voice had little to do with her getting the job. The other two girls were her height and build. The only difference was Adela was Latina and Tiff was African American. "You must be the fresh white meat," Adela said when they were introduced. "How did you get stuck with this gig.?"

"Need the money?" Jaqui wondered aloud.

"Well, you'll definitely earn it," Tiff said. "Keegan's a slave driver." The girls looked at each other as if it was an understatement. "I listened to the CD but there were only five songs. He wanted us to get together on the rest. How many are there?"

"Like, maybe, thirty at most." Adele said. "But it's really basic. Keegan's worried more about the choreography. You could be mute for all he cares. We're window dressing."

"Fuck! Really? I busted my ass learning this to the note. I really wanted to sing."

"So sing," Tiff said, "but you best be able to dance."

"Shit. Well, I was a cheerleader in high school but that's about it for dancing."

"We have our work cut out for us then" Adele said. "Tiff's pretty new, too, but she can dance her ass off. The last white girl we had couldn't pull it off. Plus, she hated Keegan. Not hard to do by the way. She lasted three weeks, never did a show."

"I'll figure it out. Don't worry." Jaqui wished she felt as confident as she sounded.

Other musicians trickled in, tuning instruments, and warming up in a cacophony of amplified noise. The drummer and bass player set up a backbeat and a couple guitarists joined in with funk-flavored riffs. The energy level rose. Suddenly the room went silent. Keegan walked in. All the energy evaporated. Folks took specific places. When the girls got up, Jaqui followed.

"Good evening boys and girls," Keegan began. "We have a new addition. This hillbilly girl is Jaqui Benderman. She's going to fill out the bitch brigade. Take a bow, Jaqui." Jaqui couldn't believe what she'd heard. She glared at Keegan. He lost all sense of joviality and stared right through her. "I said, take a bow." Jaqui rolled her eyes and performed an extreme curtsy to a smattering of applause.

"That wasn't in your best interests," Adela whispered. "You don't want to get on his bad side. Trust me."

Jaqui began to question whether this *was* any better than flipping burgers. She shifted to the polite extremes of southern manners including addressing Keegan as "sir". He seemed to enjoy it. The moves weren't difficult. She threw a little sass into her actions and put the other girls in a playful mood. Keegan was keeping an eye on her.

"Hold it. Stop." Keegan waved his arm. They were about halfway through the third song of the rehearsal. "Jaqui, what was that you did with your head and hips, end of the last chorus, like you were using your whole body to flip someone off?"

Jaqui had to think a minute. She had just been in her head; fitting moves to lyrics. "Right after 'don't need to call me no more'?" she asked.

"Yeah, do it," Keegan said. Jaqui used her body like a whip and threw her head back in defiance. "That's it!" Keegan said. "You girls get that? Eight beats and kick it, together, on four." He counted it off, the rhythm section played, he sang " You don't need to call me no more," the girls popped their hips in unison. Keegan waved his hand. "Fuckin' aye, ladies. Y'all just made half the men in the audience cream their jeans. Adela, put more head into it. Get the hair flipping. Again and 1,2,3,4,..."

They went through the move a couple more times. It did

catch attention when they did it all together. Keegan was excited. The rehearsal seemed like more fun. They spent another 45 minutes on two songs then took a break.

Adela went outside to smoke. Jaqui followed Tiff into the break room.

"Want something to drink?" Tiff asked Jaqui. "There's water, sweet tea, some cheap ass beer, couple of sodas."

"Water's cool, thanks." Jaqui's throat was getting dry. The AC in the studio was cranked down low. Probably because of all the bodies in such a small space.

"I think you're gonna be fine," Tiff said. "That was a cool move you came up with. Keegan dug it."

"I was just playing around. I figure he wants this to be like one of those Memphis show bands. I'm surprised he doesn't make us dress in costumes."

"He suggested it once. Even now he has to approve what you wear at a performance, and it better be short and sexy with a lot of leg. That was part of the problem with your predecessor. She thought this was a singing gig. Yeah, you sing, but really, we're showgirls. If you can deal with that, you'll be fine."

"It's not what I expected," Jaqui said. "I'm okay, I guess. It's not stripping and we do get to sing."

"A very fine line if Keegan has his way, and he usually does."

Jaqui was pondering that when Adela and a couple others came in from smoking.

"Who has the little blue car with no backseat?" Adela asked.

"It's mine," Jaqui said. "Do I need to move it?"

"Not likely. All your tires are flat."

Jaqui ran out to check and sure enough all four of her tires were low. She examined them and found all the valve caps removed and air leaking from the valve stems. "God damn it. Somebody loosened all my valve cores." Jaqui stomped around the car.

"Your what?" Tiff asked. She had run out behind Jaqui, as had half the band.

"The valve cores. They screw in. They let air in but not out, unless someone intentionally loosens them."

"How do you know all this shit?" Tiff asked.

"I grew up on a farm. I had to patch tires all my life, tractors, trailers, trucks, whatever."

"Damn, and I can't even change a tire."

"I've got a stem tool in my glove compartment. I can stop the leaks but I don't have any way to air them up," Jaqui said.

"I've got a bicycle pump in my truck," the drummer offered.

"It would take half the night but maybe I could the pump them up enough to get to a station."

One of the guitarist's spoke. "I can get hold of one of them compressors that clip on the battery. My roommate has one. Let me call." In a few minutes the problem was on its way to being a minor inconvenience and Jaqui had become part of the band.

The guitar player's name was Art. He was underweight to the point of looking sickly but he had a pleasant smile and unlike most guitarists she knew, had a self-effacing, quiet way to his demeanor. He called his roommate and arranged to meet after rehearsal. His roommate was Nicki, a rotund middle-aged woman with full sleeve tattoos and close-cropped hair of an unnatural red. She insisted on airing up the tires herself, after which she gave Jaqui her number and told her to call if she ever needed anything. Jaqui considered the possibility that she had been hit on but had no reference for it.

Jaqui was still excited from the success of her first rehearsal when she got home. She noticed that an inordinate number of lights were on in the house. Katrine met her at the door. "How was rehearsal?"

"It was cool. Keegan works us hard but everybody gets

along. They seem to like me." Katrine didn't seem to be paying much attention. She poured two snifters of brandy and set them on the kitchen table. Jaqui had barely sat down. "A phone call was for you, while you practiced."

"Cool, who?"

"She not say. Jaqui ...?" Katrine paused to find the words. "She was scaring me. She says she found you, now she know where you live and what you do. And Jaqui,..."

"What? What did she say?"

Katrine's hands were shaking. She was barely holding back her tears. "She say you are killer, that you kill a man. What she mean, Jaqui? This true?"

"Oh God!" Jaqui didn't know what to do.

"So, it is true?"

"No! No, well... no, it was an accident, a terrible accident." The memories came flooding back. She could feel the blood jelling, hear Randy's breathing becoming shallow, the night speeding by out of control. "God damn it, no!" She was slamming her forehead into the table.

"Who was this woman caller?" Katrine asked. "What will she do? Are you safe?"

"I don't know," Jaqui replied

Ball of Confusion
- The Neville Brothers

I t was a perfect song for this trip. Sara was singing along with "Ball of Confusion". Loud. It didn't seem to matter to her that she couldn't carry a tune in a bucket. She knew all the words. Her head was rocking side to side with each aggressive phrase, her hand was slapping the steering wheel and she had the little Civic pushed up around 80 down Highway 71. Langley was fixated. His love for her was the one thing he wasn't confused about. He worried about leaving his mom alone for the weekend, if she was alone. What was going on with his dad? Should he ask? Why did Sara just forgive him so easily for the previous weekend? She seemed to be taking it really well. She did insist on taking her car and camping gear, probably some sort of control issue. It may be just because his gear hadn't been out of the closet since he was 14. What worried him the most was he wasn't sure what his relationship with Sara was. Did she feel the connection like he did or were they just having a good time? He didn't know the answer and he wasn't sure he wanted to.

"Hey, boy!" Sara swatted his leg. "Are you going to kill us some game for dinner or should we stop before we get there?"

"Didn't bring my rifle," Langley said.

"Can't you just chase down a rabbit or two?"

"If you'll clean and cook 'em."

"Hamburger sounds good," she said, "and a lot less work."

"Yeah, but soon, I'm starving."

"Next town, whatever's open. We'll play dinner roulette."

"No chains?"

"No chains." She slowed to 60. Neither one of them liked fast food and had decided early on not to support corporate chains. They always ate local. Sometimes it made for an interesting experience.

Sometimes, on the main highways, it was hard to find a place. This time they were lucky. The burgers were pretty good but a side of fried sweet potatoes and pecan pie for dessert really topped it off nicely.

"I'm too full," Sara said. "Can't move. You'll have to carry me."

"Hey! I'm full too. The best I can do is a piggyback ride."

"Have to do, I guess," Sara said. So they left the burger bar with her mounted on Langley's back swatting his butt with her fishing hat. A table of teenagers near the back began hooting at them.

"Yee-haw," Sara yelled.

They entered the state park in time to find a spot by the water and set up camp before dark. The RV spots were full but there were enough tent camping spots left that their space was secluded. They took a dip at the swim beach then walked over to the pier. Getting wet and feeling the breeze from the lake cooled them. The sliver of sun on the horizon burned blood red.

"This is magic," Sara said "This is why I'm a Wiccan, a pagan. This, this is holy." She moved to where their bodies were touching. Langley turned and held her in his arms. As they faced each other their bodies fit together like two parts of one object. "This, the way we fit, this isn't an accident," she said.

"It feels good," Langley said, right before Sara covered his lips with hers. As they kissed, Langley smelled the lake water in her hair, felt her fingers in his back pulling him to her, felt his body temperature rise, and her heartbeat quicken against his chest.

"Let's get back to camp," Sara panted in Langley's ear. She took his hand, led him off the pier and into the darkness.

Back at camp Sara retrieved a fluffy comforter from the trunk of her car and spread it on the ground at the edge of the campsite near the water. The sun had gone down and the stars reflected off the lake. Sara faced the water and raised her arms to the sky. Langley didn't know what she was doing.

"Can you help please?" She asked. "What do you want?"

"Take off my dress."

Langley stood behind her, reached under her sundress and slid his hands along her body as the fabric gathered on his arms. He lifted it over her head. She turned to him and smiled then knelt on the blanket in front of him, removed the top half of her bathing suit, then grabbed the waist band of his and pulled him close. She laid her cheek against his stomach as she slipped her thumbs under the elastic and rolled the shorts down below his buttocks. She then stretched the front out and down to clear his erection. She let them drop and reached for two handfuls of butt to pull him against her face. She rubbed her face and cheeks against him, nuzzling around and under the protrusion.

"Shouldn't we get in the tent? What if someone sees us?" Langley asked. His voice sounded foreign to him.

"Are you scared?" She asked.

"Well, no."

"Doesn't the breeze feel good on your skin?"

"Yeah."

"You look like Apollo in the moonlight. Let's stay out here where we have room to move. We're not good with cramped places, remember?" Without waiting for an answer she took a testicle in her mouth and rolled it around with her tongue. It was settled.

"Lay down," Sara instructed. Langley stretched out on the quilt. "No, on your stomach."

Langley flipped over. He no longer had any control of the situation. Sara shucked her bikini bottom and straddled his hips. She leaned forward enough to place her fingernails at his hairline. Gently but firmly she pulled them down his neck to the center of his back, spreading her fingers just below his shoulder blades. The goose bumps on his skin let her know she was getting through to him. When she reached his waistline, she balled her fists and leaned into the sinewy muscles beside his spine, pushing back toward his shoulders. Once she reached his neck, she repeated the procedure, several times. Each pass extracted a moan of pleasure from Langley. As she leaned forward after several strokes she realized she was leaving a dampness on his butt. She made no attempt to hide it. In fact, she leaned into it. Langley's moans lengthened. On the final upstroke Sara opened her hands and slid them out along Langley's arms, examining the muscles and tendons by touch. She leaned over and breathed the scent of Langley's neck as her pebble hard nipples danced on his skin. She left a streak of wet below his waist as she slid down to meld with him. The humid words in his ear, "You can turn over now," and she dismounted.

They didn't notice the coyotes singing as they frolicked in the moonlight. The breeze no longer felt cool against their glowing skin. They were ravenous in their love without a thought to man nor beast outside their conjured world.

The tent they had so meticulously assembled got no use. They had neither the energy nor desire to untangle once spent. They cocooned in the comforter, legs laced, on the shore and drifted into the decadent oblivion of post-coital bliss.

~

"The sausages seem really small this morning," Sara said. Langley wakened to the sizzling scent of breakfast cooking. The sun was up and bearing down on his naked body. He flipped the comforter around him and struggled to his feet. Sara was back in the sundress he had peeled from her the previous night. The two-burner camp stove had coffee boiling beside the aforementioned sausages.

"How about some eggs with these?" Sara asked. She was already breaking some into a mixing bowl.

"Sure," Langley managed to shake out his bathing suit and slip it on under the comforter. He threw the blanket on the hood of the car. "Are you okay?"

"Sure, I had a blast. Okay, maybe I'm a little sore, Marathon Man, but good. Want some coffee?"

"Yeah." Langley perched on the edge of the picnic table. Sara put down her spatula and came over to give Langley a good morning kiss.

"Say, how about a hike before it gets too hot?" Sara asked.

"I guess I should get dressed."

"Wait 'til after breakfast and I'll help."

You Brought a New Kind of Love to Me

- Ruby Braff

At 2a.m. the traffic on West Sixth was brutal. *Don't
these people ever sleep?* Jaqui wondered, failing to realize she
was now one of these people. Rehearsal was stressful. Keegan's
built-in sarcastic attitude was particularly vehement this evening.
She initially bought into his prima donna credentials but lately
the asshole was beginning to show through. He was just another
egomaniac with a modicum of talent. In most circles he'd be
considered a has-been from the big hair bands, but he had the
foresight to reinvent himself as an R&B icon, a stretch, one
would think. Yet, he had a national tour of large clubs and small
arenas scheduled for winter through spring and he was paying
her quite well for her position as backup singer.

Tonight he'd made her sing the same eight bars over and
over, acapella, until she wanted to slap him sideways. There was
no point in it, just to put her on the spot in front of the rest of
the band, over and over, like this traffic that hit a red light every
block when all she wanted to do was get home, get into her
pajamas, fix a stiff drink and chill out. As she turned into her
neighborhood she took a deep breath and tried to just let it go.
She hoped Katrine was still up so she could vent. Katrine had
become such a close friend lately. It was almost like they were

sisters who understood each other down past the superficial bull-shit. Jaqui had never had that kind of relationship with a woman. It made her miss Langley, but he had his own life now and probably wouldn't want her interfering.

The green Jaguar in the driveway meant Jaqui had to find parking on the street, not an easy task in this neighborhood. Fortunately there was a spot a half block away that was rarely used due to being under a tree that was home to a flock of grackles. Her car needed washing anyway. The Jag also meant Katrine was still on her date. As per prearrangement, Jaqui walked around and entered quietly through the rear. It seemed Jaqui would have to drink alone for now. Maybe later Katrine would join her. It was rare for one of Katrine's friends to stay the night. As she reached for the bourbon, Jaqui heard a muffled but desperate scream emanate from Katrine's bedroom. She went over and tapped on the door. "Are you alright?" she asked. No reply. "Katrine!"

"Shut up and get away from here!" It was a man's threatening voice. Katrine was in trouble! Jaqui grabbed the broom out of the pantry on instinct and burst through the door. She saw Katrine, naked, lying face down on the bed with her hands cuffed behind her. A tall man with a graying ponytail had his knee in Katrine's back and held a fistful of her hair, pressing her face into the pillow. His face was red. Blood pulsed through his temples. As he shifted to face Jaqui, she saw a small but very rigid erection.

"Get away from her!" Jaqui screamed, swinging the broom handle at the man. He grabbed it and yanked, pulling Jaqui toward him. He dropped the broom and caught her by the hair, pulling violently. "Cool, a bonus bitch," he said, his face breaking into a grin. He pulled Jaqui's head toward his crotch. "How about you lube this thing up before I shove it up your little girlfriend's ass?" he cackled. Jaqui gripped his genitals and squeezed with all her adrenaline assisted strength. The man let go of Katrine and slammed his fist into the side of Jaqui's head so hard she almost lost consciousness. She yanked him off the bed by his penis. "Run!" she screamed.

"What the fuck!" Katrine hollered. "You two stop it, now! What hell are you doing, silly Jaqui? This my friend Danny. Be nice to him."

"But--- ,"

"We are playing game, you know, love game."

"It…it looked like a rape to me."

"So I guess we good at game, right Danny?" Danny pulled on his pants. He tossed his shirt over his shoulder and picked up his shoes.

"I'm out of here. You bitches are crazy. Just leave me the fuck alone." He sprinted for the door and slammed it behind him. Jaqui went to get a wet cloth and some ice for her swelling jaw.

"Are you okay?" Katrine asked from the bedroom.

"I don't know. What the hell were you doing?"

"Paying the rent. By the way, if it's not too much trouble, could you give some help?" Jaqui came back in as Katrine was sliding off the bed, still naked, still cuffed. She looked so tiny. When she saw Jaqui with the big wet towel to her face she burst out laughing. "I… thought you… were going to…. pull off his …dick!" she gasped between breaths. "A little help with the cuffs? The key's in the top dresser drawer."

"You have a key?"

"Yeah, it is my hardware. I have many toys."

"I'm sorry, I didn't… I mean, it looked like he was hurting you."

"He was, but he paid well to. I am such perv magnet, so tiny and underdeveloped, I figure why not cash in, the American dream, right? I don't let it be cheap."

Jaqui got the key from the drawer where she noticed a stack of 100 dollar bills. "Is he going to be back for his money?" she asked.

"Probably not, he may come back for something. I will take

that when it comes, these cuffs please?" She backed up to Jaqui. Jaqui unlocked the handcuffs. Katrine put on a robe. "Would you like a drink? I bought single malt scotch. You said to me how you liked whisky."

Jaqui's head was throbbing, maybe from the fist or maybe from the adrenaline, but the confusion was the main reason. "So, you're a …a …call girl?"

"I am opportunist; I think is what you would say. I get paid for what would happen anyway." She took a bottle from her nightstand and sashayed to the kitchen without ever fastening her robe. After filling two snifters, she handed one to Jaqui, then, on tiptoes, kissed her on the cheek. "You are a very fierce bodyguard, Warrior-woman. Thank you for saving me. I know that is what you were believing you to do."

"You never cease to amaze me. Whenever I think I know you I see a side of you that I can't comprehend."

Katrine sat in the chair and let the robe slide back to reveal the pale little girl underneath. "I am open book to you. Ask me, I will tell all."

Jaqui took the Scotch in her mouth, enjoying the flavor and warmth as she let it roll down her throat. Moments passed while the jumbled fragments in her head rearranged into thoughts, then questions. "What happened that made you want to sell yourself? I mean, doesn't that seem, well, somehow … harsh? I don't guess I know what I mean. It's just that I couldn't imagine myself doing something like that."

"Like what, the roughness or sex at all?"

"The 'for money' part, I think. Doesn't that just cheapen the act?"

"You must not know my going rates." A smile broke across Katrine's face as she refilled Jaqui's glass. "I have no affection for men. The one that bring me to America find that out. Well, I told him really. He was good man, but after while he knew. When he asked me I choose to not lie so he set me free. I still have to live. I am no engineer or doctor but I live well. You see that."

"But what do you feel about love, romance, that sort of thing?"

"You want honesty? I want you to not be afraid. I think maybe I say too much already."

"We're friends. After tonight I don't think there's much more you can do to scare me."

Katrine finished her drink and poured another. She stood up and walked around the table to where Jaqui was sitting and set the glass next to Jaqui's. She put her arms around Jaqui's shoulders and slid onto her lap, pressing her body against Jaqui's t-shirt. With her lips almost touching Jaqui's ear, "I do believe in love. I feel a very strong love. I feel it right now."

Jaqui stopped breathing for a moment. She felt the tension grip her. Then as Katrine's lips pressed against hers she felt the tension flow out through her body in a warm wave. She took this woman in her arms and tasted the delicious flavor of the Scotch on her lips and tongue as the heat radiated between them. This was a passion she could not understand but it was safe, and good.

Sweet Forgiveness

- Maria Muldaur

Although the last to arrive, she was not late. Time had little importance here once the sun no longer shined. She was in a very rural place; a place found after only two weeks of searching, a place so far from the rigors of daily life that it was frequented by only twelve people during the darkness between Saturday and Sunday. She parked in a spot off the narrow dirt lane secluded by brush and vegetation. Wearing only sandals and a hooded black cape, she made her way through the brush toward a single flame, a beacon to be extinguished upon her arrival. As she traversed the foreboding terrain, her body was bent into a question mark. The clearing where her comrades waited was surrounded by elm, ash and ancient oaks with long beards of Spanish moss. Sara stepped out of her sandals, shedding her robe and name. She was now Serena, a name given her by the coven in recognition of her being centered and grounded to Mother Earth. Though she took her place at the south point of the circle, tonight she did not feel as grounded and serene as her coven saw her. The moonlight enveloping the skin of her sky clad body did bring a wave of relief and belonging.

Artis, the crone-mother of the coven, extinguished the torch so the participants' eyes could adjust to the pale light of the full moon. She took a silver scepter and cut two pomegranates into twelve equal sections to pass among the members. Each devoured the fruit, allowing the juice to run down their unclothed bodies, then dropped their rinds in the center of the circle. After the sharing of the fruit, the incense burned and ceremonial recognition was given to the Creators of Light and Darkness. The members wrote on onionskin a cause or caution to be considered for action. Serena wrote: *I think I am in love.* Before handing over the note she crossed out the words, *"I think"*.

Artis placed a candle in a jar and invited everyone to tighten the circle and sit on the forest floor. She read each skin aloud and the group discussed the issue. Sometimes a spell was set prior to the skin being sacrificed to the candle's flame. Occasionally Artis would skip over a topic and put the skin at the bottom of the stack. They spoke of jobs, children, illness, issues concerning partners and other day-to-day nuances of their lives. When Artis finally came to the last skin she handed it to Serena.

"Read it aloud," Artis requested. "I am in love," Serena read.

"I see that," Artis said. "It's a new and fertile love, congratulations." Artis brushed her long, bony fingers down the front of Serena's abdomen. Serena felt like they penetrated her womb and touched the new life she was suddenly sure of. She had suspected, of course; the hunger, the nausea, the dreams. Now she was certain. She felt what Artis felt. "We have a guest with us tonight," Artis said. Everyone in the group hugged Serena.

Jaqui wanted to wait for the throbbing in her temple to subside before she opened her eyes. She was bound in damp sheets and could smell herself. It wasn't pretty. What seemed like hours passed. Long after daylight had invaded her bedroom she heard singing, beautiful singing. Katrine was in the kitchen making coffee, singing in her native tongue. Jaqui waited, afraid of what might happen if she stood up, afraid of what had happened with Katrine the night before. She knew it was wrong but she just didn't feel it.

When the noise from the coffee grinder pierced her brain she could put it off no longer. She opened her eyes and sat up, a motion akin to a carnival ride. She found that only one eye would fully open. Splashing water on her face proved painful. The mirror explained. She looked like a crash victim, but she had to talk to Katrine.

"Good morning, sweetie," Katrine chirped when Jaqui appeared. "Are you okay?"

"I think I'll live."

"That not a real good look for you. I can do make up for your face."

"Maybe later." Jaqui poured herself a cup of Katrine's strong coffee, picked up the sugar then decided against it and set it down. Then she noticed the makeup mirror on the kitchen table. A single edge razor blade lie beside it.

"What's this?" Jaqui asked.

"Breakfast. Want some? "No, I don't do that."

Katrine giggled as if it were nothing. "Okay, then, that is more for me."

Jaqui decided to let it pass. "Listen, about last night…"

"Don't worry. I don't take advantage of innocent drunk girl."

"No, I know. I didn't mean that. I mean, I liked the kiss and I like you. It's just, well, I'm not a lesbian."

Katrine sat down across from Jaqui and stared into her eyes, a wry grin on her face. "Okay" was all she said.

Jaqui wanted to explain but didn't know where to begin. Katrine reached into the pocket of her robe and pulled out a small glass vial. She poured a little pile of white crystals onto a mirror and began chopping them into powder. "You sure is not for you? Is very good with making hurt go away. It is used by doctors."

Jaqui was pretty sure that last part wasn't true but the side of her head still throbbed. "Maybe a little bit."

Katrine poured a little more into the pile. "You should sniff it up the nose hole... nostril... on side with bruise," Katrine giggled, "for best results." She demonstrated for Jaqui by vacuuming one line up with a piece of soda straw. Jaqui followed her example. The powder didn't sting or burn like she expected but slowly the numbness began to spread through the side of her head and down her throat. She was surprised by the agreeable flavor. Katrine snorted 1/2 the remaining line and handed the straw back to Jaqui.

"What the hell," Jaqui said and finished off the line. She noticed most of her pain and all of her hangover had dissipated.

"Do you do this a lot?" Jaqui asked.

"No, too much money. It is like champagne, sometimes to celebrate. This is tip from customer. Very good to clean up house by. My room is mess after fool last night."

"I'm sorry."

"No, it is okay, not your fault."

"I'll help you clean it. I need to wash my sheets anyway," Jaqui offered. "let me take a shower first."

Jaqui turned the water as hot as she could stand it and scrubbed until she was pink. As she rinsed, she felt the water cascade over her shoulders and slide down her body. She was tingling. She thought it was probably from the powder but then she found herself wishing the house had only one bathroom so Katrine would have a reason to come in. She imagined asking Katrine to wash her back or just watch her shower. When she noticed that her hand had lingered between her thighs she yanked it back and shut off the water. She dried quickly and pulled on jeans and a t-shirt. She ripped the sheets from her bed and tossed them in the laundry room.

Katrine's bedroom still held every trace of the battlefield it had been the night before. Her "toys" were scattered everywhere. Pillows were on the floor. The cosmetics on her dresser were all pushed to one end and the mirror had a huge smudge right in the middle. There was a small spot of blood on the sheets that made Jaqui queasy when she saw it.

"You are better now?" Katrine asked as she tossed an empty laundry basket on the floor.

"Oh yeah. The shower was wonderful."

They began picking up the clothes that were strewn around the room. Katrine found a single man's sock. She laughed as she tossed it in the garbage, then stripped the bed and grabbed the dirty towels from the bathroom. Katrine removed her robe and threw it in the basket. She yanked a white lace nightie over her head and tossed it in the basket. As she turned to get clean clothes from her dresser, she noticed Jaqui had stopped cleaning. Her movements slowed.

Jaqui watched Katrine shuck the nightie and noticed how tiny and vulnerable Katrine looked; the thin line of muscle down her back, diminutive but firm buttocks riding high above slender thighs, almost nonexistent breasts with large almond colored nipples. Katrine slipped on some board shorts and a tank top. Jaqui began to breathe again. It was all she could do not to act. She wanted to hold Katrine on her lap, slide her hand under the tank top and touch those nipples, feel Katrine's talented tongue dance with hers again, but she knew it couldn't happen. It was wrong. She just needed a man to get her centered again. It was probably just the coke making her feel like this.

"Earth to Jaqui," Katrine said and grabbed Jaqui's bicep.

"What...? Oh, yeah. I'm cool." Jaqui replied. The place Katrine had touched her felt like melted chocolate.

"We should do this so we can have fun time," Katrine said. "Maybe go shop."

～

At Brenham City Park, Sara sat at a picnic table. She'd finished off a corndog and was working on a big dill pickle while she waited on Langley. He'd handled her religious preference pretty well, she thought. For a supposedly devout Presbyterian, he had about as much interest in religion as a dog has to fashion trends. The nude worship bound him up a little but once she related it to their weekend in the park, he accepted, if not wholly supported, her position. As she finished off the pickle she saw his truck pull into the park. She stood on the table and waved until he spotted her and honked his horn.

Langley picked her from the table and hugged her, then placed her on the ground. "So, what's the big news that we couldn't meet on campus?" he asked.

"I went to the doctor today."

Langley became concerned. "Are you alright?"

"Oh yeah," Sara said. "I'm also five weeks pregnant."

Langley grew pale and dropped to the bench. "The camping trip?"

"Had to have been."

"What are we going to do?"

"I'm going to have a baby."

"I mean, I guess we need to get married, pretty quick, too."

"Need? You fucker, I wouldn't marry you now if you drug me to the altar with your stupid pickup truck!"

"Oh my God! That's not what I meant. I want our child to have two parents."

"It's my child and it does have two parents, but I'll be damned if I'll marry you just 'cause you knocked me up. I'm not going to have you saying I trapped you."

"It's not like that," Langley said, but he couldn't find any more words. He wanted to tell her how much he cared about her, but his heart was in the way of his tongue.

Sara started to cry. "I didn't know what I expected," she moaned. "I don't want our marriage to start this way. Can you understand?"

"Yeah, but I don't think I agree."

"It's got to be this way, going to be this way. If we get through this in one piece maybe we can talk about it after the baby is born."

"You sure I can't change your mind?"

"You know, while I sat here waiting for you, I wasn't sure what would happen, but now I know. It's got to be this way, for both our sakes."

"What about the baby?"

"He won't care."

They sat at the table in silence intent on their dilemma. All thoughts of going to lunch vanished. Finally, Langley spoke. "What do you think he'll be like?"

"Or she," Sara said. "I hope it has your blonde hair and blue eyes."

"I hope he has your brains."

"Or she!" Sara repeated. "You know there's a better than 50/50 chance we'll have a girl."

"That's okay I just don't like referring to it as 'it'."

Sara laid her head on Langley's shoulder.

"We'll be alright," she said.

Jaqui stared at the phone. Katrine had an out call. A limo had picked her up leaving Jaqui rattling around in the house alone. She thought about making dinner but wasn't really hungry. The thought of her friend in the clutches of some pervert made her queasy. The odd people she knew were making her crazy; Keegan with his misogynistic personality, Adam stalking her and for what? Whoever the woman was that was calling and making threats, and why? What woman would have a reason to threaten her? Life was topsy-turvy in the most disturbing way. She knew who she needed to talk to but she was ashamed to call. She had just baled on him with no explanation. If she called her dad his answer would just be to come home. That wasn't going to happen. She desperately needed to talk to someone, someone who really knew her, someone she could trust. She mixed herself a bourbon and coke, saving the Scotch for her time with Katrine, and dialed Langley's house. "Hello?" It was Langley's dad. Jaqui didn't know what to say.

"Hello, is anybody there?"

"Hi, Mr. Scott. It's Jaqui, Jaqui Benderman. How is Marjorie doing? I miss y'all."

"She's doing a lot better, getting movement back in her arm, talking more. We're very pleased with her therapy. Where are you living?"

"I'm in Austin. I got a job singing with a band. It's not great pay but it's what I want to do. Is Langley there?"

"He's in the back yard with Sara, barbecuing. Let me get him. I know he'll want to talk to you. He's been worried sick." That wasn't what she wanted to hear. He should know that she could handle damn near anything.

"Hey girl! Where the hell you been?" Langley sounded happy.

"Austin. Who's Sara?" Jaqui asked.

"She's my girlfriend. Can you believe that? Me, with a girl-friend? So what have you been doing? Rumor is that you've been sick but I didn't believe it."

"I'm singing in a band. You remember the band, Frostfire, from the late eighties? The singer is doing this R&B thing. I'm singing backup. We're supposed to go on tour in the fall. He's kind of a jerk but the band is fun. So, a girlfriend,? Tell all."

"She's so sweet and funny, really smart. I can't wait for you to meet her. She lived all her life in Lockhart. I can't believe she was only 15 miles away and we never met."

"So how did you meet?"

"We have a couple of classes together at SACC. She's in my criminal justice class. She wants to be in social work, like a juvenile probation officer or CPS, something like that. I'm going to catch 'em, she's going to fix 'em, a team effort."

"That's funny. I'm glad you're happy."

"What about you? How's your love life?"

"It started out weird and it's gotten even stranger. I'm really confused right now. I don't have a boyfriend. All the guys I've met here are either deadbeat slackers or jerks or really creepy. I even had a stalker. I had to move. It's OK, though, I'm living in a really beautiful house in West Austin with another singer. She's Romanian and sings folk music, an amazing guitar player too. The thing is though, I think we might be becoming more than just friends."

"What do you mean?"

"Well, okay, well, the other night we were talking and, well, she's always been super friendly, you know, one of those hugger, touchy-feely people. I'm okay with that. I am, too, in a way, but we were talking the other night and she more or less told me she was attracted to me and she kissed me and I guess I kind of kissed her back. Anyway, the next morning I told her I wasn't a lesbian, so nothing else has happened, but now I'm not so sure. I think about her all the time. She's so pretty and small and I just want to hold her and kiss her some more. I don't... I mean, is there something wrong with me? I'm sure I still like guys. If Keegan wasn't such a jerk I could get something going with him. He's buff, kind of old, but he works out. I'm pretty sure he thinks I'm sexy. I'm sorry, I'm just rattling. I'm so confused. None of this feels wrong, just different. What should I do?"

"I didn't see that coming. I don't know, Jaqui. I don't think there's anything wrong with it. A lot of people do, though. I'd just say be true to your feelings but, if you decide to have a girl-friend, be ready to get some grief from a lot of folks that don't understand."

"Don't tell my daddy, okay?"

"I won't, but you should call him and let him know you're

okay. He's your dad. You owe him that. He's going crazy worrying about you."

"Yeah, I should. I will. I'll do it now. It'll be good to talk to him. I've got to get past the accident. Really, it wasn't his fault anymore than mine. Take down my number, okay? We need to stay in touch."

"I've got it. I miss you, Jaqui. We need to get together soon." Langley hung up the phone. When he turned around Sara was leaning against the door jamb with her arms folded across her chest.

"Who was that?" she asked. She wasn't happy.

"It was Jaqui, probably my best friend in the whole world. She's awesome. I can't wait for y'all to meet."

"She your ex?"

"No, sweetie. I don't have an ex. You're my very first girl-friend in the whole world."

Sara snorted. "I find that a little hard to buy. It sounds like bullshit to me. So, when are you planning to get together with her and when were you going to let me in on it?"

"Sara, please, you're way off base here. Jaqui's like a sister to me. Besides, she lives in Austin and she just called to let me know she thinks she might be a lesbian. So, really, just let it go."

Sara trudged back outside. Langley came up behind and put his arms around her. "You've got nothing to worry about," he said. "I love you."

He'd been trying to mention that tidbit of information for a couple of weeks, but it kept getting stuck in his chest. This time it just rolled off his tongue. Sara turned around and looped her arms around his neck. He noticed the wetness in her eyes as she leaned her face against his chest.

"I love you, too," she said, "but I'm not sure how this can work."

Everything I Have Is Yours

- Julie London

Jaqui had her first check for working with Keegan's band and she felt a celebration was in order. She invited Katrine to the Four Seasons. It was partly an excuse to dress up, but she also needed to see Bruce. She owed him a gig. She'd agreed, way before the pageant fiasco, to sing at a wedding he'd booked. In the back of her mind, hidden in a secret compartment of her psyche, was a desire to flaunt her beauty for Katrine. Ever since Katrine's kiss she'd been unable to completely block the desire out of her mind. It danced around their friendship like an unspoken poem with a shared meaning. Tonight, she thought the poem should be spoken. If she got the chance to perform, she'd direct her performance to Katrine.

They were dressed to the nines as they left the house, both girls in evening gowns. Jaqui's royal blue gown came just above the ankle, Katrine's red one, just above the knee. Their hair was swept up and held high with elegant jewels, exposing their slender necks. They'd helped each other with the hairdos. It tested Jaqui's will not to nuzzle Katrine's shoulders.

In the car Jaqui flicked on the wipers to knock away the fallen elm leaves. She noticed a business card under her wiper blade and retrieved it. The handwritten side just said, "call me". The printed side was for Spring Street Redeeming Spirit Church - Adam Wolf, pastor. It gave a phone number and a strip mall address in East Austin. A cold shiver gripped Jaqui. "It's Adam, the blues guy. He didn't tell me he was a preacher."

"Shit," Katrine said. "I was hoping for him to leave you alone. I should have told you. He called twice for you. I not tell you. Remember when I say he want more from me than singing? You think probably sex, and probably that, too, but I think he want to steal my soul. He want yours too, I think. That's why I not say about calling. I'm sorry."

"No, it's okay. He creeps me out. I don't know if he's dangerous but I don't plan to find out." She threw the card in the back floorboard. "Let's just have fun tonight. Don't even think about that idiot." Since it was a weeknight, and early by nightclub standards, Jaqui wasn't surprised by the small number of patrons. The bar itself had a crystalline sparkle against the drastic black and white elegance of the club. Several groups of businessmen took immediate notice as the girls chose a table near the piano where Bruce deftly manipulated the ivories. Instead of a welcoming smile Bruce greeted Jaqui with a gaze of total confusion.

The waitress remembered Jaqui. "I'm so sorry to hear about your boyfriend," the waitress said. "How are you holding up?"

"I'm working through it, thanks," Jaqui replied. "I'll need to…" The waitress began.

"As always," Katrine said, placing her driver's license on the waitress's tray. "Are two double shots of Glenlivet 18 available for us please?" She placed an American Express alongside the license. "Can you do also a… I'm sorry, run a tab."

The waitress smiled. "I'll have those right out."

"Hey, it's supposed to be my treat," Jaqui said. "Besides, I'm fine with the cheap stuff."

"Let me pay first one. Just watch. We will not pay any more."

"I know what you're thinking. I'm sure we can get guys to buy our drinks but I don't want to obligate to them, and really, I just want to hang out with you, anyway."

Katrine's eyes sparkled. "We can have both, watch. You dance, yes?"

"Sure, I'm okay at it."

"After our drinks we dance, me and you, then watch what happens."

The thought made Jaqui blush, not just her face. A very warm blush enveloped her body. "Sounds fun, even if we buy our own drinks."

The Glenlivet was the smoothest Scotch Jaqui had tasted. Several of the "suits" kept eyeballing the girls. Soon the waitress came with another round and pointed out two very tall gentleman at the bar. The girls raised their glasses to them in a salute of thanks. Katrine took Jaqui's hand and led her to the little dance floor near the piano. The song was a slow rendition of "Ain't No Two Ways About It, It's Love". Katrine slipped into Jaqui's arms and wrapped a hand around her neck. She nuzzled her cheek against Jaqui's breast and began swaying to the music. Jaqui slipped into a dreamlike state at the smell of Katrine so close, their bodies absorbing each other's motions. The Scotch magnified the glow of the crystal bar. Jaqui felt the evening flowing in the direction she'd hoped. When the song ended Katrine gazed into Jaqui's eyes and kissed her lightly on the lips. Jaqui took Katrine's hand and led her back to the table. They had no sooner set down than the two men from the bar were asking to join them.

"We should join you at bar instead," Katrine said. She looked at Jaqui. "If that's okay with you, Baby."

Jaqui played along. The game promised to be a lot of fun. "Sure, Sweetheart, the light's better and you look so pretty tonight." The girls stood and headed toward the bar. The guys tripped over each other trying to give the girls space to lead the way." I'm Jaqui and this is my roommate, Katrine," she told the taller of the men.

"James, I'm James and this is. Lawrence," the tall one said. "Call me Larry," Lawrence said. "You ladies are stunning."

"Thank you," Katrine replied.

"We don't get out much. We figured we'd do it up right," Jaqui said. "We're glad you noticed. Thanks for the drinks by the way."

"No problem," James said, "Just let us know when you're ready for another."

Bruce announced he was going on break. "Excuse me for a minute," Jaqui said. "I need to speak with the pianist. I'll be right back." She intercepted Bruce on his way to the bar.

"Hey, Jaqui," Bruce said. "I didn't expect to see you here."

"Really? Why not?"

"I,... I heard you were in rehab."

"No. Why would I be in rehab? Who told you that?"

"Lilah. She gave me a ride home after you had your accident. We've been staying in touch. That's where everyone in your hometown thinks you are."

"Fuck! That lying little bitch. No. No, I'm definitely not in rehab. There's no reason I should be. She set me up. She's the one who planted the liquor and pills in my suitcase. The bourbon was hers. I have no idea of where the pills came from."

"That doesn't sound right. She seems really concerned about you. She stopped by last Thursday, said she'd driven all the way into the city to visit you in rehab, bring you some clothes."

"I never saw her and I'm obviously not in rehab. She's a conniving slut."

"Hey, no need to be that way. She cares about you."

"Okay, listen. Last Thursday I was at a rehearsal. I got a gig singing backup for Keegan Stone. We were… son of a bitch, that explains a lot! Look, you have no idea who you're dealing with. You should be careful. She's not what she seems. That's all

I'm saying. Anyway, you still want me to help with that wedding?"

"Well, no. I thought you were in rehab. I made other arrangements." Jaqui just shook her head and turned to walk away. "Jaqui?" Bruce was tentative. "Would you like to sing a couple? I'm sorry about… well, everything."

Jaqui thought about her real reason for being here tonight. "Sure. What's a good, sexy song with a lot of longing in it?"

"Do you know 'Everything I Have Is Yours'. Julie London made it famous back in the late fifties. It's a real torch classic."

"Oh yeah, I know that one, not all the words."

"Well, you're in luck. I just happen to have the chart. Let me break it out and you can look it over."

"We can do that one and a couple that we worked on before. Cool?"

"Cool," Jaqui said. "I'll look over this while you're on break."

She went back to her group and found a fresh Scotch waiting for her. "Are you guys trying to get us drunk? Katrine, I think these are very naughty boys. I don't think we should trust them."

"I know this one is being naughty. I gave him my number. He needs therapy appointment. Other boy here is either dead-beat or secretly married. Are you married, deadbeat boy?"

"Busted," James said. "Married and deadbeat, but I'm still here for a good time tonight."

"Sweetheart, I think these boys have ulterior motives. Maybe we should go back to our table," Jaqui said.

"But Baby, they buy good drinks. I think if they are behaving maybe can come."

"Hmm, no touchy-feely, right, boys?"

"Okay, no touchy-feely," Larry said.

"No promises," James said.

"I will slap you silly," Jaqui said.

"Okay, I'll be good."

"Well, all right then, y'all can come on down," Jaqui said.

"I'm going to have to start getting my Scotch with soda. It's still early." Jaqui said. She had a long-term plan. "I'm driving." Bruce resumed playing. After one song he invited Jaqui to join him.

"You want to do the Julie London song?"

"Yeah, but last."

"Okay 'Summertime' then?"

"Sure."

Once again Jaqui had the small crowd enraptured. She walked around the dance floor as she sang, projecting her strong voice out across the room. All conversation stopped. She owned the room. Then it came time to sing "Everything I Have Is Yours". As Bruce played the intro, she walked in a slow rhythm toward Katrine and held her gaze. She moaned the words, *"Everything I have is yours, you're part of me. Everything I have is yours, my destiny."* Katrine fixated on Jaqui. She was having trouble swallowing. Jaqui circled the table. The room slipped away. The girls were the only bodies floating in the universe. The hairline above Jaqui's temples moistened when she noticed Katrine's nipples accentuating the front of her gown. When the song ended, Katrine stood and looped her arms around Jaqui's neck. Jaqui felt the humid breath as Katrine nuzzled her neck. "Can we go home, please?" Katrine asked.

Jaqui said goodbye to Bruce and led Katrine toward the door. "Y'all want some company," James hollered from behind.

Katrine shook her head.

"In your dreams," Jaqui shot back.

Once they got to the car Jaqui pulled Katrine to her. Their warm lips met. In overwhelming moisture their tongues teased and tangled. Jaqui took the back of Katrine's head to pull their lips even tighter together. They stopped to breathe. "I've been thinking about this since our first kiss. I want you so bad," Jaqui whispered.

"I, too," Katrine said and nuzzled between the exposed tops

of Jaqui's breasts. "I touched myself when you sang song, very wet and needing for your taste." She slipped a tiny finger between Jaqui's lips. Jaqui found a new flavor, the taste made her moan, salty candy.

"We have to get home."

∼

Sunday dinner, the family all together in a Norman Rockwell print, but the photographer was too lazy to use the dark room. The negative was on display. Dad, mom, son, but no pop-culture trivia, no *"how was school?"*, *" what's going on at work?"*, *"how about those Cowboys?"*. Obligatory Sunday dinner is how Langley felt about it. Dad was a virtual ghost in his absence. Mom was struggling just to function. Langley had a life no one cared about. Obligatory. Dad had hired help so Mom wouldn't have to care for the house. Obligatory. Momgraciously accepted even though not being able to be a homemaker was eating away what was left of her essence. Obligatory. Langley squelching the rumors of Dad's affair with Jeanine Buckholtz. Obligatory. Since Wednesday, anyway, when he'd stopped by his dad's office to… to what? He couldn't remember. It didn't matter now.

It was dark, the blinds open. He was halfway to the building when he saw Jeanine come behind and rub Dad's shoulders. His dad took her arm and pulled her into his lap, kissed her mouth and slid his hand under her skirt. Langley turned back toward the truck, angry, not because his dad was cheating on his mom, not because he had abandoned his family. It was too late for that. Langley was pissed because they didn't even have the decency to close the blinds.

The vocal void at the dinner table was deafening. The more there was to say, the quieter it became. Screw it, Langley thought. He had important news and nobody wanted to hear it.

"Sara's pregnant," he said. It's not like the room could get any quieter. His dad took another bite of roast. From the corner of his eye Langley saw one side of his mother's mouth crack a wistful smile.

"When's she due?" His mother mumbled.

"Not sure," Langley said. "She's only like six weeks in. We're going to the doctor on Wednesday."

"I'll talk to the pastor," his dad said, "schedule a wedding for the end of the month."

"We're not getting married," Langley stated.

"Yes, you are!"

"No, not now, anyway. We'll see after the baby is born."

"The baby needs a father. You can't just have a bastard child!"

"I'm the father. I'll make that decision."

"You must get married. It's the only right thing to do."

"Don't fucking talk to me about what's right. You won't,— can't, tell me what to do. You're in no position!"

Before he could react, Langley felt his father's fist against his jaw. It shocked him more than it hurt.

"Stop it!" Marjorie said, "Please, this should be a happy time." She began to cry, Langley went to his mother, ignoring his father, who seemed to be in shock from his own actions.

"It's okay, Mom. Everything is going to work out. I should leave now, though."

"Langley, wait," his dad said.

Langley turned on his father. "Right now, I'm out of here. I'm not talking to you. I'm pretty sure you don't want to hear what I have to say."

Langley drove into the night, generally toward Sara's house without realizing it. What did he expect? His jaw was beginning to ache. He'd never been in a fight, not even a play fight. He had no way to respond and no desire to retaliate. It didn't matter. Dad was wrong, he was right, simple as that, but it wasn't.

The truck turned into the subdivision Sara lived in without any coaxing from Langley. The front of her house was lit up. The garage door was open and a couple of older pickups were in the drive. Langley parked across the street. Before he got out of the truck, he could feel, more than hear, the low rumble of her dad's motorcycle idling in the garage. As he stepped out, someone twisted the throttle and a window rattling blast of sound shook the neighborhood.

"Hell yeah, that's what I'm talking about!" came a shout from the garage. "EVO, 130 plus horses. She screams"

Langley angled for the front door. "Hey Langley, come check this out." It was Sara's dad. Langley ambled over. "We just dropped a tricked-out EVO in this baby. What do you think?" He twisted the throttle again. Langley thought his ears might bleed.

"It's loud," Langley said.

"Fast, too," her dad said. "I can't wait to get this baby out in the hill country. Hey, this is Robb and Crow." He motioned to the two bearded guys in sleeveless tee shirts. Robb had a red bandana around his head. Crow was wearing a Harley Davidson trucker's cap. "Guys, this is the fine young man that knocked up my little girl. Should we kill him or give him a beer?"

"Kill him," Crow said.

"Give him a beer," Robb said.

"I guess I'm the tiebreaker," her dad said and handed him a Budweiser. "Look at this kid. That's going to be one good looking baby."

Sara's mom stepped into the garage. She was barefoot and wearing a sun dress. "Guys, I know that shit gets your dicks all hard, but you need to shut it down before the neighbors call the cops. It's getting late. Take it home to mama. Oh, hi, Langley. Does Sara know you're here?"

"He just walked up, checking out the machine. Give him a minute." Her dad reached under the tank and turned off the ignition. "Chill out, finish your beer. She ain't going nowhere." He kicked a stool toward Langley.

Langley opened the beer and took a sip. He didn't drink but he wanted Sara's dad to accept him. "Sweet machine, how long have you been riding?"

"Since before you kicked the slats out of your cradle. You ride?"

"My mom would have a heart attack, probably from seeing my dad shoot me."

"I reckon you'll be leaving the nest pretty soon."

"It may have just happened."

"That why your jaw's fucked up, duking it out with Daddy?"

"Sort of. I couldn't hit back."

"Yeah, me neither. He'll get over it when the grandbaby shows up. I went through the same shit with my dad."

"I hope it doesn't take that long."

You're welcome here if it comes to that. It's a little late to try to keep you two kids apart."

"Thanks Mr. Sloane."

"Bud. Call me Bud, should be easy to remember." He held out his arm to show off the marijuana leaf tattooed just above his elbow.

"I guess you won't be working at the bank, Bud."

"I hope not."

Sara came part of the way into the garage. She was gripping the door frame as if it were a long-lost toy. "Hey, baby."

"Are you alright?" Langley said. "You look pale."

"The morning sickness has jet lag or something. I never know when it's going to hit. I'm getting tired of crackers and 7-Up but if I even think about real food I toss my cookies."

"Bud, I'm going to get her settled in," Langley said. "Thanks for the offer." He took Sara by the arm and led her inside, fixing her a spot on the living room couch.

"What happened to your face?" She asked.

"Long story."

"I'm not about to run off."

"Basically, I told my parents you're pregnant. Mom's cool but Dad wants us to get married. I told him no and he punched me. I don't think I've ever told him no before. It felt pretty good, worth getting punched for."

"Oh Langley, I'm sorry, but you know what?"

"What?"

"That wasn't really a very long story." She kissed the bruise on his jaw.

"There's more to it. Let's just say I'm glad you live here in Lockhart instead of over in Luling. Dad's porking his secretary, has been for a while apparently. Mom's probably the only person in town that doesn't know. I didn't believe it until the other day when I saw it firsthand."

"Eww!"

"Not the act! Oh my god! But more than I ever wanted to see, and it was like he didn't even care who knew."

"So you told on him? That's why he hit you?"

"No! Of course not. I would never hurt my mom like that. I just left."

"What are you going to do? "

"Not sure, your dad offered to let me move in here."

"So you and Bud are drinking buddies now?"

Langley looked down at the Budweiser in his hand. "What? This, I don't drink. This shit is nasty. I guess I just wanted him to accept me."

"I'm going to give you a hint. You and Bud, not a good fit. He's nice enough most of the time but he can get in your face if he doesn't get his way and his way means everybody in the house. You should stay tonight, though, and we can work it out in the morning. Okay?"

"Sure, thanks, that would be cool. Think he'll let us sleep together?"

"He can't really say no. He's not even married to mom. She'll be cool with it. The way I feel, though, sleeping is all you can count on."

"That's fine. I just like hanging out with you. I should call Mom and let her know."

∼

Jaqui picked the broken pieces of her coffee cup out of the sink. If the crash awakened Katrine there was no indication. She looked over and noticed clean water dripping into the carafe. *Shit, I forgot to put the coffee in the basket.* She found it still in the grinder. *I've got to get it together,* she thought as she began the morning coffee process anew. The smell of Katrine permeated her nostrils. It was all she could do to untangle their limbs without waking the girl. She needed time alone. Jaqui had no point of reference to understand what she experienced in Katrine's bed. She'd participated willingly, even enticed Katrine. It was a mutual seduction. Who was this woman inside her that needed this? She looked at her reflection in the dark kitchen window. She saw herself, maybe a frantic, wild version, but not the woman who teased and tantalized another woman; but she was and she liked it. It was too early to call someone. Besides, who would she call? Who could understand when even she couldn't? The reflection had no answer.

"You are early rising today," Katrine said. She was standing in the doorway, disheveled, but smiling. "You have plan for today?"

"No, I... I just need to think."

Katrine came to Jaqui and slipped her arms under Jaqui's robe. She laid her cheek against Jaqui's breast. "You are pretty, even in morning with tangled hair. I love these, make me wish I had some." She kissed Jaqui's nipples and nuzzled her under her breasts. Jaqui shivered. The feeling was beginning again.

"Want some coffee?" Jaqui asked. Katrine took a seat at the

table. "Yes, please." Katrine contemplated Jaqui as she fixed the coffee, the way she moved so tentatively and prepared the drink with just the right combination of ingredients without asking. "I am not... without clue, you know. This scary for you, this new feeling. I feel it, though, from when I first see you. I want you to feel it too, not be afraid. It is not game for me."

Jaqui dropped the sugar spoon on the floor. She grabbed the counter with both hands. "I am scared. I don't know what this is. I want to hold you and kiss you and touch you, like last night. I want to share my secrets with you. I trust you, but you do scare me. What you do... scares me. How you make your money. I'm afraid I will lose you. I'm not sure I can do it. I don't know how. I've never felt this way."

"We can be slow with this," Katrine said, "be friends first, be lovers when it is right. You stay, I will stay. We will find good life for us, okay, Baby?"

The tears began as Jaqui brought the coffee to Katrine. She touched Katrine's hair and pulled her close. "I love you, too, Katrine."

The phone on the wall behind Katrine rang. "It is your boss man," Katrine said and handed Jaqui the phone.

"Hey Jaqui, Keegan here. Could you plan on staying late after rehearsal tomorrow. I was considering a duet, one of those 50 style things and I wanted your input." This was so far out of character for him that Jaqui froze up for a minute. "Well, what do you think, you in?" Keegan asked.

"Yeah sure, I guess. Tomorrow?"

"After rehearsal, I'll buy dinner. Bring some ideas. Cool?"

"Cool." The call ended.

"What that douche want? Katrine asked. Jaqui giggled at Katrine's slang.

"Input, of all things. It seems he wants me to pick a song for a duet. The only thing that comes to mind is Ian and Sylvia so I've got to do some research."

"Be careful. He is slimy bastard. Do not trust."

"Hey, you hooked me up with him."

"Because you want job. I know Mr. Stone in other ways, too. I just say be careful."

"It's just a song, Darlin'."

~

Langley called home to let his mom know where he was and wasn't going to be. His dad had left in a huff after declaring Langley a hopeless sinner.

"Don't worry, he'll settle down. He just loves you so much.He wants you to do the right thing," she said.

"I am doing the right thing. Sara and I are in for this for the long haul."

"I know, son, but you know how he is."

"He'll have to get over it. This is my decision."

"Try to be patient. Your father is a good man."

If she only knew. "Are you going to be alright?" He asked his mother.

"You and Sara have fun. I'll be fine."

After Langley hung up, Sara took his hand and led him to the back of the house. "I bet you're tired. You look totally stressed out," she said.

"It's been a weird day."

"Let's crawl in the sack and take it easy."

Langley could hear the raucous party outside winding down. First one truck and then another pulled away. Sara's parents were still loud but it was a playful loud, an adult relationship foreign to Langley's experience. "Your folks seem to really have fun together."

"Yeah, most of the time," Sara said. "When they get pissed off they go at it just as loud though."

"I like it. I see some of that in you. At least I don't have to guess what you're thinking."

"We'll see. Let's don't get too heavy in the head right now."

Sara stripped down to her bra and underwear, white cotton, no frills, and stretched out on her back. Langley pulled off his boots and jeans and lay beside her.

"Lose the shirt," Sara said. "I know we can't really do anything but I'd like to feel you next to me."

Langley smiled and pulled his tee shirt over his head. Sara snuggled against him. His hand gently caressed the little fertility dome that had appeared on her lower abdomen. He was overcome with a wondrous realization. "We did this together," he said, "a new life. We created a little person."

Sara laughed. "Yeah, 'we' did. Next time I need to toss my cookies how about you handle that for me." Then she took his hand from her abdomen, kissed his fingertips and pulled his arm between her breasts, rolling over and pulling him around her like a comforter.

"I love you, Langley" she said.

He kissed the back of her neck. "I love you, too."

She snuggled closer under his arm. As he lay there listening to her parents' laughter he realized this was the first time they had slept in a real bed together. He fell asleep knowing a level of happiness and contentment he'd never experienced.

Chain of Fools

Aretha Franklin

Jaqui spent Thursday afternoon researching R&B duets. She was surprised how many good ones there were, some she recognized but most were obscure "B" sides. She had a list of several she felt would work with her and Keegan's voices. She packed a blouse and some make up in a handbag to change into after rehearsal. Practicing the choreography usually made her sweat. She looked in on Katrine who was sitting on her bed playing intricate finger style guitar.

"I may be back late, Babe," Jaqui said. "Keegan wants to take me out and discuss working up a duet or two for the tour. Could be the break I'm looking for."

Katrine put down her guitar and invited Jaqui in, patting a spot on the mattress. "Watch Keegan, he is…complicated man. He might say one thing, mean another, if you are in my drift."

Jaqui smiled. "It's 'getting my drift', but it's cool that you're learning the slang. Don't worry about me. I'm a big girl. I'm taking my brain but I'm leaving my heart here with you. Besides, Keegan's my dad's age. That would just be creepy."

Katrine slid an arm around Jaqui. "That is sweet thing to say. My heart goes with you, too."

Jaqui gave Katrine a kiss. "See you tonight. Are you workimg?

"Not likely. It is late for call and is weeknight."

Jaqui headed out. She'd parked on the street under a tree. Her car was covered in bird droppings and another of Adam's cards was under the wiper. It read: "We really need to talk!" and had a number written on it that wasn't his church's number. It disturbed her that he kept coming by the house but wouldn't just knock on the door. She figured she'd deal with it later and put the card in her purse. As she pulled away from the curb, she failed to notice the beige sedan pulling out of a side street a block behind her.

The show began to jell. Keegan seemed to be less of a jerk during this rehearsal. They went through the first half without stopping. The few comments he made before the break were constructive, even asking the band members for suggestions. It was so rare no one dared offer any.

On instinct, Jaqui went straight to her car. The tires were up. There were no notes under the wipers. All the doors were still locked.

"Everything okay?" Jaqui hadn't noticed Keegan come out behind her. She flinched at his voice.

"Keegan! You startled me."

"Sorry. We on for dinner?"

"Yeah, sure. I brought some ideas."

Keegan leaned against her car. "We'll talk shop later." He sniffed the air. "Stinks out here. Too damn hot for September. Not sure I'll ever get used this Texas weather."

"Where are you from?"

"All over, Army brat. Spent a lot of time in Europe growing up. When I started in music I based out of LA. Spent a lot of time in Washington State. Love it around Seattle. The dreariness works for me I guess. You?"

"Texas farm girl, black land prairie, grew up about 70 miles from here. I've only been out of Texas twice on school trips."

"Well this tour should be an eye opener then. We're hitting 12 states, east and west coasts plus Chicago and Denver. You'll see some stuff. We booked it with some days off between shows."

"Yeah, I'm pretty excited."

"You'll have fun. I'm going back inside before I melt."

Jaqui scanned the area. There was nothing unusual; all the band members vehicles, the equipment van, a few random cars parked here and there including a nondescript beige sedan.

After rehearsal Jaqui stepped into the restroom. She rinsed her face and arm pits then applied fresh deodorant before putting on a green silk blouse. The careful addition of eyeliner and lip gloss added the illusion of maturity to her face. She didn't want to be carded at dinner. Keegan had never asked her age but she didn't want him to know she was only eighteen, though she wasn't sure why. By the time she was spiffed up the other musicians were gone and Keegan was listening to a recording in the sound booth.

"Have a seat." He motioned toward a swivel chair in the corner. "Listen to this, the horns. Their tuning sucks, sounds like some fucking high school marching band." He played a segment of a Motown cover.

"It's just the trombone," Jaqui said. "The other horns are good. Do they have a monitor?"

Keegan played the tape again. "Damn, you're right. I didn't catch that. There's a monitor for the drum and bass. They work off that but the 'bone is farthest away. I should probably set up an extra monitor just for the horns. Thanks, Jaqui. You're sharp, picking up on that."

"No problem."

"Think you could go over some of the tapes? You've got quite an ear."

"Yeah, but later. I'm starving and you promised me dinner."

"Okay, you're right. Let's go."

While waiting for a table Keegan suggested sitting at the bar. "So, who do you think you sound more like, Smokey Robinson or Marvin Gaye?" Jaqui asked while waiting for her second scotch and soda. "I see you as more of a Smoky sort of guy."

"So you want to go Motown, I guess?" Keegan replied. "That's where all the really good R&B duets hang out."

"I guess you're right...again. So you probably have something in mind. Care to share?"

"Well, there's Smoky and Gladys Knight's 'Ain't Nothing But the Real Thing' or 'I Want You 'Round' with Mary Wells. He did a couple with Tammy Terrell, some with Diana Ross, even Aretha. I'd love to sing some Aretha. I could seriously belt out some Aretha." The scotch was getting through to her quickly on an empty stomach. Keegan found the girl entertaining. She knocked back the last of her second drink and started in, "Chain, chain, chain, --- Chain of fools." Her voice was spot on but loud enough to get the attention of several patrons and the bartender , who came over and shushed her.

"Really? You don't like Motown?" she asked the bartender a bit too pointedly.

Keegan laughed. "Bring her another scotch and soda."

"You sure you don't want to eat first?" The bar man asked. "Don't worry. I'm driving."

"Hey, Bar boy, I'm sitting right here. Is there a problem?" Jaqui said and smiled her most innocent smile. The bartender walked away shaking his head. The next round took a while to appear.

"So I was thinking, open the second set with the duets so you don't visibly pull me from the backup singers then maybe you do a couple of acoustic songs while the band resets. It shows off your versatility and I don't have to be obvious about where I fit. What do you think?" Jaqui said.

"Looks like you thought it out. You want to be stage manager, too, while you're at it?"

"Sure, why the hell not? What's it pay?" Jaqui was riding high on a wave of scotch fueled manic joy.

"How about we just start out by picking some material?" Keegan thought it might be time to rein the girl in. "You've got some great ideas but we don't actually have a stage manager."

Just as Jaqui received her third drink, a table miraculously be- came available near the back wall of the dining area in a dark alcove. The waiter offered menus. "Could I start you off with an appetizer, a shrimp cocktail or some Russian caviar?"

Ooh! Caviar!" Jaqui said. "I've never had it. What is it?"

"Fish eggs." Keegan proffered.

"Oh, no, nope, I think not," Jaqui said and shuddered visibly. "I'll go with the shrimp cocktail."

"I'll have the caviar," Keegan said. Jaqui crinkled her nose. "I hope you weren't planning on trying to kiss me." She felt

a wave of shock. Where had that come from, she thought. She felt herself blush. Keegan glanced at her then pretended not to hear.

"So, anyway," Jaqui said, "there's other well-known stuff like those famous songs or we could pick out some more obscure stuff. Diana Ross and Marvin Gaye did the Burt Bacharach song called 'Things I Will Not Miss'. It's kind of silly but it would show off the band's talent if you arranged it right. There's all sorts of stuff we can do." Jaqui was trying to distance herself from the comment about kissing.

"We should stay with songs most people are familiar with. 'Ain't Nothing But The Real Thing' would be a great crowd pleaser. Then maybe a slow ballad like 'Endless Love' or 'I've Had the Time Of My Life'."

"Can we get arrangements for these or how do we adapt?"

"Art does most of the arranging. We just pick out what we want and the key."

Jaqui was enjoying the shop talk when the main course came.

It was all she could do to keep from wolfing the meal down. Hunger had a hold on her. After dinner they had another drink, his second, her fifth. She excused herself to the restroom on rubber band legs. The mirror told the story. She had drunk herself into a corner. She had to sober up by the time she got back to her car.

After freshening up, she returned to the table. "Well, this has certainly been an enlightening evening," she said. "We should probably get back to the studio now so I can pick up my car."

"Sure you don't want another scotch?"

"Oh no, I can barely walk, and I'm supposed to drive."

Back at the studio she poured herself out of Keegan's Porsche and stumbled toward her car.

"Jaqui, wait. I have something inside that will help sober you up."

Jaqui considered her inconsistent gait and followed him inside. She was sitting in the sound booth, in the same chair where she had picked the out-of-tune trombone player from the mix, while she watched as Keegan chopped some white powder into lines with a single edge razor blade.

"I suppose you know how this works," he said as he rolled a twenty into a short tube. She snatched the bill from him and vacuumed up a line with one nostril. Since there were three lines left, she used the other nostril to make a another one disappear. The numbness was already beginning in her palette. The pleasant taste jogged her memory and she thought about Katrine and how comfortable she was with the odd relationship.

Keegan raised his eyebrows. "Getting a bit greedy, are we?" He snorted one line and scooted back from the counter.

"I'm sorry," Jaqui said. "There were four, I just figured two apiece."

"No reason to get in a hurry. You don't have a day job, do you?"

"Well, no, I guess not."

"Let's go over one of the songs, then. I think I can work out the chords to 'Ain't Nothing Like The Real Thing'. Goes pretty well with the coke, don't it?"

Jaqui could only giggle at his joke. Her heart was beating faster. She could feel the blood charging through her veins, alternating between cold and hot. She watched Keegan sit down at the piano, unbutton his top shirt button then roll his head around on his shoulders. It caught her attention.She walked toward the piano, trying, but failing, not to put any slinkiness into her stride. She wasn't sure what was happening but every movement, every word, had multiple meanings.

"I don't remember all the words," she said. Her voice sounded like a lost child. Keegan went back into the sound booth and opened a computer file. In seconds, the printer came to life. Meanwhile, Jaqui was admiring the perfection of the piano's black lacquer finish. When Keegan handed her the words, she felt his breath on her neck. Her skin sizzled where his fingers brushed against her arm.

He sat back at the piano bench. "Let's do this." He began the intro.

What had he meant, *Let's do this*, dual meaning again or was it just her? She could see the muscles rippling under his shirt. She realized she wasn't a lesbian, at least not now, not completely. She missed her cue.

"Jaqui?" Keegan said. "Are you okay?"

"Yeah, sure, I'm sorry. Start again." This time she nailed it. She kept the lyric sheet handy for a reference but mostly closed her eyes and leaned into the song, letting it take over. Suddenly the music stopped.

"Damn, Jaqui, that was incredible. Only problem is, you're singing both parts. Give me a shot at it. C'mere, let me see the lyrics." He took a pencil and underlined her part then drew a circle around the parts they would sing harmony on. She could smell him as he leaned beside her. "You want to carry the melody here or sing harmony." He was pointing to a circled area.

"It's up to you," she said.

"Let's alternate then. I'll take the lead on the first chorus. You can have the second."

Was he clueless? She wondered. *Could he not feel this energy between them?* He was so close she could taste his breath. She brushed her hip against him. He looked startled but a hint of smile touched the corners of his mouth. She saw it. She was watching.

"From the top." He sat back down at the piano. Jaqui made every effort to concentrate on the song. It worked, but it wasn't great.

"Let's try it again," he said. "This time I'll do the harmonies.

You seem more comfortable with the lead."

She was beginning to perspire. She felt it in her armpits and her crotch. "Can we turn the air on?" She kicked off her shoes. Without waiting for an answer, she adjusted the thermostat. "Okay then, I'm ready. Start again." Each time was a little better. On the fourth try she saw that Keegan was enjoying the song. It brought out her best effort.

"Well I think we nailed it. That sounded pretty good. What do you think?" he said. "It's a start. It'll kick ass with the whole band... and someone who can actually play piano." She was sparring now, just having fun. She sat beside him on the bench. "So where did you learn piano?"

"I didn't, as you just pointed out. I use it to figure out arrangements and harmonies when they don't come to me."

She caught herself watching his eyes. They were glancing at her cleavage as he revealed his musical inadequacies. She bent over and slipped on her shoes, intentionally pressing her thigh into his. When she sat back up he had finished talking. She looked in his eyes, then closed hers and leaned into what she knew was happening. He grabbed the back of her head and pushed her face against his, thrusting his tongue between her lips. She gasped at his forcefulness then ground into him as he wound her hair around his fist.

So this is how it's going to be. You like rough. I can do rough. When he withdrew his tongue, she took his lower lip between her teeth, biting and sucking until he pulled her loose by the hair.

"This isn't right," he panted, "very unprofessional."

"Who'll know? I'm good at secrets." She grabbed his crotch and felt his erection through his pants. "You know you want me. This don't lie." She gave a little squeeze and bit his earlobe. She took his head between both hands and pulled it down between her breasts, then pulled him away. "You can have it all, but you have to say 'please'."

Keegan felt like he'd won the lottery. Had this girl figured him out so quickly? "My lovely lady, may I please enjoy your pleasures?" She stood up and stepped back. "That was kind of a prissy way to ask. Face the wall in I'll think about it." As soon as he wasn't watching she shucked her clothes and hopped onto the top of the piano. She threw her panties past his head. "Turn around."

He was stunned by her picturesque pose. She was stretched out on her side, her head propped on one hand, the other hand covering the part that could engulf him. One finger was hidden behind the others. "You may approach. No touching. This is some grade A stuff. Want a taste?" She pulled her middle finger out of her vagina and poised it, arm extended, as if she was flicking him off. "Lick it!"

He treated the finger as if it were the last Dreamsicle on earth. "No hands!" she demanded. "Want more?" He nodded. "Get undressed, shirt and shoes first. While you're doing that, tell me what your tongue has planned for me."

He tried to arrange his thoughts as he unlaced his boots. "Keegan, Baby you need to talk. I'm not going to trust a tongue that can't make syllables. Look at me while you take off your shirt." She rolled onto her back and began running the wet finger over the hard nibs of her nipples. "C'mon, speak!"

"I thought you might enjoy it if I started behind your knees and slowly kissed, licked, and nibbled my way up to the juicy part. I'll slide my tongue in as far as possible then flatten it out and drag it straight up. I know where the sweet spot is. I'm not an amateur, you know."

By now, Jaqui's wet finger had found its way back to the "sweet spot". "Not an the amateur? You mean you've done it for money? You whore!" She couldn't help but giggle.

"No, I mean I know what I'm doing."

"Pants now, slowly, I'm watching." Her breathing was getting shallow. The finger was undulating in a circular motion.

"I thought I would bring you to the edge and hold you there," he said.

"Not unless you want to get smothered between my thighs."

"Beats getting hit by a bus."

"Boxers, really? Those have got to go. Throw them in the trash."

"But there brand new."

"Now they're trash. That's a deal breaker, a secret I won't keep twice. You're pretty damn hot looking, though, for an old fart." She slid her legs off the side of the piano, "Come show me what you learned over the years. Remember, no hands." She laid back with her hands fondling her nipples and spread her legs. Although she enjoyed the way he brought her to the edge and then pulled back, she couldn't help but think about how Katrine was so much more in tune with her body, so gentle and passionate. Keegan was more like a human sex toy than a lover.

"Bring it," she said when she was near a peak. He did. It was like a low voltage localized wave of electricity, effective but not really satisfying. She slid off the piano and fell to her knees. She noticed his erection was diminished slightly. "What's wrong? Wasn't that fun for you?"

"You're delicious," he replied, avoiding a direct answer.

At the first touch of her lips the erection problem disappeared.

She sucked his testicles, popsicled his erection. She attempted to get it all in her mouth without gagging. She almost could. He wasn't very large. When his hand went to the back of her head, her teeth bit down lightly. The hand retreated. She felt the tension begin in the throbbing between her lips and his shortness of breath. "I know what you want," she said. She stood and leaned over the piano, spreading her legs.

"Holy shit! Is that a watermelon? I was in Alabama once and I heard a story about young boys plugging melons to get off. Girl, that's some seriously hillbilly shit," Keegan said.

"What's wrong, Baby? You don't like watermelon? You missed out as a kid. But, hey, I can take it home untouched."

"No, I'm cool with rural." He slipped in from behind and started hammering away at her, full force. She remembered to moan a couple of times during the 90 seconds it took him to finish. She noticed some of her fingernail polish had chipped.

When they were done she dressed without looking at him. If he checked her out, she didn't notice.

"You want that other line?" he asked.

"No, I should get on home. You were right though. I feel wide awake and stone cold sober."

He didn't respond. As she left, he was bent over the counter with a rolled bill up his nose.

Langley opened his eyes to sunlight streaming through the window. He was in bed alone. He pulled on his jeans and went to look for his little love. She was at the kitchen table finishing off a bag of microwave popcorn. A jar of pickles sat on the table in front of her. It was half full, or half empty depending on your perspective.

"You snore ... loud," she said.

"I'm sorry."

"No problem. I was hungry anyway."

He pulled out a chair.

"Get a shirt," she said, "house rules. Bud will have a conniption fit if he comes in here and sees you half naked at the table. It's bad enough that you knocked me up."

"He seems okay with that."

"It's a lot easier for him to deal with than coming to the table without a shirt. Why don't you grab a shower and I'll fix you some breakfast."

"You don't have to do that."

"Just be a good boy and lose the stink. I'll be a good little wifey and whip up some bacon and eggs. Now go."

This is going to be fun, Langley thought, then he realized that, as much as he wanted to stay here, he had to go home and take care of his mother. He couldn't count on his dad. What about after the baby? He was only a few weeks from starting at the police academy. Something had to give.

Okay, maybe not quite sober, she thought as she walked to the car. The keys jingled in her trembling hand and a dull ache lingered behind her eyes. She slammed the car door and rolled all the windows down to let the air circulate around her head. *What the hell was I thinking?* The guilt began to set in. Katrine. What would she tell her? Would she tell her? Had she trashed her career? She chirped her tires as she pulled onto East Seventh street, running for the comfort of home. It seems like every light is red when you're in a hurry. At the second light, a beige sedan pulled beside her on the right. Something about the slow way it stopped, too close to her car, made her look over. The driver was wearing a clown mask and staring at her. Just as the image registered, an arm came out. The hand held what could only be a pistol. Jaqui floored it, red light be damned, but the sedan kept pace. The clown took aim. She hit the brakes. The shot clipped her hood. The sedan pulled in front of her and slowed. Jaqui saw an opportunity. She made a hard left, slipping across the path of an oncoming city bus. She raced down the block and cut a hard right onto East Sixth nearly pulling her little coupe up on two wheels. Ignoring lights and stop signs she gunned it toward the Interstate. If she could just get to the highway the police station was on the other side. This time in the morning there wasn't much traffic. She took a breath and looked around. She wasn't being followed. When she reached the highway, she turned turn right and hit Seventh again. The beige sedan was waiting. The clown tried to pull beside her. She didn't see the gun but she knew it was there. She swung the coupe into the Austin Police Department's parking garage and parked between two cruisers. She ran to the door of the station but found it locked. Terrified that she may have been followed, she thrummed on the steel door. "Please, please," she screamed, "somebody's trying to kill me!" It seemed like forever but eventually the door opened. She stepped inside.

"Hold it!" The officer said. "Personnel only."

"But they're shooting at me!" Jaqui said.

"Okay, put your hands behind your head and step in. Face the wall."

Now she was angry, but she obeyed. "Look, God damn it, I'm not the criminal here."

"I'll need to see some ID." The policeman called for backup with one hand on his weapon. Almost immediately, a female officer appeared and frisked Jaqui.

"Okay ma'am, what's the problem?" The first officer said. Jaqui slipped her license from the pocket of her jeans and described the incident as best she could. She wasn't much help identifying the vehicle, just an older four door that she didn't recognize. "Maybe a Chevy or Buick, definitely not new," she said.

"What were you doing out east?" the female officer asked, as if white girls shouldn't be on the east side at night.

"Rehearsing. I sing backup in a show band."

The male officer rolled his eyes "How much have you had to drink?" Not, "Have you been drinking?" They weren't going to give her the benefit of the doubt.

"What the hell does that have to do with being shot at? You know what, just forget it. I'll take my chances on the street." She doubted her assailant would hang around the police station waiting. It had to be random anyway.

"Suit yourself, but before you leave we would like you to take a Breathalyzer test. You appear to be intoxicated."

"Seriously! Are you shitting me?"

"No ma'am. We can't let you drive in your condition."

"My condition? What condition? Human target? Sure whatever, I'll blow in your box if it will make you feel better. I can't believe this. I came in for help, and this?"

The officers led her into an oversized closet connected to booking. An electronic device was humming away with what looked like ticker tape attached. The female officer unwrapped a disposable plastic mouthpiece and slid it over a corrugated hose. "Take a deep breath and exhale into the tube," she said. Jaqui obeyed. "Again." Jaqui raised her eyebrows. "We didn't get a reading." The officer sounded disaffected. Again Jaqui exhaled.

"Point oh nine," the male officer said. "That's legally impaired. We could arrest you, but considering the circumstances, can you have someone pick you up? We can't let you drive."

"What about my car? What about the guy who shot at me?"

"We have a bulletin out for the shooter. Your car can stay until tomorrow. Officer Sanchez will put a temporary parking permit on it. You'll need to have it gone by noon."

Jaqui considered her options. Keegan was the obvious choice since Katrine only had the little scooter. "My phone's in my car" Jaqui said. "I don't have any numbers memorized."

Officer Sanchez accompanied her to the car for her phone and purse.

"No backseat?" Officer Sanchez began examining the vehicle more closely.

"Long story. It got trashed." Jaqui preferred not to elaborate. She pulled up Keegan's number and hit send. It rang twice and went to voice mail. She hung up. You bastard! She dialed again, this time it went to the mailbox after one ring. "Fuck him," she said and began digging through her purse for numbers. The businessman from the bar, James? Bad idea. Adam Wolf, the preacher, Oh, hell no! Jaqui was surprised at how few real friends she had. She found the number of Art the guitarist's roommate, Nicki. Well, she said if I ever needed anything. She punched in the number. A sleepy woman answered.

"Nicki?" Jaqui asked.

"Just a minute," then in the background, "Nicki, it's for you, a woman. Do you know what time it is?"

She put on her best cheerleader voice. "Hi Nikki. It's Jaqui, from Art's band. I'm in a pickle and I didn't know who else to call. I'm sorry about it being so late. I need a huge favor. Can you or Art give me a ride home from the police station?"

"What kind of shit did you get yourself into now?"

"Well, that's a story. Pick me up and I'll tell you."

"Shit, okay. It's going to take a minute for me to get it together. I'll probably be bringing a friend."

"Cool, I'll see y'all in a while."

Jaqui stood in the front yard staring at the house. The ride home had been surreal. Nikki showed up with her friend Angela. There was so much tension in the car that it was hard to breathe. Jaqui felt she'd done something far worse than asking for a ride home. Apparently she had picked up the nickname "Black Cloud". That's how Angela referred to her, repeatedly, the whole trip. Jaqui hoped it only referred to the run of bad luck she'd had.

It was time to go in, still an hour before dawn. Maybe Katrine was still asleep. Maybe she hadn't been missed. She slipped her key in the door and eased into the dark sitting room, clicking the door closed behind her"You fucked him!" Katrine's voice came out of the dark. "I knew it. You bitch! How long you were going to stand out in the yard for excuse making? Did you think I not know?"

"Really? No, 'Are you alright?' No, 'where's your car?' Kiss my ass! Yeah, I fucked him and I liked it! Well, kind of, it was more that I liked making him do shit." Jaqui heard Katrine begin to weep. Jaqui's eyes adjusted to the darkness. Katrine sat in the antique rocker, her outstretched hands were dwarfed against the wide wooden arms of the chair. Jaqui realized she'd worried and disappointed the one person she truly loved. She was heading over to coax a hug when she noticed the sobs were actually subdued chuckles.

"You think that you want, we can be making the big dollars doing the double team," Katrine said. "I still kind of am kicking your ass for fucking the loser. I think, though, you know now something of yourself."

"I'm sorry. I really am. You trusted me and I let you down."

"Cowshit, I know you will fuck him before you leave today. He give you coke?"

"Yeah, how did you know?"

"Is his favorite thing, he mix with X to make him hard. Only way old fucker make it happen. Put your sugar ass in love spell, too. I know the trick he uses."

"Why didn't you tell me?"

"I say be careful. You say you big girl, so I leave you alone. Better to know from experience. Now come to bed, tired girl. Shower first. I am not large fan of his taste. What he thinks of art work?"

Rural, the fucker called it rural." Jaqui went for the hottest shower she could stand. She began by vigorously scrubbing her snatch. By the time the shower curtain opened, the bathroom had become so steamed that Katrine's hair was beginning to uncurl even before it got wet. The fun started early, or late, depending on your perspective.

Just down the street from where the two women frolicked in the steaming shower, a beige sedan was parked under a grackle infested elm tree. The only sound emanating from the car was the rhythmic tick - tick - tick of the engine cooling. In the dimness of the dome light, teeth gripped two ends of a blue bandanna looped around the occupant's bicep. A hypodermic needle pierced the pale skin of the forearm and a whorl of crimson spun in the cylinder as the needle found the vein.

The occupant spit the rag, slowly depressing the plunger. As this was the third time in as many days that the poison had been introduced, there was no rush of euphoria, no enlightenment, only a slight gasp and a tightening of the facial muscles. The poison had burned all humanity, all emotion from the occupant, all but vengeance. No food or shelter was necessary to sustain the occupant; no love, lust or desire. The occupant had become pure vengeance and vengeance does not sleep.

"*Vengeance is mine sayeth the Lord*", but Vengeance knew better. Vengeance had an epiphany. It was wrong to kill Jacquelyn Benderman, as had been planned and attempted. The dead did not suffer. There are better ways to inflict suffering. Vengeance knew about suffering.

La Pistola Y El Corazon
- Los Lobos

The iron of the gun barrel tastes a lot like blood,
Vengeance thought. An hour had passed since the porch
light darkened. The occasional plop of bird shit hitting the car
caused a start. In the lap of Vengeance lay the 45 caliber
revolver. One round had been placed in the cylinder, the
cylinder spun, then the sharp gray flavor of iron as the hammer
fell - twice. The eyes of Vengeance never left the porch of the
little white house with pastel blue trim, all just shades of gray in
the stifling darkness. No matter, this would not end well. It
couldn't.

"Are you sure you won't have any trouble hauling me on
your scooter?" Jaqui asked.

"Is good. Put down foot when we stop. All okay."

"Okay then, I'm going shopping after you take me to pick
up my car. Want to come?" Jaqui hollered from Katrine's
bedroom as she pulled her black dogging boots up over the legs
of her jeans. She yanked a tank shirt over her head, barely
enough to cover her sports bra.

"What are we shopping for?" Katrine asked. She was at the
bathroom mirror futilely attempting to brush the tangles from
her tumble dried and slept on hair.

169

"A pistol, semiautomatic, nine mil I'm thinking. Not too big but big enough. The next asshole that takes a shot at this chick is going to have only a moment to regret it."

"You could shoot someone?"

"If they shoot first? Oh yeah. It ain't like the cops in this town are going to help."

"This is new girl I don't know. Maybe you think about it first?"

"I had plenty of time to think about it when I was standing in that closet giving the Breathalyzer a blow a job. Don't worry I'll license and register, take a class, whatever it takes."

Katrine gave up on the hair and came into the bedroom with her robe hanging open. Jaqui snort giggled, "Oh my god, Baby! What happened to your hair?"

"You did. Is like our love, not knowing which way is up. You look like woman soldier in movies. I put mascara under your eyes and you are a big tough alien ass-kicker."

"Arrrgh!" Jaqui howled, picking up Katrine and body slamming her into the feather top mattress. They rolled around until Jaqui let Katrine pin her. When Katrine raised her arms in victory, Jaqui tickled her ribs. Katrine crashed down on Jaqui and kissed her deep then bit her nipple. Jaqui yelped even though it didn't hurt much through the two layers of cloth.

"Watch for the little girls, we bad ass bitches," Katrine said and jumped out of bed. "We better go. Only 40 minutes is noon."

"I want a rematch when we get back."

～

You would think a tiny girl hauling an Amazonian warrior woman around on a little pink scooter would bring a chuckle or two from the circus fans out on the roads. It did draw attention. The pair was indirectly responsible for causing the near crashes of frat boys and beer-bellied construction bosses, especially when Jaqui leaned over and whispered directions in Katrine's ear. Brakes squealed.

In the police garage, Jaqui pulled the parking permit from under the windshield, wadded it up and threw it on the ground. Once in the vehicle she exited slowly, saluting the security cameras with an expressive middle finger.

~

"I'd feel a lot better about your job if you had protection too," Jaqui said.

"I am always having protection," Katrine replied.

"Not that kind. You know what I mean, like this." Jaqui handed Katrine the Taurus 9 mil she had just decided to buy.

"Is too heavy. When I need something like it, is nowhere to hide."

"How about something you can put in your purse. Look around."

Reluctantly Katrine checked out the selection of pistols in the display case. "Oh look! Here is pink. Little, like me!"

"It's a 22. It would just piss off your attacker." Jaqui motioned for the salesman who responded in a few nanoseconds. "Do you have this in a 38 caliber?"

"Similar," he said, pulling out a case. He made a production of opening the leather bound box as if it contained precious gems. It contained a flat angular nickel silver 38 caliber with onyx grip inlaid with pearlescent pink in the shapes of the suits in a poker deck. Both of the girls gasped.

"It's beautiful!" Katrine said. Her eyes burned with desire.

"Want to hold it, get a feel for it?" The salesman asked. The sale was made, four digits. He could take the afternoon off.

"Now we can go to range together," Katrine said.

Jaqui raised an eyebrow. "Sure."

The Stalker

- Nick Curran

Jaqui **arrived late on purpose.** It didn't help, even though the musicians were more or less in place and warming up. Keegan motioned Jaqui into the control room. "Look, about the other night--," Keegan began.

"I'd just as soon we kept it professional from now on," Jaqui said. "I don't appreciate being drugged, although I did it willingly. I wish you'd have taken my call later. I needed help. You're kind of a jerk but I can live with that. I really need the gig."

"And I need your talent, singing and helping with the mix. I'm still up for the duet if you're cool with it."

"There won't be any more --- encounters."

"No, you're too, um, assertive for my tastes anyway."

"Bullshit, you know you loved it."

"Whatever."

"Anyway, I'm a lesbian."

"Sure you are."

"Just shut up," she said. "Let's get to work."

"So we're good?" Keegan extended his hand.

Jaqui shook it, gripping very firmly. "We're good."

When they entered the studio, Keegan explained that Jaqui

would be helping with the sound during rehearsals until they had a sound guy.

"We need to get the horns their own monitor," she said, while stringing out a cable. She turned to the trombone player, "Jack, can you drag one of those cabinets over from the front of the stage?"

"Sure," Jack said, "about fucking time."

Jaqui drug the other stage monitor in front of Keegan. "Boss, you'll have to use this until we can pick up another one. Now let's rock." She took her spot with Adela and Tiff.

"How'd you rate that gig?" Adela asked.

Tiff snorted. "Probably fucked him."

"Yep, fucked the shit out of him, but the extra gig don't pay and he's a crappy fuck." Tiff and Adela laughed. The girls were still a team. We'll see what happens when they find out about the duet, she thought. By the time they took their break it hadn't come up. Jaqui went to the parking lot to check on her car and avoid Keegan. Everything was okay; the tires were up, no beige sedan around, that she could see. Half a block down was a van with "Heaven's Gate Locksmith" on the side. In a string of rental spaces that wasn't unusual. The tenants were mostly musicians and artists, folks who tended to be somewhat transient. Adela, Art and a couple of the others came out to decompress or smoke or whatever. Jack wandered over to where Adela and Jaqui sat against the building gulping cans of energy drink.

"Thanks for the monitor," he said. "I can finally hear what's going on."

"No sweat. It had to suck trying to hear with the drums pounding away next to your head."

"Yeah, but it'll be better now."

"It's all about visuals for Keegan. You guys should be on a riser in the back for the best sound. I'm going to talk to him about it."

"Good luck with that," Jack said. "He only listens to his own ideas."

"We'll see." Jaqui got up and stretched. "I'm going back inside."

When Keegan handed out charts for three new songs he mentioned that Jaqui would be singing duets with him. Everybody took it in stride except Tiff.

"I guess he thought you were a pretty good fuck after all." Tiff sneered.

"I am. He's the one that sucks," Jaqui said, "but I had the duet gig before that." Tiff just shook her head.

The band enjoyed the old Motown tunes. They sounded pretty good for a first run through. Jaqui's voice was spot on and Keegan was trying to blend. It worked. Most of the band probably thought the two had something going on.

"Can you stay and listen to some of these rehearsal recordings?" Keegan asked as everyone was packing up.

"Not tonight, I'm beat. Can you e-mail the files to me? They're digital, right? Katrine has a good system I can listen at home and make notes."

"No problem. Get some rest. I'll get up with you in the next few days." He leaned over to kiss her cheek but she ducked away.

"You don't like me that way, remember?"

The night was a sweet, earthy kind of cool as she walked toward the car. It made her think of home. She should call Sarge in the morning. He would be sleeping in, preparing for the hibernation of the farm. "Battening down the hatches," he called it. The days were still warm but the nights, these nights lately, made her homesick. She had only called him once since she left. It hadn't gone as well as she'd hoped. He'd all but bribed her to come home; coerced, far beyond begging.

It wasn't just the promise of fall that put a spring in her step. She figured she'd dodged a bullet with Keegan. She'd managed to bring her relationship with him back to a professional level with no hard feelings.

The breeze picked up, knocking a few loose leaves from the trees across the street. She pulled the barrettes from her hair and shook it in the breeze. Facing into the wind, the perspiration around her throat and temples dried to a cool contentment,

Out of the corner of her eye she saw the locksmith's van back out and turn in her direction. She knew she was the last one to leave except Keegan. Too much had happened lately for her not to react. Sliding behind the wheel of her car she reached in the glove compartment for her pistol. She released the safety and placed it on the passenger seat. Sure enough the van stopped behind her, preventing her from leaving. Picking up the pistol, she stepped out of the car, gun first.

"Whoa, easy Jaqui, it's me," Adam Wolf said. "I've been trying to talk to you."

"What? The weird notes under the windshield? You could have called or just come to the door. You were there anyway."

"You're in danger. I thought I should talk to you alone."

"I'm not talking to you alone. You're creepy and you broke into my apartment. Just leave." She waved the pistol toward the exit of the parking lot.

"I didn't break in. The other thing, well, I'm sorry. It's the devil. I'm fighting him."

"Just go." She steadied the gun's aim just below his naval. He retracted into the van.

"Look, you really are in danger, but not from me."

She thought about what she'd been through lately. "Okay, there's a coffee shop on West Sixth just past Lamar. Go there. Get a table in the middle of the room. I'll be there in a minute and I'm bringing my little buddy here." She nodded toward the pistol. The van pulled away. She followed shortly, the pistol on the seat beside her. After she left, the beige sedan pulled in the parking space she had vacated.

Jaqui drove past the coffee shop and made the block after locating Adam's van. She circled twice before a space became available near the entrance. She saw Adam at a table near the door but didn't acknowledge him.

Partly for the flavor, partly for the heat, she ordered a large dark roast, the secondary, less lethal weapon. She went to the table where Adam sat nursing a glass of pale tea. She pulled out a chair, spun it around and straddled it backwards.

"So, first off, what the hell were you doing in my apartment. Don't try to bullshit me, I know it was you."

"My job."

"Really? Who pays you to masturbate into women's underwear?" she said, loud enough to turn a few heads.

"Damn it, no, I told you, that was the devil. I was there to rekey the back door to match the front. I'm sorry, I just saw those lying there when I used the bathroom. The devil took over. I remembered you had mentioned the name of the apartment at the open mic. Your voice, the way you look, I just lost it." He slumped over the table, staring into his glass.

"Is that why your ransacked my closet?"

"I didn't. When your roommate showed up I tossed the panties in the sink and went to work on the locks. Look, I'm sorry. I'm really trying to get a handle on this."

"Bullshit, I don't have a roommate."

"Yeah, blond girl, shorter than you. Pretty, but not as pretty as you, kind of flighty."

"Nope, no roommate."

"She said she was. She knew you. I gave her a key."

"Jesus Christ! You fucking idiot! Did you even check her ID, get a name?"

"She knew you, said y'all grew up together."

"God damn it!"

"Not the Lord's name again, please."

Jaqui thought for a moment that maybe she wasn't the best candidate for gun ownership. All she wanted to do was empty a clip into this fool.

"That's not why we're here though," Adam said.

"What could be more dangerous than giving a key to my apartment to a total stranger?"

"Katrine."

"Look, I know y'all had issues but she's one of the sweetest people I know."

"She's not what she seems."

"Really, how so?"

"I did some research. Her father is a known enemy of his own country, for one. She may be in the country illegally. Could even be a terrorist!"

"Wow, seriously?" Jaqui rolled those baby blue eyes.

"She's also known to have homosexual relationships in the past. She never repented. I asked her. She actually thinks that it's okay."

"And I take it you have a problem with that?"

"God has a problem with that. You're a Presbyterian. You know that. She also sells her body for sex."

"Yeah, she did mention that you didn't want to pay."

"Jaqui, it's not like that. I wanted to be her friend. I was trying to bring her to Jesus. I had her best interests in mind."

"You certainly sent my panties to meet Jesus."

"I don't claim to be perfect, it's a process."

"Look, I don't like what Katrine does for money; not because it's wrong, but because it's dangerous. I know her better than you do. She's a wonderful woman, and yes, we share a bed and a lot more. Think about that the next time you run across a pair of nylon panties. I hope it's as good for you as it is for us." Jaqui left the full cup of coffee on the table and headed for the door.

"Wait, Jaqui," Adam called. She turned "You should pray

about this, ask for forgiveness. You don't want to end up in Hell."

"I'll see you there." She left. So that was the danger? she thought. A chuckle began escaping from deep in her chest.

~

Jaqui had never been so glad to pull into the driveway. The porch light was on as were most of the other lights in the house. *Katrine must be up.*

The door was unlocked. As soon as Jaqui was in the house, Katrine was in her arms. "You're okay?" Katrine said.

"Yeah. Thanks for waiting up." Jaqui saw something desperate in Katrine. "How about you? Everything okay here?"

"The woman call again. Scaring me. She say 'tell your roommate she's fucked now.' I'm so scared for you."

"I'm here. I'm fine. See." Jaqui did a pirouette for Katrine. "I don't know who this crazy bitch is but I'm going to have to figure it out. Boy do I have a story to tell over breakfast tomorrow, but right now I just need to get tangled up with you and fall asleep. Shit, it's almost 3:00 AM."

"Okay, but we talk tomorrow. I am scared for you."

De Natura Sonoris No.1
Krzysztof Pederecki

Saturday, the only day Langley got to spend with family, family now being Sara. The DPS training was physically and emotionally brutal. Sara picked him up, took him to her house and fixed breakfast. If she felt okay, they slipped into the back of the house and made love. Today they drove over and took Marjorie out to lunch. It had been three weeks since he saw his dad, not since the incident. No great loss, he figured.

Marjorie stayed silent as they gathered around their regular table in the corner of Dean-O's dining room. On Saturday, Dean-Os featured a steam table buffet, the only cafeteria in town.

"So, Mom," Langley said, "it looks like you're getting pretty good with your hands again."

"Better," she said. "I'm cooking again, not that it matters." Sara looked away. Langley stared at his plate. "I can function on my own now you know."

Langley looked at his mother. "Good, that's good, getting back to normal."

"What's normal?" She paused. "I'm going to divorce your dad. I think he's having an affair, not that I blame him."

"No, Mom, do blame him. You've been --- well, you've always been there. It's him, but yeah, you should."

"There's nothing there anymore, between us, I mean. You know what I mean?"

"Yeah Mom. I don't know what to say. I understand though. How did he take it?" Langley asked.

"I haven't told him yet. He doesn't believe in divorce. It's going to be hard. I was hoping you could be there when I tell him."

"Sure Mom, no problem. What are you going to do, I mean, where will you stay?"

"Right where I am." She pulled herself up in the booth and clasped her hands on the table. "He's the one who strayed. This is Texas. I won't get alimony but I'll get the house. It's paid for, and I'll file for disability, plus my teachers' pension. It's not a lot but I don't need much. I'll get half of what ever savings he hasn't squandered on that bimbo."

"Looks like you thought it through."

"Yeah, I've had a lot of time to think about it. I'll be okay."

"So when do you want to tell him."

"After lunch."

"Okay, I guess. Sara can take me to pick up my truck."

"I can stay with you if you want," Sara said. "I'm kind of part of the family now."

"Okay, sure," Langley said, "maybe he won't be such an asshole in front of you."

"We can stop by his office. He's almost living there, I guess." Marjorie said.

"If not, I know where he is."

"Jesus, Langley! You knew about this?"

"Mom, I'm sorry. It's Jeanine Buckholtz. I thought you knew. He's not really keeping a low profile."

Marjorie wilted, her strength oozing from her unclenched hands. Silent tears trickled from her eyes. "How long have you known? Why didn't you say something?"

"Mom, I didn't want to see you hurt. I haven't known long, since the week we last had dinner maybe. I'm sorry, I didn't know how to tell you."

Marjorie took a deep breath and forced a halt to the water-works. "It's okay. I've known at least that long. I just didn't want to admit it. Let's eat."

It was dark. Vengeance had nothing but time. Time being linear, a necessary path from gunpowder and lead to blood and bone. While waiting for the parking space to clear, Vengeance had taken another shot, just to steady the hands, you understand. Vacating the beige sedan for the cover of the tree line, Vengeance waited. The timeline was short. The man exited the studio, *all puffed up with ego*, Vengeance thought. *A 45 slug will pop that balloon.*

He got in the Porsche, threw the satchel into the passenger seat and buckled the seat belt. The irony drew chuckles from Vengeance. At about the point Keegan shifted from reverse to first gear the Porsche was frozen in space. A single shot rang out. No one heard. Keegan slumped over the steering wheel as the Porsche made a slow arc into the back of the building. The crunch of metal, the tinkling of broken headlight, Vengeance stepped back into the beige sedan and pulled away.

"You're going to love this," Jaqui said as she placed the steaming cup of Ruta Maya dark roast before Katrine's nodding head. She positioned behind Katrine and began massaging her neck and shoulders, trying to pump some life into the waif's body. "We've got to do something about this hair," Jaqui said, pulling her fingers from the tangles.

"Shave it, whatever" Katrine mumbled. It was almost noon.

Sleeping in was not Jaqui's strong suit.

"So, I ran into a mutual friend of ours last night."

"All friends in city are mutual."

"Right, but this particular one thinks you are Satan's own terrorist."

"You mean Adam? I say to stay far from him. You see?"

"Yeah well, he kind of blocked me in."

"Him you could shoot."

"You have no idea how close I came to doing just that. Instead we had coffee."

"Now you are idiot."

"He admitted to being a sexual pervert while professing his Christianity, and, the asshole gave a key to my apartment to some girl posing as my roommate."

"How he get key?"

"He's a locksmith for his day job."

"I thought he was preacher?"

"Preaching must not pay very well for perverts."

"So you think girl with key is crazy woman calling?"

"Probably, he said she was a blonde but smaller than me. I don't know anyone here like that, at least not anyone who has it in for me. Tiff doesn't care much for me but she's not blonde. Nikki's girl friend, Angela, doesn't like me much but I was already deep in this shit before I even met her."

"Maybe a person from your past?"

"Even my dad and my best friend don't know where I am, besides everyone back home seems to think I'm in rehab."

There was a pounding on the door. "Who the hell knocks like that?" Jaqui said.

"City of Austin police. Open the door please." It was a female voice, a rather authoritative one.

"I'll get it," Jaqui said. "Get dressed and stay in your room for now." She opened the door. A fairly large young redhead in a business suit and a chubby older Hispanic man in a rumpled blazer stood with two uniformed officers flanking them. Another pair of policemen sat in a patrol car blocking the street with their emergency lights flashing. *Great,* Jaqui thought, *we'll be big hits with the neighbors.*

"Are you Jacquelyn Benderman?"

"Yeah, why?"

"We need to ask you some questions."

"Fine, ask, and can you shut down the circus out there?"

"Ma'am you'll need to come with us," the Hispanic cop said.

The uniforms put their hands on their holsters.

"Shit, can I at least get dressed first. I'm still in my pajamas. What's this all about? Did you catch the guy that was shooting at me last week?"

"Ms. Benderman, do you have any weapons?"

"Yeah, I have a nine mil in my purse on the kitchen table. You want me to get it?"

"No ma'am, please don't move." He motioned to one of the uniforms who motioned to the cops in the street who brought a suitcase to the porch and opened it.

"We'll need to take the gun in also." The detectives motioned again and the uniform pulled on some rubber gloves and bagged the gun.

"Are you here alone," the female officer asked. "My room-mate's asleep, or was."

"What's her name?"

"Katrine."

"We'd like to speak with her also."

"Katrine, the cops want to talk to you," Jaqui yelled. Katrine appeared, fully dressed.

"What this is about. I am citizen of America. I know. You not just come and take us. We have rights."

"Yes ma'am. You're not being arrested. We just need to ask some questions."

"About what?"

The female detective stepped inside near Jaqui, the male, near Katrine. "Keegan Stone was found in his car outside of his recording studio this morning. He'd been shot."

"Oh my God!" Jaqui said. "Is he okay?"

"He's alive, for now."

"Adam, that sick fucker!" Katrine said.

"Let's go down to the station and sort this out." The officers escorted the girls out and put one in each of the patrol cars. Several of the neighbors looked on just as a local TV news team arrived.

"We missed you at lunch, Dad." Langley spit the words through Jeanine Buckholtz's screen door.

"I'm sorry. We have to get a commercial policy finished by Monday."

"Just stop," Marjorie said. "This has gone on long enough. It has to end."

"What?" Langley's dad tried the old surprise innocence routine.

"I'm cutting you lose. Move in here if you want, live in your office, but tomorrow your belongings will be packed and on the porch. I would appreciate a call before you come so I don't have to be there. What's not picked up by Monday goes to Goodwill."

"Marjorie, you're not thinking straight. It's probably the medicines," Langley's dad began.

"Dad, don't start with that. We know. I know. I've seen it. The whole town knows. Don't you even try blaming Mom. Just pick up your shit. Come on Mom. Let's go."

Langley's dad came through the screen door. "Watch your mouth, Son. I won't have you talking to me like that. This is between me and Marjorie."

"Get in the car Mom. You too Sara. I've got this," Langley muttered then turned on his father. "It's over, leave her alone. Just go back where you belong."

"I don't think so."

Langley blocked the sidewalk. "Back off. The lawyer's can handle it from here."

Langley's father stopped but puffed up like a rooster. "There will be no lawyers. There won't be any divorce."

"It's no longer up to you," Langley turned and walked toward the car, fully expecting to be attacked from behind. When he heard the screen door slam he breathed a sigh of relief.

As they drove away Sara said, "Well, that went better than expected." There was no reply.

~

"Can I get you a latte or something?" The young redhead asked Jaqui.

"Just black coffee is fine." Jaqui sat in an interrogation room.

The large mirror on one wall left nothing to the imagination. No handcuffs, the door wasn't even closed, but Jaqui knew better than to leave. Besides, she was innocent and curious about what happened. When the detective returned, she placed a Styrofoam cup of coffee on the table and sat across from Jaqui. " I'm detective O'Daniel. You can call me Bess. It sucks to have your heart broken, don't it?"

"I wouldn't know," Jaqui answered.

"Really? I heard you in Keegan were an item."

"He's my boss. We fucked once. It was a mistake. He's an okay guy though. How is he? What happened?"

"He's alive. The wound wasn't that bad. The bullet ricocheted off the door frame. He lost an eye. He'd be okay except he bled for a couple of hours before he was found."

The blood drained from Jaqui face. The image of Randy

flooded her mind. It was too late by the time she knew it was coming. "Sorry," she cried just before throwing up all over the interrogation room. Bess didn't quite know how to read this.

"I'm so sorry," Jaqui said. "I don't react well to blood."

"Let me see if another room is available." It wasn't, but housekeeping cleaned up while Bess and Jaqui chatted about music and police work. Bess was trying to bond. Jaqui was trying to not think about Randy. Once the mess was cleaned up they resumed.

"So why do you have a gun?" Bess asked.

"Well, I could say 'single girl alone in the city', but, as I'm sure you know, I had someone shooting at me from a car last week and I've been getting weird phone calls."

"I didn't know."

"Figures."

"So what happened exactly?"

Jaqui explained about the clown mask, the car chase and the Breathalyzer.

"Exactly what is your relationship with Keegan Stone?"

"I'm a backup singer in his show band. We've been rehearsing for a national tour. He's bringing me up for some duets and I'm helping with the sound. So it wouldn't be in my best interest to shoot him."

"What about your personal relationship?"

"Like I said, we fucked. It was a mistake. We both realized it. That's about the size of it."

"Pretty mature for an 18 year old."

"Just the facts, ma'am." Jaqui raised an eyebrow.

A uniformed officer came in and whispered in Bess' ear.

"Why didn't you mention that your pistol had never been fired?" Bess asked.

"You didn't ask. I know I didn't shoot anyone. I figured you'd catch on."

"I'm going to release you. Don't leave town without letting us know, okay?"

"Fine, I'm guessing the tour will be delayed. Is it okay if I stop in and check on Keegan?"

"Sure."

"How about a ride home?"

"I'll get you and Katrine a ride."

"What about the guy who's shooting at me."

Bess put her thumb up to her eyebrow, a look of frustration on her face. "I'll see what I can do. Here's my card. Let me know if anything else happens, okay?"

Jaqui shook her head. "Sure."

Langley and Sara stayed to help Marjorie pack boxes and bags. It wasn't a lot to pack. Marjorie seemed energetic, almost gleeful.

"Look at all this room in this closet," she said. "Sara, we're going to have to gang up on a couple of shopping trips. You're going to need a maternity outfit or two and I'm going to have to spruce up my wardrobe if I'm going to be dating again."

"Mom, really!" Langley said.

"Did you think I was going to sit around and raise cats?"

"Well, no, but ---"

"One thing I'm going to do is, when I go to court I'm going to be hotter than a two dollar pistol. He needs to know what he tossed away."

"You sure that's what you want to do?" Langley said.

Sara grabbed Langley by the waist and put a hand over his mouth. "Don't listen to him, Marjorie. That's a great idea. Rub his face in it. Let him know he screwed up."

"Okay, okay," Langley said, breaking free from Sara. "I can see when I'm outnumbered and outsmarted here. I give up."

"Good move, Darling," Sara said, "before you get in too deep."

It took about an hour to complete the packing and goodbye hugs.

"I'm going to stay at Sara's tonight if that's cool with you, Mom." Langley said.

"Sure, I'm fine. How long until you're finished with training?"

"All next week and then we graduate on the following Wednesday and get our assignments. Depending on where they send me, I'll probably go on patrol the following week."

"Any chance you'll be local?"

"Possibly. There's a couple of openings in Caldwell County and one in Bastrop. I told them about my pregnant fiancée. They're trying to work with me. Of course, it would be much easier if we were already married." He shot a grin toward Sara. She answered with a happy little single-fingered birdie. "But I don't reckon that's going to happen."

"Don't worry, Babe. I'll follow you to the ends of the earth," Sara said, "as long as you support me in the manner to which I've become accustomed."

"So we have to move in with a couple of hard partying hippies?"

"No, sweetie, just a roof and a bed will be fine, maybe a kitchen with pickles."

It was getting dark as Sara drove home. Langley noticed she'd lost her jovial demeanor.

"What's wrong, Sara. Something's bothering you."

"Just thinking."

"About what?"

"Us. What happens to us when we're on our own, when you get tired of me, to coming home to the same woman every day? I don't want us to end up like your parents."

"I don't see that happening. It's different for us. We're in love."

"They were too, once."

"Maybe, but they were never like us."

"Are you sure?"

Langley brushed his fingers against Sara's cheek. "I can't imagine ever not loving you. We'll be fine."

Sara took his hand and kissed his fingers. "We've just got to keep it exciting and fresh." She took the next little dirt road into the surrounding fields. The night was cooling quickly but the hood of the Honda was warm against her naked back as she guided Langley in.

Even though the police drove Jaqui and Katrine home in an unmarked car, it fooled very few of the neighbors as they were pulling back their drapes to spy on the girls.

"Not hoping for this kind of fame?" Katrine said.

"Fuck 'em, it's not like we hang out with anybody around here anyway."

"Still, is good to feel safe at home."

"You know they'll be watching our house. That's pretty safe, even if it is a little bit creepy."

"Not so good for business. Maybe I just do out calls for now."

"You want to visit Keegan with me? I think I'll wait until morning. It's already late for today."

"Sure, I go tomorrow. Tonight we sit on porch and watch people who never leave house take first evening walk. I'll make tea."

"You're one crazy ass chick," Jaqui said, "but I like your attitude."

So the girls cuddled under the comforter on the porch swing and greeted about 50 of their closest neighbors who suddenly decided to start an exercise regimen. It was almost dark when Katrine realized the porch light was off. She pulled the blanket up around their waists and put her head on Jaqui's shoulder. "My dear, may I diddle your twat?"

When Jaqui's outburst of laughter subsided she replied, "Dare you, my love? What if someone should observe us?" They opted to go inside and frolic instead.

Feeling Good

- Nina Simone

Langley missed church for the third weekend in a row using DPS training as his excuse. His dad knew the real reason. It was only right since Sara missed her meeting the night before, saying the alternate encounter they shared was equally as magical. They pledged not to neglect their spiritual lives in the future.

"My spiritual family is important to me," Sara said. "I need it to be part of my life."

"Go then," Langley replied, "but I don't feel that way about my church. With my dad on the church council I can't see myself ever going back. I guess I could find a different church."

"Do you believe in your God?"

"I don't know, it's just something I've always taken for granted." Langley rolled out of bed and pulled on his jeans. "I've got to pee." When he returned Sara was lying naked on the bed. Her eyes were closed and her head was tilted back. Her left hand was gently massaging the small mound that was now her abdomen. Her right hand cupped a breast.

"What are you doing?" Langley asked.

"Praying."

"For what?"

"For our baby --- for you to find peace, Gods or Goddesses you can trust."

"Do you have that?"

"Yeah, but I don't think we're expecting the same thing."

"What do you mean?"

"Can we talk later? Right now I need some quiet time."

"Sure. I'll go make breakfast." Sara smiled but did not open her eyes.

When Jaqui and Katrine arrived to visit Keegan, a uniformed officer was at the door chatting with a balding blonde guy wearing a Hawaiian shirt and Dockers. He was slightly overweight with an infectious smile and a pair of those wire-rimmed sunglasses that turn clear when out of the sun.

"Can I go in and talk to Keegan?" Jaqui asked.

"They just sedated him, but you can try," the officer said.

You must be Jaqui Benderman," the blond guy said.

"Yeah, and this is Katrine. You are?"

"Bill Billings. You've seen my name at the bottom of your paycheck. I'm Keegan's agent and manager. We need to talk, but go see if you can catch our boy before he passes out." The uniform held the door open for Jaqui and Katrine then stepped in with them.

"My dream team. Hey ladies!" Keegan slurred. He was clearly out of it. Without his trademark diamond stud earring he looked like an overgrown newborn from Area 51. "You guys crawl on up in here and let's have a party."

"Easy boy, you're in no shape for any calisthenics. Besides, you don't like me that way remember?"

"Aw come on, I like both of you anyway I can get you but together would be sublime."

"You are needing rest and healing, then we'll see," Katrine said. "Anything is possible."

"Keegan, I just want to say, I'm sorry this happened. It might be someone that wants to get to me. I'm just so sorry." Jaqui felt hot tears on her cheeks.

"Don't worry," Keegan said. "I get a cool eye patch out of the deal. Arggh, Matey."

Jaqui chuckled through the tears, "We love you. Hurry and get better, okay?"

"For you, Baby, anything. But I think I have to sleep now, Okay?"

"Sure."

"How's our boy," Bill asked as soon as they stepped out of the room.

"Sleeping," Jaqui said.

"Good, so we need to talk, little miss person-of-interest."

"Hey, I'm cleared."

"I know. Keegan knows. The cops know. That's not the point. The media is busting loose with this. The story is, you shot him because he drugged and raped you. Some say it's jealousy over of one of the other backup singers. I personally don't give a fuck. The fact is your trending and so is Keegan. I was thinking of canceling the tour due to weak ticket sales but now the first three East Coast shows are suddenly sold out and we just raised the prices in the West. So here's the deal. I want you to sign with me."

"What do you mean?" Jaqui's head was swimming.

"I mean me be your agent. Your name's in the news. I want to put your voice on the radio. You ever hear of the Bluebirds?"

"Yeah, kind of. Some crappy all girl bunch of thug, pop star wannabes."

"Hey! Those are my girls. Two were high school honors students, one is valedictorian at the New York School for the Performing Arts. They don't even take aspirin without a prescription. The deal is, they're almost good. They need a bad-ass lead singer. That's you. What do you think? You ever make six digits in a year, clear? You still sing with Keegan's band, the

Bluebirds open with you in front. We take it from there. Just to let you know I'm serious, you sign with me you start with this." Bill handed Jaqui a check for $50K. It wasn't signed. "You sign with me, I sign that check."

"Holy shit," Jaqui said. "What does it mean, 'sign with you'?" she asked.

"To start with you stay with Keegan on the same deal you're on. You front the Bluebirds for at least a year. What you make, I get 10% of. I can't guarantee six figures but it's realistic. I'll bust my ass for you. The more you make, the more I make. We've got to move while you're in the news. I need an answer."

Jaqui's head was reeling. "When would I start, with the Bluebirds I mean, and where are they?"

"I'll move 'em here. They've been on the road anyway. As soon as we can get studio space, maybe next week. You'll just be Jaqui B, drop the Benderman, it's too country, okay?"

"Shit, this is a lot to take in. Katrine, what do you think?"

"Is your dream, right?"

"Well not exactly. I never wanted to be a thug or famous for shooting somebody that I didn't even shoot."

"But the singing," Katrine said. "You can make it about that. You are strong. The people, they will see."

"Will you come with me on tour?"

"Sounds like fun. It is a thing we can speak of when we know time and place"

"Okay," Jaqui said. "Where do we do this, Bill?"

He held out a card. "My office, 4:00 PM today, sound good? I'll have the papers ready. Bring a lawyer if you want, but I'm being straight up with you."

"Okay, okay, I'll be there then."

"Oh shit, oh shit, Holy shit," Jaqui mumbled as they headed for the car. "I've got to call Dad. I don't know. It's sounds too good."

"For sure is good. We must celebrate."

"Right, how do you want to celebrate?"

"Is America, American dream come true. We shoot off guns for sure in Texas."

Jaqui laughed. "I love you, you crazy little bitch. Sure, we'll go home. I'll call Dad, then we can go to the range, okay?"

"Yee Haw!"

∽

"Hey Dad, it's Jaqui."

"What the hell have you gotten into? I heard you shot a guy who raped you. Then maybe not. Jaqui, I need a way to reach you. I'm worried sick. What's going on?"

"Well none of that. A guy I work for got shot. He's okay and I didn't have anything to do with it. The police have cleared me."

"That's not what I heard."

"Trust me, Dad. I'm not calling you from jail but I need your advice."

"My advice is to haul your ass back home."

"I can't Dad. I'm a singer. Singers live in cities."

"Not all of them."

"This one does. I really need your help. Please, Daddy?"

Sarge let out a sigh. His little girl had the better of him again.

"Shoot!"

Jaqui giggled.

"Sorry," Sarge said, "bad choice of words."

"There's this agent that wants to sign me. He says I can make a lot of money singing with this R.&B. band, touring and stuff, nationwide, maybe overseas too. He wants to pay me fifty grand just to sign on. I'm supposed to meet him at four this afternoon. Can you please, please, please come? I don't know anything about contracts."

"It sounds too good to be true."

"I know, that's why I want you to check it out."

"Okay, where?

"Can you meet me at three at a restaurant just north of UT called Trudy's? Remember from when we toured UT? I'll buy you lunch. There's somebody I want you to meet."

"Well ain't you full of surprises?"

"You have no idea. So will you?"

"Sure, what's this guy's name, the one with the contract."

"Bill Billings."

"I'll be there."

"Thanks Daddy."

It was hard for Sarge to read the monitor as he Googled Bill Billings, until he wiped the tears from his eyes.

The weekends are too damn short, Langley thought as he aimed his pistol at the paper silhouette across the field. It was only Monday afternoon and he already missed Sara. His mom also had him worried. She seemed a bit too happy about the divorce. He squeezed the trigger, imagining the silhouette was his dad. A hole appeared in the neck. He squeezed again. This time light shone through the forehead. Then he realized what he was thinking and the nausea forced his hands to his knees. He retched but caught it before it came up.

"Scott, are you alright?" His instructor yelled.

"Yeah, must be bad baloney or something. I'll be okay." He took aim again, thinking only of the paper target and put a couple through the lower torso. "I need a break, boss. I've got to reload anyway."

"Take 5 minutes then get your butt back out here. Good shooting by the way."

"Thanks," Langley wondered if he ever had to shoot a real person, could he do it? Statistically it wasn't a likelihood. Many DPS employees retired without ever firing a shot at another human. *I'm sure I could if it was a matter of life and death,* he thought. Then he didn't think about it anymore. He just wiped his face with his bandana, hit the water cooler and returned to the range.

⁓

By the time the girls were set up at the firing range they only had about an hour before they had to head back toward the restaurant. It turned out to be ample time to burn through all the ammo they brought and another box each they bought on site.

"This could be an expensive habit," Jaqui said.

Katrine put a fresh clip in her 38. "Yes, but is really big fun. Who would think?"

"You seem to be a natural at it. You never miss."

"Maybe is geneticle."

"I don't think that's a word."

"Yes, means in your family. My mother was soldier. I did not know her but I hear of her shooting. She killed many enemies. See, genetical." Katrine put a couple more holes in the middle of the paper target. "Don't fuck with this little girl."

"We need to get ready to go meet Dad. I don't really know how he'll deal with our relationship."

"Not to worry. I am very charming girl and you're not lesbian, remember? Just have woman for lover."

Jaqui grinned. "Yeah well, I hope he sees it that way. After what he's been hearing in the media he'll probably be glad that's the only problem."

"Oh, I am problem now?"

"Not for me, Darling, but him? We'll see." The girls said little on the drive. They waited in front of the building as Sarge found on-street parking for the farm truck.

"Ain't room to cuss a cat. I don't see how y'all live here. Too damn crowded for me," Sarge said as he approached.

Jaqui grabbed him and gave him a long hug. "I miss you, Dad."

"Well you know where I live."

"I know and I'm going to start coming out occasionally. Dad, this is Katrine. We live together. I love her." Jaqui had decided that glazing over the truth just wasn't something she did with her dad.

"You mean like you're a couple?"

"Yeah Dad, that's what I mean."

"I'm glad to meet you, Katrine. You don't look old enough to be running loose."

"I am by six years older than Jaqui. I am just being lucky like that. Many years it will be good thing."

"She's Romanian, Dad, but she's been a citizen for a while now."

"Isn't that where the vampires and werewolves live?" Sarge said. Jaqui winced and rolled her eyes.

"Yes," Katrine said, "is why I have to leave, very scary there."

Sarge laughed. "Okay, Sweetie, I can see why you go for this girl. So, Katrine, do you sing too?"

"I do sing. I am in entertainment business."

"Let's go grab a table," Jaqui interrupted. "I need to get you up to speed before we meet with Bill." Katrine bought a round of margaritas while they talked about Jaqui's career opportunities.

The waitress came to take their order. "Hey, aren't you Jaqui B, the girl who shot Keegan Stone?"

"I'm her but I didn't shoot him. I wouldn't be sitting here if I had."

"But he raped you."

"No, it was consensual."

"Yeah, I'd consent," the waitress said.

"Okay, okay let's just order," Sarge said.

Jaqui leaned over and whispered to the waitress, "You didn't miss out. He's not that good."

"Jaqui!" Sarge bellowed, "Your girl is sitting right here."

"Oh she knows, Dad. She's had him too."

"Jesus! I'm getting too old for this shit. Things are a lot different than they used to be."

"So who shot him?" the waitress asked.

"They're still figuring that out, but it wasn't me. I was having coffee with my stalker." She had thrown that in for Sarge's benefit but even the waitress was shaking her head. Katrine was sitting across the table using all her will to stifle an outburst of hilarity.

"I'd love to be able to tell my buds I bought you a drink," the waitress said. "The next round is on me."

"The star power is already paying off," Sarge said.

"I'm not a star." Jaqui said.

"Yet," Katrine added.

"Be careful with the media," Sarge said, "It can make you and it can break you."

Sara sat in the back of her Sociology II class on the edge of tears. The tears were without logical instigation but were brimming, nonetheless, when the universe shifted on its axis, the axis being centered in her abdomen. She gasped, loud enough that her classmates pivoted at once. Their eyes all fell on her. The tears burst forth but were accompanied by a subtle laughter. Her baby, the life she carried, had awakened, stretching and gaining its bearings. She felt it testing the size of its quarters and, after extending an appendage directly toward her bladder, decided it had established a suitable position.

"Excuse me," Sara said as she slipped from class, bound for the nearest restroom. She peed, but only a little. Remaining seated in that laminate enclosure she spoke a prayer of thanks to Anu and Oanara then a bit louder she praised and petitioned Brigid, daughter of the Dagda. Immediately she experienced an energy she could neither deny nor define. She dropped to her knees and threw up her lunch. Rising, she washed her face and strutted back to the class, empowered with a glowing energy completely new to her experience. Her radiance so illuminated her countenance that her mere presence in the classroom elicited smiles from her classmates.

The break of day marathons were over. The obstacle courses done. The firing range was quiet. The final two days of training were academic testing. Langley could do these in his sleep. Wednesday he would get his uniform. Thursday he would graduate. Monday he reported for duty at the DPS station in Caldwell. After that he wasn't sure. One thing for certain, he planned to find a place where he and Sara could live and raise their family, if she agreed, of course. His stomach was cramping. Acne was spreading from his face, down his neck to his torso. Since he no longer hit the rack exhausted, sleep had eluded him. He wasn't worried about his mom. Her decision seemed set in stone. But Sara, he wasn't so sure. Where was he in her future? Would she marry him? Did she even believe in marriage? The dissolution of his parents' marriage hit her hard. He longed to talk to her about it, this weekend, maybe. If she didn't see it his way, could he convince her? He looked down at the number two pencil twitching in his hand. The taste of bile rose in his mouth. He squeezed his eyes shut. Just focus, he thought, see the goal, weigh the options. Focus, for now, with this test. He took a deep breath, squared his shoulders and placed pencil to paper.

Sarge's reading glasses hung halfway down his nose, still he squinted over the 12-page contract. He grunted occasionally as the girls looked on and Bill tapped his pencil impatiently. Twice while Sarge turned back a couple of pages, Bill rolled his eyes.

"Are you late for something, Bill?" Jaqui asked. "We can do this another time if it's a problem."

"No, no, I'm good. Can I get you guys anything to drink?"

"Bourbon and coke would be great," Jaqui joked.

To her surprise, Bill hit the intercom. "Lucy, can you fix Jaqui a bourbon and coke?"

"Me, too,?" Katrine said. Sarge held up three fingers.

"Make that three, Lucy," Bill spoke into the device, "and a Vodka Collins." He sat back in his chair, crossed his ankle over his knee and smiled at Jaqui. "You're going to fit right into this business."

"I knew she was star when I see her very first time," Katrine said. Lucy brought the drinks. Sarge continued reading. The girls had almost finished their drinks when Sarge finally placed the contract on Bill's desk. He removed his glasses and turned to Jaqui. "Well, by the time the expenses and the vultures are paid you might clear a buck or two. You get to keep the job you have as long as this Keegan Stone guy wants to keep you on. The good thing is, as far as I can tell, it's impossible to end up any worse off than you are now. As long as you complete one tour, 11 shows I believe, all your living and travel expenses are covered."

"That's the gist of it," Bill said. "You're welcome to have an attorney look over it."

"No," Jaqui said. "I trust my dad."

"One thing I noticed," Sarge said, "is there's no time limit to renegotiate. I would think both partners would benefit from it."

"Actually, if you check page two the contract ends after the tour with an option to renew. We want to see how Jaqui works with the Bluebirds. My feeling is she will eventually become a solo act." Bill said.

"Wow!" Katrine said, "I will be groupie for you, Baby, when you are big star."

"Let's don't jump ahead too far. When do I get to meet the Bluebirds?"

"I'm getting them a place here. They're in New York, but if everything works out they'll be here by the end of next week. We're co-opting with Keegan on his studio. So as soon as they get here you guys can get to work. It's important to get an album in the stores before the tour."

"This is cool," Jaqui said. "Let's sign this sucker so we can go celebrate." Jaqui grabbed the nearest pen. Bill hit the intercom and Lucy brought more drinks.

"Daddy, can you stay in town tonight? I want to show you our house. We have plenty of room. We can drive over so I can show you the studio, too."

Stomp and Holler

Hayes Carll

Langley's dad missed the graduation, probably because Langley neglected to share the details with him. Marjorie came and Sara brought her folks. If there was any doubt about Sara's mom getting along with Marjorie it vaporized. Ten minutes after the introductions they were conspiring like sisters on various methods of spoiling grandchildren. Even Bud was beaming as if it was his own son graduating.

"Do me a favor and don't bust all of my buddies the first week, okay?" He laid his big paw on Langley's shoulder and thought how odd it was not to be intimidated by a DPS uniform.

"Don't worry," Langley said. "I'll just be on patrol for a while, at least until I finish school. Tell 'em not to speed and they'll be okay. By the way, it's unofficial, but we give a nickel. You'll never get stopped for doing 65 in a 60 unless, of course, you look like you."

Bud laughed. He'd grown fond of Langley. "The kid's a little serious but he's got a good head on his shoulders," he told his running buddies. "He bit off a pretty big chunk hooking up with my little girl, but if anyone can handle her, my money's on him."

203

After graduation Langley's dad treated the entire party to a dinner at the Olive Garden, a fact that he was unaware of. Marjorie still retained one credit card in her husband's name until the divorce was final. Langley had no appetite. Sure, he was glad to have graduation behind him but it only meant real life was ahead and he wasn't sure what real life would be like. Right in the middle of dinner Sara took Langley's hand under the table and pressed it to her abdomen. Langley felt his offspring kick his hand.

"When did that start happening?" He whispered.

"Yesterday. He started out by punching me in the bladder." As Langley's hand rested on Sara he felt another poke from inside his girlfriend.

"Wow," he said.

"Yep, a rowdy little guy," Sara said. "It's been like this most of the day. I tried to take a nap but he tap-danced on my back bone. That was loads of fun."

"He?"

"Speculation, but if we want to know I can make an ultrasound appointment in about two more weeks."

"Do we want to know?"

"I don't know, do we? Maybe we can talk later." She said. Langley breathed a sigh of relief and took a bite of his chicken alfredo. At least they were going to talk.

Jaqui gave Sarge the grand tour of the house then showed off the elegant backyard where Katrine was sitting enjoying the sunset with a snifter of El Presidente. They joined her at the patio table

"You can use my room. It has its own attached bath," Jaqui offered.

"Where will you sleep?" Sarge said.

Katrine and Jaqui beamed at each other and smiled.

"Where I usually do." Sarge's weathered cheeks turned pink but that was his only response. Meanwhile, a locksmith van slowly cruised down the street.

Looks like a party, Adam thought. Behind Jaqui's car was a huge four-wheel drive pickup, and behind that, hanging halfway into the street was a beige sedan. Adam was almost past when he noticed someone in the sedan. He made the block. When he came back around he pulled to the curb. As he stepped out of the van the sedan shot backwards, spun around and peeled down the street. spraying him with tiny chunks of gravel. *Was that a clown?* he asked himself. He jumped in the van in a futile attempt to pursue the sedan.

Ten minutes later, an unmarked patrol car stopped across the street long enough for the officer to call in the plate number of the farm truck parked in the driveway. Satisfied with the results, the patrol car pulled away. In the back yard another round of drinks was passed.

"I think I need to wait till morning to show off the studio," Jaqui said. "I'm catching a significant buzz."

"What buzz is that?" Katrine asked.

"Sinficant," Jaqui repeated. Her tongue stumbled over the syllables this time.

"Not for me to say at this time," Katrine said. Her eyes were starting to glaze over. "I'm hearing the mattress calling."

Oh Baby, stay up with us," Jaqui pleaded. Sarge stared over the fence to where the sun had been earlier. The faintest glow remained.

"No, you kids have big fun," Katrine said. "I sleep now." She stood and walked around to Jaqui. Leaning over to kiss her she tumbled into Jaqui's lap. Jaqui grabbed the opportunity to give her a "significant" kiss and helped her back to a vertical position.

"I'll be in soon," Jaqui said. Sarge shook his head ever so slightly as he continued to observe the darkening horizon.

Bullets didn't always work. Anyway, this time it was personal. It needed to be face to face. Vengeance laughed at the fact that he never saw it coming. That was a hell of a look of surprise as the knife pierced his abdomen. Even a bigger one when he watched his intestines spill out onto the asphalt. Had to get it right this time. Finish it. *"You can't talk about her that way,"* Vengeance hissed as the knife penetrated the chest cavity repeatedly. *"You can't talk about me that way."* Over and over the knife perforated until the last vestige of life flickered from his eyes. *"You won't be needing these."* And the knife sliced through bone - ten times. Now everything was red, slimy red, hot red, sticky red. Ten trophies were collected, Vengeance got in the beige sedan and reached under the seat. Blood dripped and smeared. Vengeance dumped the contents of the bag, set up the spoon and emptied almost a ½ gram of meth into it, mixing it with barely enough water to liquefy it. Still, it almost filled the syringe. Vengeance used the paper bag to wipe away enough blood to find a vein one last time. The needle found home. Vengeance made no attempt at care or control, just pushed the poison in; but Vengeance didn't die. Breath choked the dehydrated throat. Heart pounded a pre-war drum circle as clear bile spewed from digestive depths to mix with the slimy blood. Vengeance screamed and jumped from the car, running around it, beating on the trunk and hood, fists flailing. "God damn it, God fucking damn it." A guttural subhuman wail rose and mixed with wrenching sobs. Vengeance jumped back in the sedan and sped out of the parking lot, side swiping as many cars as possible.

Sara finished off Langley's take-home box of chicken alfredo. It was still almost warm. "You eat in your bedroom?" Langley asked. Sara looked around then down at the Styrofoam container and shook her head as she crossed her feet on the mattress. "Okay, stupid question. I guess we have to get used to each other's eccentricities."

Sara continued eating, asking herself why she didn't order the chicken alfredo. The shrimp scampi she'd put away at the restaurant had been little more than a tease. She watched Langley while she gobbled the goodies. Obviously the boy had something on his mind.

"I was thinking we could look at houses this weekend." He waited. She waited. Nothing.

"Why?" she asked between bites.

"My job is 110 miles away. I can't very well commute from here. Caldwell is about the same distance from Blinn College as you are now from SACC, plus you only go two days a week."

"Are you asking me to shack up with you?"

"We're already living together."

"Not officially. You're a refugee."

Langley closed his eyes, took a deep breath and started over. "Sara, in a perfect world you would marry me. Right now you won't and I understand that. I hope someday you'll change your mind."

"Probably, on some level."

"The thing is, I love you. I want to be with you forever, starting as soon as possible."

Sara smiled, forked in a piece of chicken and waited.

"So if we're going to live together, even eventually, I want you to have some input on where. I want you to be comfortable."

"You're cute," she said. "I love you so much. Of course. It sounds like a fun way to kill a weekend."

"So you'll move in with me?"

"Could be. It sounds like a lot of work but, yeah, if we can find a decent place." She performed an enormous belch. "I can't finish this, want some?"

Langley found his hunger had returned. "Sure, thanks." Baby steps, he thought. It's a start.

~

Finger On the Trigger
- Bleu Edmondson

Jaqui watched the tennis shoes tumbling in the dryer.
Then she was the tennis shoes tumbling in the dryer. The
dizzy world spun outside the window. She pounded against
the metal tub, pounded, and spun, spun and pounded, pounded,
pounded. Then she opened her eyes and the spinning stopped---
almost. But the pounding, the incessant pounding, continued.
She looked over as Katrine groaned and pulled the pillow over
her head Still the pounding, someone was at the door. She
looked at the alarm clock: 7:45.

"Fucking idiots!" She pulled on a robe and stumbled into
the living room. "Just a minute." The pounding stopped.

"APD, we need to talk to you."

She was a disheveled mess, inside and out. When she pulled
the door open, she faced the same two detectives as before.
"What now?"

"Ma'am, do you know anything about these?" The chubby
male officer asked.

Jaqui looked at the plastic bag with severed human fingers
inside and threw up all over the front porch. The detectives
caught her limp body just before she hit the puddle.

"Nice work, Juan," Bess spouted.

The knocking woke Sarge too. He stumbled into the living room. Upon seeing his unconscious daughter being handled by strangers he was fully awake. "What the hell?" Sarge bellowed, as he leaped across the room. When he saw the detective reach for her gun he froze and locked his hands behind his head. "Whoa, easy. I'm good. What happened to Jaqui? What did you do to her. I've heard about your 'shoot first, ask questions later' style of law enforcement in this city."

"No sir, she just fainted."

"Bullshit, Jaqui doesn't faint."

"Extenuating circumstances." Bess' eyes rolled toward her partner. "Can you help us get her to the couch?" By the time they had her inside she'd come to.

"Daddy, can you get me some water, maybe an aspirin. They're in the kitchen cabinet next to the stove." As soon as he left she asked detective Juan, "Did you just show me a bag of fingers?"

"Do you know a Bruce Lane? He played piano at the Four Seasons." Juan asked.

"What do you mean played? I just saw him there a couple weeks ago. He's like a fixture there. He *is* the Four Seasons bar."

"He was murdered last night. His body was found in the parking garage. We found your number in his wallet."

"Yeah, we've worked together."

"Working with you seems like a bad idea for musicians around here," Juan said.

Sarge came back in. "You don't have to answer their questions without an attorney."

"It's okay, Daddy, I didn't do anything." She looked back to the male detective. "What about the fingers?"

"We think they're his. We didn't find them with the body." Jaqui stomach danced again.

"Where were they?"

"In your front yard."

"Oh, Daddy!" She burst into tears and reached for Sarge.

"What the hell is going on here?" Sarge asked"

We're trying to figure that out. We don't think Jaqui has anything to do with it but she may have some information."

Jaqui's mind was muddled. By now Katrine was up, standing in the bedroom doorway, staring at the surrealistic scene. "I'll make coffee," she said.

Jaqui's face was buried in Sarge's shoulder. He took the reins. "Y'all need to give her a minute. This is a lot to wake up to. I'm sure these girls will be happy to help you. Just let 'em regroup, okay? Katrine, darling, can you make enough for the detectives too?"

Katrine shuffled to the kitchen.

"So, get me up to speed, can you?" Sarge looked to the detectives as Jaqui swallowed the aspirin and leaned back into her father's shoulder. The sobs reduced to sniffles.

The female officer took a seat in the rocker. "According to security footage in the Four Seasons parking garage, someone, probably female judging by the size, although camera angles weren't definitive, came up and gave Mr. Lane a hug then they disappeared down between the vehicles for several minutes. The perp then got in a beige Buick, sat for a couple minutes, got out of the car and ran around it beating on the vehicle in a crazed frenzy. She then got back in the vehicle and left at a high speed, hitting several parked cars on the way out. That alerted a passerby who found the eviscerated body of Mr. Lane."

Jaqui quit crying and faced the detectives. "I'm pretty sure I know who did it, not sure why, but who."

"This is more like it," Langley said as they stepped out of the property manager's Tahoe for the fourth time. It was an older neighborhood but the houses and yards were immaculately maintained. A raised bed of vincas, marigolds and assorted culinary herbs greeted them at the entry. Sara reached down and pinched a few leaves of oregano, crushing them between her fingers. She sniffed and then held her hand to Langley's face.

"Okay, now I'm hungry," he said.

"You're always hungry."

The agent opened the door. Sara stepped in first. "This is too cool, the first one without carpet. His toys will roll easier and it will be easier to clean." Sara rubbed her pronounced tummy.

"It's a boy?" the agent asked.

"We don't find out until Thursday."

"You want a boy?"

"Doesn't matter really," Langley said. Sara had already wandered into the kitchen. Langley followed. "What do you think, Baby?"

"Give me a minute. I'm going to be the one hanging out here all the time while you're out saving the world, at least for a while."

"Take your time. I'm going to check out the back yard."

The agent stayed with Sara as they explored the two small bedrooms at opposite ends of a short hall. The pastel green and pink tiled bathroom took up the space between.

"It reminds me of the house I grew up in," Sara said.

"There were tens of thousands of these post war floor plans built in the fifties and sixties," the agent explained. "There's real wood behind the sheetrock here. You can hang a picture anywhere. The owners put polyurethane on the hardwood floors so they can be mopped just like the tile if you want. This house is easy to maintain."

"It looks like fresh paint too."

Langley's voice rang from the back yard. "Honey, come here, you've got to see this." When she got outside, she found Langley staring into the belly of a black barrel barbecue pit. "This thing looks like it's brand new."

"It is," the agent said. "The owners are barbeque aficionados.

The old one had seen better days so they replaced it."

"We used to barbeque almost every weekend when I lived at home," Langley said, mostly to Sara. "I know, I was there for a couple of them."

"Y'all like this?" the agent asked.

"I love it," Sara said.

"How much is it?" Langley asked.

"Twelve hundred a month."

"Ouch!" Langley winced. "I don't know. I'm just starting with the DPS and with a baby coming and all, I'm not sure we can do that."

"Let's talk to the owners. Since you're a first responder, they may give you a break. I know they like the idea of having newlyweds who're starting a family as tenants."

"We're not" Langley began. Sara twisted his fingers.

"Give us a minute." She gave the agent her sweetest smile and towed Langley to the kitchen. "Don't you dare tell her we're not married."

"But we're not. They're going to find out."

"We will be," Sara said. "I want this house. Just let me do the talking."

Langley nodded. He doubted he could form words anyway. All his dreams had just come true. He looked around but Sara was gone.

"The most we can possibly handle is a thousand a month plus electric." Sara was saying when Langley found her. "If that can work we can move in on the first. Talk to the owners and get back to us okay."

"You'll need to fill out a credit app," the agent said.

"We will, if you can make the deal."

Give me a couple of days. I promised I wouldn't bother them on the weekend."

Vengeance drove. What else was there to do? Suicide hadn't worked out. She could blow her brains out but that wouldn't be very pretty. Besides, there was one more task to perform first. She drove northwest roughly parallel to the chain of LCRA lakes. By the time she reached Lake Buchanan, the population had dwindled, as had her fuel supply. The inside of the car had begun to stink, and there was the blood. She had to do something about this blood. She turned onto a rural road, then a county road, then an unmarked caliche road where she began searching. Within a couple of miles she found it, just visible from the rutted lane was a travel trailer parked out in the pasture near some trees in waist high prairie grass. She checked the gate, chained but not locked, someone's deer lease. She saw the utility pole sticking up behind the RV and figured she'd struck gold. After parking behind the trees she found the doors locked, a temporary setback. There were canned goods in the cabinets, beans and soup, and several gallons of water on the counter. She turned on the faucet. The water pump groaned but all that came out was a trickle of milky liquid with a strong odor of plastic. She shucked her clothes and washed her arms and face with some of the bottled water. When she caught her reflection in the mirror stuck to the bathroom door she thought damn chick, you look hot! You must be down to a size three now. The dark circles under her eyes, thinning hair and gray green bruises down her arm didn't register. She looked at the bed above the fifth wheel. Not yet. She sat on the couch and stared out the window as the day began. It wasn't sleep, that didn't happen anymore, but there were these trances, "little blessings" she called them, where her brain checked out for a time. The longer she stayed up, the longer the trances. This one lasted quite a while. When she came to, she was exhausted. She rummaged through the cabinets and found a bottle of liquid cold medicine. After chugging half of it, she crawled up into the bunk and waited. Finally.

Keegan Stone sat in the sound booth editing rehearsal tapes into a workable format. The left side of his face was still bandaged but the Percocet was taking the edge off his pain and improving the quality of the music. The figure in the dim space behind the window startled him. At first it appeared to be an apparition. The man with the dark hair and sea blue eyes stood motionless in a black duster. As Keegan caught his breath, the corners of the stranger's mouth twitched into the briefest grin. Keegan shivered as he removed his headphones to let the stranger in.

"You're a blessed man," the stranger said. "God is watching over you."

"Yeah right, just fucking peachy. Who in the hell are you?"

"Adam Wolf, one of the few surviving male acquaintances of Jaqui Benderman."

"You a musician?"

"Amateur, acoustic delta blues, but that's not why I'm here. I'm here to warn you. She had me fooled too."

"Fooled? What do you mean?"

"She's a killer. I've been looking into her past. She killed her boyfriend before she moved here, pushed him under a moving trailer."

"I doubt it. That doesn't sound like her. Besides, the police cleared her."

"Wasn't she the last one here the night you were shot?"

"But she was having coffee with some preacher when it happened."

"That was me."

"You? You don't look like a preacher."

"What do preachers look like?"

"Not like you. Anyway, she didn't shoot me."

"I was outside with her. She said she would follow me to the coffee shop, one she picked, but it took her about 15 minutes to get there after I arrived, plenty of time to take you out."

"But there's no motive. Hell, I'm going to help make her the next Beyonce'."

"No motive for the boyfriend either. Have you heard about her tattoo?"

"I've seen it, kind of strange, but so what?" Keegan, losing patience, stood up and prepared to eject this oddball from his studio. The guy obviously had an agenda. Keegan preferred to focus on the future looming before him; the upcoming tour, the other band sharing studio space, the surgery necessary to remodel his face.

Adam paused before responding. "That trailer she pushed her boyfriend under; it was loaded with watermelons."

Keegan felt the room tighten around him. He fell back into his chair. Nothing made sense. "Have a seat, Adam," he said. The preacher continued to stand. "So what are you here for? You don't even know me."

"We have to stop her. I just found out that the police are questioning her for another murder."

"God damn it!"

"Please don't."

"What?" Keegan said.

"Use the Lord's name like that. He's the reason you're alive today. He has a plan for us."

"You need to leave. How the hell did you get in here anyway?"

"The door was unlocked. I knocked but you couldn't hear so I just came in."

"Bullshit! You think I wouldn't lock it after this?" he said, pointing to his face.

Adam shrugged and turned to leave. "Think about it. She needs to be stopped." He dropped a card on the console. Keegan watched until Adam was gone and dead-bolted the outer door and locked himself in the sound booth where he spent the night.

"Lilah Snipes," Jaqui said.

Detective Juan scribbled in his notebook. "Where can we find Ms. Snipes?"

"Luling. My hometown. We were friends growing up, sort of." "No," Sarge said. "She disappeared a few weeks back. They found her car in the parking lot of a Mexican flea market out on highway 290. They put out a bulletin but that was the last I heard. Word was she'd been running with a rough crowd since the pageant fiasco."

"She didn't win?" Jaqui asked.

"No, after your accident the judges tested all the contestants for drugs and alcohol. Over half were dirty. They decided not to award prizes and canceled the pageant indefinitely. At first everyone thought Lilah just split, but when they found the car they thought maybe abduction or she pissed somebody off."

"I had no idea," Jaqui said.

"It's not like I could tell you. You made yourself pretty scarce too."

"If it's not her, then who?"

"We're not going to have to get naked are we?" Langley asked.

"No, silly boy. Handfasting is a public ceremony. Just because we're Wiccan doesn't mean we run around sky clad every time we get together. Besides, our parents and friends will be there. You don't really want to see them naked do you?"

"Your mom's kind of cute," Langley said. "But if I ever see Bud stripped down it will be way to soon."

Sara's eyes mocked shock. "Boy, you best leave my mama alone!"

"All I'm saying is that you'll probably look like her when you're older too, so that makes me a lucky man."

"Nice save. So how about your parents, will they come?"

"Mom will. Dad, probably not. He wants us to get married in the church. I haven't even mentioned the Wiccan thing to them yet."

"Will your mama be okay with 'the Wiccan thing'?"

"It doesn't matter. She likes you and that's what counts to her. Is there a Wiccan priest or something? How does that work?"

"Artis will perform the ceremony and, yes, it's legal. We have to get a license and register with the county clerk just like any other couple. The ceremony is a little different is all. We should do it outdoors in a natural setting. We can even have a party after. Bud said he'd put one together if we wanted. The cool thing is," Sara said, "we get to make up the entire ceremony from scratch."

"You think we can pull it together in a couple of weeks? We should hear back on the house tomorrow. Wouldn't it be great if we could come home from our wedding to our own house?" Langley said.

"Handfasting."

"What?"

"Handfasting, not wedding." Sara said.

"Same thing."

"No, with handfasting the union can be dissolved in a simple ceremony. There's no divorce necessary."

Langley rolled away from Sara and stared at the ceiling. "I want this to be permanent."

"I do too," Sara said, "but if something goes wrong the split doesn't have to be messy."

"That doesn't sound like much of a commitment."

"It's as much of a commitment as we make it. Look at what your parents are going through. It sucks. We don't want that."

"We're not them."

"Sweetheart, when they were first married, I'm sure they felt the same as we do now."

Langley thought back to his childhood. There had been a time when his mom and dad were playful and loving toward each other. That was years ago. How many years had they wasted just going through the motions? "Okay, but don't expect me to ever stop loving you.

"I don't." Sara rolled onto Langley and took his earlobe in her teeth. He felt their child adjust to the new position inside his wife to be.

Slip Inside This House
- 13th Floor Elevators

Vengeance **awakened in total darkness** with her ears
ringing. She had no clue as to her location except she was
in a bed. She felt around. As usual she was alone. She sat up and
bumped her head on the low ceiling. Her forearms ached and
her mouth tasted like a toxic spill. An unfamiliar sense overcame
her - hunger. The fog began to clear and she realized where she
was. It had not been a nightmare. She fumbled for a toggle
switch and a dim light flooded the cramped space. She stumbled
to the toilet and peed a stream of stinking acid before realizing
there was no way to flush. Pushing the handle only caused the
pump to moan and hiss.

Trembling hands fumbled through the cabinets until she
found a can of chicken noodle soup. She dumped it in an
aluminum saucepan and lit the burner on the stovetop. While it
heated she rummaged through the drawers for a spoon. As she
stirred, she caught a glimpse in the mirror. A corpse stared back
from the shadows. Crying didn't work. The tears wouldn't come.
She remembered having felt something once; some love, some
hate, lust, even pride. It was all gone and Jaqui Benderman's
was to blame. She'd given Jaqui the finger times ten. How she'd
love to be a fly on the wall while that uppity bitch tried to

explain it to the authorities. *I'm not done with you yet, Jaqui Benderman.*

Time wasn't important. It was the middle of some night, not sure what day. She still had a little money. She could probably find some stuff in here to pawn. The car was a liability in Austin, out here, not so much. What she needed was more fuel; for the car, for her body. The soup danced on the top of a stomach that was unfamiliar with solids, but she knew she had to hold it down if she wanted to survive long enough to fulfill her mission. She'd use her assets to acquire the rest. The clock in the car said 10:20. It was either Friday or Saturday night, she wasn't sure. It didn't matter. She dug through her bags until she found a leather skirt, and a sheer cotton blouse with bell sleeves long enough to hide the damage to her arms. Rawhide boots with pointy toes finished off the disguise. She splashed herself heavily with the perfume her dad had bought her last Christmas. The beige sedan was nondescript but when she stopped to gas it up she made sure the body damage faced away from the cashier.

"Where's a good place to party hard?" She asked the girl behind the register.

"Not from here? The cashier asked. She fingered a blonde streak that had fallen from her mostly brown locks.

"Nope, just passing through and lonely as hell," Vengeance said. "Looking for a quickie with candy if you know what I mean."

"There's a biker bar north of here on 29 if you're up for it. It's a little rough, but fun. I wouldn't go alone though."

"Thanks, I'm a big girl. It sounds like what I'm looking for."

"Take 29 north to the next major intersection. Good luck." Less than 10 minutes later she pulled the beige sedan into Fuzzy's Corner. She strutted in with the smooth intensity of a runway model. Head's turned toward her, fresh meat. Her scowl and obvious attitude shut down about half the onlookers. The rest watched for her next move. She straddled a bar stool and ordered a longneck. When it arrived she took a swig, spun around and hooked her elbows on the bar. With her boot heels on the chair rail she spread her knees and cradled the longneck between her breasts. She tried her best to smile. It came off as more of a sneer.

She noticed several men check her out. They ribbed their buddies but none approached. While she eyed the crowd a woman in a black sleeveless Harley Davidson t-shirt sat on the barstool beside her. Black Tee Shirt had close cropped hair, tight jeans and full lips. She clipped her words as she spoke. "S'up, girl. You gonna find trouble putting it out there like that."

"What's it to you?" Vengeance said.

"Chicks got to stick together. You looking for company?"

"Yep, but you're one appendage short for my taste."

Black Tee Shirt licked her lips. "Don't knock it 'til you've tried it. I'm Vera and I can at least offer protection, maybe more if you're feeling adventurous."

"Adventure is my middle name. A girl like me, well, I might try anything if I had some candy to loosen me up."

"I got nothing but a six pack and a magic tongue, Miss Adventure. What's your other name?"

"Lilah."

"Sweet little Lilah. What kind of candy you looking for?"

"I was thinking maybe an eight ball of crank."

"Eew, nasty. I don't fuck with that shit. It'll steal your soul." The girl stood to leave, then turned. "See that guy shooting pool; skinny guy, chain wallet, pizza face. He can hook you up. You ought not go there. You're too damn pretty to take that road."

"That's my highway."

"If you change your mind, let me know."

Vengeance ambled over to the pool table and slipped four bits on the rail. "I've got the winner." She picked out a questick and leaned against the wall, the stick gripped snugly in her crotch. "Well boys, where does a nice girl go to have fun around here?"

Pizza Face shot her a look of disgust. "I ain't paying!"

Vengeance looked confused.

"He thinks you're hooking," Pizza's burly companion announced.

"He's dreaming. You can't buy this." Vengeance spun like a runway model. "But I do like cute skinny guys and so far the only interest has been from a dyke."

Be nice, Vera's this dork's sister," Pizza said.

"Fuck you, Jimmy. She's your mama!"

"She's your mama's pet muff diver."

"You guys shut up. Vera's sweet. She didn't say anything mean about you."

"We're just messing," the big guy said. "We've known Vera since high school. She's cool. She's in here every weekend trying to get lucky. By the way, I'm Lester. Folks call me Snout - don't ask. This useless little fuck is Jimmy and if you're really a nice girl you probably better run away."

"Been there, done that. That's why I'm here. I've got the hots for little old Jimmy, but first we need to shoot a game to see who starts out on top."

"I'm down by four balls," Snout said. "I'll go by a round. You lovebirds can have this table. Just ain't my night. Maybe if I get Vera drunk enough ---."

"You'd have to Rouphy her you ugly fuck," Jimmy said.

"Like I was saying---." Snout wandered away.

Vengeance sidled up so close to Jimmy that she could smell the methamphetamine in his sweat. She hooked a thumb in his belt loop. "Looks like we've got the table to ourselves." Jimmy picked up her quarters and put them in the slots. "Rack 'em," he said.

After calling his house and getting no answer, Jaqui reached Keegan at his studio, odd for noon. She needed to try to explain what was going on, that he might be in danger. He was evasive when she wanted to drop by.

"I just want to show my dad where the magic is made," Jaqui explained.

"I've got some errands to run. Why don't we meet at EL Azteca around four for an early dinner. Then we can hit the studio after." Keegan didn't really believe Jaqui was the killer, but Adam's theory wouldn't leave his mind.

Jaqui brought Katrine and Sarge with her. When they walked in, she was surprised to see Bill Billings at the table with Keegan. "I see how it is," Bill joked. "My two main players here together, I guess I know who's picking up the tab."

"I've got it," Sarge offered.

"No, seriously," Bill said, "I can write it off."

Jaqui ran to hug Keegan. He stiffened. "Are you okay?" She asked. "I've been so afraid for you. I don't know what's going on but I feel like it's all my fault somehow."

"I'm blind in one eye," Keegan said, as if it were an accusation.

"I know, I'm so sorry. I thought I knew who did it. Now I'm not sure. Please be careful."

"I talked to a guy you know named Adam,"

"Yeah, he's pretty weird but I don't think it was him. It could be though."

"He thinks it was you."

"What? That liar! I was with him when it happened." She started to tear up. The paleness in her cheeks burned red.

"What about that Bruce guy you worked with. He's dead now, right?"

Jaqui lost it. The realization of his death and that none of her friends were safe body-slammed her to the table. The ensuing moan turned heads and brought waiters from across the room. She found it hard to breathe, so hard in fact, that when she sat up the room began to spin and her world turned black.

Sarge caught her just before she hit the floor. He glared at

Keegan. "You know damn well she wouldn't hurt anyone, you little shit! She looks up to you."

"What about her boyfriend back home, the one she pushed under the trailer?"

Sarge flushed magenta. His fist clenched and unclenched repeatedly as if grinding Keegan's bones. "That - was - an - accident," he spit. "The kid wasn't paying attention. She's suffered enough for that."

Keegan got the gist of the situation, deciding to back off. "No, I don't think she did it. I've just got a lot of questions."

"The police do too." Sarge tried to calm down. "Instead of throwing accusations around maybe you can help us find an answer. What about this Adam guy? What's his story?"

"He is odd boy," Katrine said. "Is possible to be him but I think not. Still, is not to trust. Very crazy with God ideas. He hates me. Probably think I did all killing and shooting. I would only shoot him, or anyone trying to hurt Jaqui."

Sarge was kneeling on the floor with Jaqui's head in his lap. Tears were forming in the corners of his eyes. He pushed a strand of her hair from her face. "How did we get here, little girl. What the hell happened to us?"

Jaqui opened her eyes and saw that Sarge was about to cry. She took a deep breath and allowed him to help her to her chair. "Let's eat," she said. "We can figure this out."

"You guys better pay off," Bill said. "I've dealt with some flakes in my time, but you guys take the cake." He turned to the waiter who was a couple of shades paler than when his shift started. "Vodka Collins, make it a double, and whatever these guys want."

Okay, so police work is boring, maybe not boring, but mundane. Langley thought. His first week he'd ridden with a partner. Due to staffing, he was already on his own, in a cruiser that was pushing 150 K miles. He mostly ran radar and stopped speeders. If things got really slow he would break out the binoculars and check for expired tags and inspection stickers. Most of the people speeding knew they were doing it. The others he gave a warning if they were apologetic. The ones that knew it pissed him off a little, especially the guys in the $60,000 cars that thought they were entitled and the better than average looking women who thought they could flirt their way out of it. These folks were sadly mistaken. He tried to be fair and mostly he was. Sometimes it was tough. Like the guy with the expired inspection driving from one job to the next. He knew his inspection was out. "As soon as I can afford to get the horn fixed," the guy said. He got off with a warning. The pregnant lady with four kids in the back of the minivan, late for an OB-GYN appointment; another warning. He really did try to be fair. It's not like there were any quotas, right? At least not officially. He was just glad to go home at the end of the of whatever shift he was on. Sara was stuck unpacking and decorating the house, not that they had much, but she was also putting together the handfasting. She also had to find time to transfer her credits at SACC to Blinn before the semester break, determined to finish her associate degree before the baby came in late June. Her tenacity was almost scary.

The sun was low in the sky. He was working highway 36 out toward Milano. It had been slow. What he really needed was a DWI. Almost everyone in his graduating class had at least an assist on one. Now was the time they came out of the woodwork, guys stopping for one too many on their way home from work. He had the radar on. A cargo van came from behind the rise he was sitting beside. It wasn't speeding, 67 in a 65, but when he was spotted the driver dropped his speed by about 20 miles per hour, something a drunk would do. Langley decided to tail him a minute or two, just for grins. He ran the plates, nothing outstanding, but the van was registered in the valley, a good 200 miles south. The driver maintained 50 miles per hour but drove fairly straight. Something wasn't right. Langley could feel it, so he kept a distance. The driver of the van turned on his lights. Jackpot, Langley thought, burned out license plate light. He hit the siren for a second and turned on the light bar. The van eased to the shoulder. Cargo vans could be risky, poor visibility. He took the safety off his weapon and walked a wide arc. There were two people in front. The driver kept his hands on the wheel. There was a female passenger. They looked like ag workers.

"Do you know why I stopped you?"

"No habla Ingles," the man said.

Langley noticed a *Houston Chronicle* on the dash. It was in English. He stepped closer. The woman was holding *People* magazine, also in English. "So you read English but don't speak it? No! Speak English! I stopped you for a faulty taillight. I need license and insurance." The van had liability only but it was in someone else's name. "Step out of the vehicle, sir." The driver kept one hand up and opened the door with the other. "Anybody with you but her?"

"No sir."

"Can you open the back for me please?"

"No sir."

"Put your hands against the side of the patrol car." He called for backup. "This could go badly for you. I'm going to ask once more. Open the back of the van, please?"

The driver held his hands at shoulder level and went to open the van. There were only several cardboard boxes but there was an odor of vegetation Langley had learned at the academy. He drew his weapon. "Hands against the vehicle! Spread your feet!" He cuffed the driver and frisked him. As he was putting him in the patrol car, he heard the van's passenger door open. The woman was running toward the fence line. "Stop!" He shouted. She kept running. He put the driver in back and followed. When he reached the fence he could still see her. The lights of the backup cruIser approached so he returned to the scene.

"I think we have a significant cache of marijuana." Langley explained to the officer. "Should we get a detective out here?"

"Just call a hook," the sergeant said. "You follow and we'll process it at the yard. Let's bust one of these babies open to make sure it's a good collar."

They ripped open a box. It was full of compressed marijuana bricks. The sergeant lifted it. "If these are all like this you've got about 1000 pounds here. You'd better call your old lady, Scott. You're going to be late getting home."

Langley looked over at the field then down at his spit polished boots. "Sergeant, sir, one got away, a female."

"On foot?"

"Yes sir."

"You want to bring out the dogs?"

"We can't just leave her out here. It's going to be in the low forties tonight and a good chance of rain."

"You got the driver, right? My gut tells me to let it go but it's your collar."

"She's probably on the dash cam. I know I am, running after her."

"Shit! Damn it, Scott. Call it in. It's going to be long night."

Jimmy laid a couple of lines of homemade meth out on the console of his truck. Vengeance snorted one, not her favorite method of ingestion, in fact it burned the shit out of her sinuses.

"You can have the other one if you want." Jimmy had unzipped his jeans to explain the terms of the transaction. "As long as you're down there anyway." He pulled out his semi-erect member. Vengeance lollipopped it a couple of times. "So you never did tell me your name," he said.

"It's Lilah, and you need to put that thing away. I've got much bigger plans for you."

Jimmy forced his now rock solid erection back into his pants. "Where to? You want me to follow you?"

"No, you can bring me back later. Let me get a bag out of my car and I'll ride with you." She cupped her hand over his crotch. "Wait here."

Vengeance picked up her backpack that held her syringes and supplies then she spotted a favorite scarf and slipped it around her neck. "It's primitive," she said, jumping back in Jimmy's truck. "I'm kind of holed up. I'm running from a bad situation, hiding out, but it'll be fun. Just pretend you're camping, upscale camping, but camping."

"Sergeant Goodwin, could you do me a favor?" Langley was already getting his flashlight and GPS from his patrol car. "I saw which way the woman was heading. If you could wait for the wrecker guy, I'm going to try and locate her. Save some time. She's probably just waiting this out. Hit the horn when the hook shows up. I'll come back."

"Was she armed?"

"I doubt it, but I'll be careful." Langley climbed through the barbed wire and set out down a game trail. The remaining hint of light left from the day was obscured by the trees and brush. As he traveled deeper into the forest he began to rethink his decision to pursue the suspect. Though he was concerned for the woman's welfare, he realized his chances of locating her were slim. When turning to leave he heard a rustling by a fallen tree. He drew his weapon. "Police! Show yourself, hands first!" Two dainty hands appeared from behind the stump. The woman stood. Langley's stomach two-stepped into his throat. The woman's abdomen protruded at almost the same angle as Sara's.

"Step around to the path and get on your knees!" The

woman obeyed. She was a girl really. It appeared unlikely she had reached her twenties. "When are you due," he asked.

The look she gave him fell somewhere between defiance and suspicion, "March."

Langley took the handcuffs from his belt then put them back. The forest seemed at once familiar and claustrophobic. The light had completely faded, as had the hardness in the girls eyes. Langley glanced over his shoulder. "I'm going to have to bring out the dogs. I know a little about the terrain. If you walk deeper into the woods and then downhill you'll find a creek. I don't know how deep it is but if you walk in either direction in the water for 100 meters or so you'll trick the dogs. After that you're on your own. It's going to be a cold night. Your other choice is that I can take you back and arrest you and your child will be born in jail. It's your choice."

"Will I see my brother?"

"That's not your husband?"

"No, my brother made me come. In case we were caught, for good feelings."

You probably wouldn't see him except maybe at your trial."

"You won't shoot me?"

"No, of course not."

"For escaping?"

"No." She turned and continued to follow the game trail. "Good luck," Langley said. She kept walking.

"I lost her. Got too dark," Langley told the sergeant. "She's long gone. By the time we get the dogs there probably won't be much point. You want to wait on the hook. I'll take in the perp if that's okay?"

"No dogs?"

"I don't see the point."

∾

By the time Sarge parked behind the studio Jaqui had made a full recovery. She harmonized with Katrine and Loretta Lynn on Don't Come Home From Drinkin' With Lovin' On Your Mind".

"Damn, girls" Sarge said. "I can see why they want to make y'all famous."

"Only Jaqui is to be famous," Katrine said. "I am only her big fan."

"Y'all should sing together. It sounds like angels."

"Not a place for angels in music today."

"You're forgetting about Nashville. There's always a place for angels there."

"Cowboy music get the meat from the bone," Katrina said, "but it is not good songs for Jaqui's voice."

"Well, it sounded good to me," Sarge said.

"I think Katrine could be a star in her own right. When I get some credibility I'm going to make sure that happens," Jaqui pulled Katrine close and hugged her.

"If someday I get lucky it will be on me," Katrine said. So much for fun and frolic.

Once inside, Sarge took in the sights. "This looks like some space explorers hang out."

"It's the magic kingdom," Bruce explained. "Thanks to your daughter."

"She'll be almost living here starting Monday," Bill said. "The Bluebirds should be settled in by then. In fact I'm planning a little introductory party on Sunday. I hope all of you can make it. Jaqui and Keegan, for you, it's mandatory."

"No problem," Jaqui said. "Until then we need to lay low."

"Y'all want to come out to the farm?" Sarge said.

"We can't leave town without telling the cops," Jaqui took Katrine's hand.

"Bullshit, y'all come on out," Sarge said. Jaqui looked at Katrine. Katrine shrugged.

Gods and Monsters
- Lana Del Rey

"Turn off your headlights," Vengeance instructed. "Drive by moonlight."

This girl's a little freaky, Jimmy thought, but that usually worked to his advantage so he complied. "Where are we headed?"

"Quarter mile up, look for an iron gate on the right. I'll make an exception this time and do gate duty." She slid toward the door.

"It's just a pasture," Jimmy said. Vengeance huffed but jumped out and opened the gate. Jimmy followed a trail of knocked down grass to the camper parked in the pasture. "Does this thing have a bathroom?"

You're a guy, pee outside."

"That's not going to do it."

"I don't have water, except jugs. Pull around back."

"There's a fucking pump house right there. Why don't you have water?"

"I don't know."

Jimmy went over to the pump house and turned a valve. He heard the pump click on. "Go inside and try it now."

In a few seconds. Vengeance came running out and jumped

on Jimmy, wrapping her arms around his neck. "You're my hero, you saved the day."

It was too dark to see Jimmy blush. He usually paid for this level of appreciation. The evening kept getting better.

"Enter my lair," Vengeance said, holding the door for him. While Jimmy relieved himself, she took off her boots and blouse, leaving nothing on but a black lace bra and her leather skirt. When he came out he burst into a grin. "So have you ever shot meth?" Vengeance asked.

"Fuck no! I hate needles, anyway you get AIDS from needles."

"You get AIDS from people who have AIDS. Just don't share needles with faggots and you'll be okay. Want to give it a try? You'll never go back to frying off your nose hairs."

"I don't know."

"Come on, I've got a fresh rig, never been used. I'll help you."

Jimmy would probably have thrown himself under a stampede at this point just to tap this wicked little honey in her love shack. "What the hell."

She grabbed a couple of fresh spoons from the cabinet. "You're going to love this. Then you get dessert." She ran her hand up the inside of her thigh, barely pulling up the hem of the skirt. "Put about an eighth of a gram in each spoon." She prepared the product and handed him her scarf to wrap around his bicep. "Okay, pull it tight and hold both ends, release when I tell you." She slapped his forearm with her fingers a couple of times until a vein stood up. As she pierced it a drop of red appeared in the cylinder. She pulled back on the plunger and the drop expanded into a whorl. "I'm in, release." He let the tension off the scarf and she slowly depressed the plunger.

He could swear he saw her eyes glow cherry red as the warmth overtook him. It started in his knees and mouth and met in the middle of his groin. A power surge hit his heart. She was smiling.

"Fucking aye. That's awesome," he said between gasps. "You want me to do you?"

She shot him a sidelong glance. "I've got it. You need to get naked." She laid the prepared syringe beside the bed, shed her skirt and bra, wrapped the scarf around her arm and lay back on a pile of pillows. "How good are you with your tongue?" she asked.

"Pretty good, I've been told."

"Let's find out."

He pulled her knees up over his shoulders and started at her anus. He slid his tongue up, stopping to flick the tight spot between the front and back a couple of times. He then used it to scoop as much juice from deep inside her is it could reach. By the time he reached her clit it was engorged. He wrapped it in his lips and nursed. Occasionally he pushed it out with his tongue and slipped it back in. Her breathing was becoming shallow. It took all her concentration to give herself the shot in the midst of this. Once the needle was in, she waited for the next wave of energy to the press the plunger. The orgasm burned through her like a blast furnace, combining with the rush from the meth. She lost all control. Everything was hot and wet. Something oozed from her and Jimmy licked it up. She began trembling and shaking. She pulled out the syringe, dropped it and grabbed Jimmy by the head forcing herself into his face. She began twitching like an animal in the throes of death, then, as blackness spun in front of her eyes, she pissed herself. Jimmy came up sputtering.

"God damn it, Lilah. That's some bullshit! You could have fucking warned me."

She was still twitching, but realizing what had happened, pulled his head up between her breasts and wrapped him in her arms. Her wet crotch was still involuntarily humping his abdomen.

Things returned to some semblance of normal. She was sobbing an apology. "Oh baby, I'm so sorry. I'll make it up to you. I'm sorry. That was so good. I've never had anything like that."

They tore the sheets off the bed and Lilah threw them outside while Jimmy dug around for a fresh blanket.

"We can shower now, thanks to you figuring out how to turn on the water," Lilah said. "I'm really sorry about that peeing thing."

There was no way they could share the tiny shower stall. "You go first," she said. "You got the raw end of the deal anyway." While he showered she checked his pockets to see how much he was holding. She was surprised to find another full vial stashed in his pocket with the one they were using out of. He had a wad of bills in his wallet too, but she didn't risk taking the time to count it. *I found my new best friend,* she thought. She had just dropped his britches back on the floor when the bathroom door opened. She gave him a coy smile. "My turn." She took her purse in the bathroom with her.

He was splayed out on the blanket when she returned. Her long blond hair was wet against her neck; her pink nipples tight little nubs on her full breasts. The sight of her brought him back to attention. She slithered into the bed next to him and put his earlobe between her teeth. Her breath in his ear warmed his whole body. His erection was already echoing his heartbeat when she wrapped her fingers around it. He leaned into her but she pushed his shoulders back down on the bed. "I won, remember?" she said. "I start out on top." She lay beside him for a bit, kissing his neck and dragging her fingers from his chest to his balls in slow easy strokes, cupping and squeezing firmly on the down stroke, almost to the point of discomfort. She was legs and arms and hair and breasts. The rest of her body was diminished. Jimmy was okay with that.

When she finally rolled on top of him, she had the scarf around her shoulders. She straddled him, her hands on his chest, and lowered herself onto him. When he tried to thrust inside she retracted,

"Relax, let me handle this," she said. "I want this to be as good for you as it was for me. "She crawled down and wetted him thoroughly with her mouth then straddled him again and lowered slowly onto him until he was completely immersed in her. She clasped her hands behind her head and began grinding in a circular rhythm, him buried to the hilt. She used her lower half to grip as firmly as she could. He put his hands around her waist and shoved her down harder.

She took the scarf from her shoulders and fell forward, wrapping it around his neck. As the ends of her hair lashed his face she began riding him, sliding his full length.

"Do you trust me?" She asked."

He was panting. "What do you mean?"

"I'm going to make you come harder than you ever have."

"What?"

"Can you trust me?"

"Yeah, sure."

She pulled the scarf snug around his throat but not tight. He was pounding into her.

"I've heard of this," he said.

"Let's do it." Her eyes glowed.

"Okay." He thrust harder. She began tightening the scarf. He had her by the hip bones shoving into her. He felt his breath stop.

She could feel a trickle of heat inside and she tugged at the scarf. His face flamed red and his eyes began to bulge as his member inside her burst, flooding her thighs. He was pushing her arms now, grabbing wildly, causing the scarf to tighten even more.

She was almost there. The liquid heat aroused her. The fading light in his eyes aroused her. His death twitching finally caused an orgasm to form from deep within, where it had never started before, and radiate outward. His arms had dropped from her waist but his erection remained. She continued to ride it, yanking the reins of the scarf as his lifeless body flopped beneath her. She hoped it had been good for him. She'd lost herself in it. The total power of fucking him to death made the tremors last for many minutes. She rode it out from atop his body until he finally faded from within her.

She arranged his body in the center of the bed with his hand around his freshly washed, flaccid penis. She took the belt from his pants and tightened it around his neck. She rummaged through his truck and found an empty vial. After taking all her belongings from the RV, she laid his syringe on the bed beside him, washed one spoon and left the other on the table. She kissed his cold lips. "I'm sorry."

The money from his wallet totaled $680. She also found a film canister 2/3 full of meth in the truck's glove box. What a sweetie, she thought as she drove his truck to the gate. She closed and chained it carefully. Deer season didn't start for almost a month.

Langley stared at the mirror. The man staring back had all the teenager wrung out of him. After a 14-hour shift and 6 hours of sleep, he had a couple of hours before he had to be back on duty. He scraped the stubble from his face

"You need to check out the paper," Sara said as she handed it to him. A cup of fresh coffee was already steaming at the table. "You'll be the talk of Texas." Langley glanced at the first page and saw himself staring back from behind several open boxes of pot with Sergeant Goodwin by his side. His captain was shaking his hand.

"It's my job. I can't wait to hear Bud's take on it, though."

"Since there was also the 1/2 pound of heroin in the van, he'll understand."

"No, there wasn't."

"Says so right there in the article."

"Must be a misprint. I helped process the whole load."

Sara brought eggs, a slab of ham and buttered grits. "We
need to get the invites out for the handfasting."

"I don't have many folks. Let's see; Mom, Dad. He won't
come but we should invite him anyway, but not Jeanine. Jaqui,
her dad, Sarge and her girlfriend. I'll have to get her name for
you."

Sara stiffened. "Why them? You haven't seen her in half a
year."

"She's still my best friend. I've known her all my life."

"Don't you think that's a little weird? I've never even met
her."

"You will. Y'all will be best friends. You're going to love
her."

"Why, because you do?"

"Well, both of you love me, so you guys have one thing in
common."

"How would you feel if I invited my ex-boyfriends to this
handfasting?"

"Like the winner, but she's not my ex-girlfriend. I may have
mentioned that a couple of times."

"I heard you talking to her. I have trouble buying it."

Langley was too tired to continue this interrogation.
"Thanks for breakfast. I know it's mid-afternoon. You take such
good care of me."

"You're right, Boy, and don't you forget it." She leaned over,
kissed his forehead and snatched a piece of the ham he had
already cut from the slab.

He turned to the paper. Sure enough, they reported 1100
pounds of marijuana and half a pound of heroin. It didn't
make sense. When he read the final paragraph, his heartbeat
quickened. He read the sentence twice. "A female suspect was
apprehended at a nearby farmhouse. She is also charged with
delivery of controlled substances." This couldn't be a good
thing.

I am missing appointments for this?" Katrine said. "One I can reschedule, the other maybe next time in town, no big loss. We leave your car and my scooter in driveway. Cops think we are here if they check. We should not tell anyone where we go. Just be at Keegan's house Sunday."

Sarge waited in the driveway. He noticed there was very little traffic in the neighborhood. One pickup and a locksmith van were the only vehicles in the 1/2 hour he waited for the girls to pack. When they finally came out they piled in the front seat with Sarge.

"I brought a CD of some of our rehearsal tapes if you want to hear what the band sounds like," Jaqui offered.

"Put 'er in and turn it up," Sarge replied. The music blasted from the speakers and the girls harmonized with the backup singers. When the duets came on they stopped singing. Katrine took Jaqui's hand, kissed it and held it in her lap.

There'd been enough of a drizzle that the dirt roads weren't billowing dust. In fact everything was rinsed clean and the freshly tilled soil was a liquid shade of amber. Conservation easements sparkled in multihued greens. Mirror still surfaces of clear water lay deep in the irrigation ditches. As the farmhouse came into view Jaqui's breathing slowed, the muscles in her neck and face became pliable once more. Katrine felt the tension dissipate. It was contagious. Sarge began singing along; poorly, but with gusto.

The girls hadn't packed much as they had no intention of leaving the house. With backpacks strapped on, they traipsed through the damp grass. The smell of southern home cooking filled their lungs as they entered. Brenda Bartlett emerged from the kitchen in full chef's regalia.

"We'll hey there, Jaqui. Oh good, you brought a friend. Y'all hungry? I fixed a roast and we have corn bread and butter beans."

"Dad, you didn't tell me about Brenda. This looks serious. What's up with you guys?" Jaqui asked.

"With you gone she kept me from starving to death."

"Seems to be working."

"Well there is a little more to it than that. Show her, Baby." Brenda stuck out her left hand to show off her ring, white gold with a significant diamond flanked by two smaller emeralds.

"Wow, Dad! Way to go. I'm going to have a mommy." Jaqui grabbed Katrine's hand and pulled her into the group. "Katrine, this is Brenda, my new mom. Brenda this is my girl-friend, Katrine. We can't get married. This is Texas."

"Okay, then." Brenda said. She didn't seem to understand or appreciate the irony.

"So Brenda," Jaqui asked, "are you living here now?"

"I still live in town when Sarge can get by without me, which ain't much lately. How long y'all staying."

"We have to leave early Sunday. We've got to be out west of Austin by two."

"I was hoping y'all could make it to church. Everybody would love to see you."

"Shit, with what's been in the paper lately they probably wouldn't let me in the door."

"Aw, they ain't like that." Brenda said. "They'd love for you to sing one."

"Langley still playing bass?"

"No, the DPS put him over in Caldwell. It's too far. Y'all going to his wedding?"

"I didn't even know about it. When is it?"

"Not sure. Marjorie said sometime in the next couple of weeks. He knocked up his girlfriend."

"Sara?"

"Yeah, I think that's her name. They're having some kind of ritual shit out in the woods. She's a little weird." Brenda's face contorted as if she was choking down an unpleasant dose of medicine. "The world's going to hell and we just sit and watch."

Katrine pulled Jaqui aside. "Where we are sleeping?"

"I'll show you," Jaqui said and led her to her bedroom.

"Give the kids a break," Sarge told Brenda. "It's a different world than we grew up in. That don't make it bad."

"It don't make it right, either." Brenda sulked into the kitchen leaving Sarge alone in his living room.

Heroin
- Velvet Underground

Langley sat in his pickup in front of headquarters. The heroin thing had him baffled. The arrest of the sister had him worried. How thoroughly would they interrogate her? With only two minutes left until his shift started, he decided to face the music.

"Scott, the captain wants to see you." Sergeant Goodwin said before he was even in the door.

"Great, more debriefing." Langley headed for the captain's office. Goodwin followed.

Captain Nopalito was decked out in a gray yoked wool suit. The high-backed leather chair added to the image of authority, not that his face alone couldn't have handled the job. The sun lines on his weathered face, offset by the streaks of gray in that black hair, made it obvious he was the one used to asking the questions. "Come in gentlemen. Have a seat." Two low office chairs waited directly in front of the desk. Sergeant Goodwin took the one on the driver's side.

"Impressive work guys, really put our little outpost on the map. We have to make damn sure we have an airtight case here. Right boys?"

"Yes sir," came the answer in unison.

"Problem is, though, our ducks are not quite in the proverbial row." Captain Nopalito stood to his full 6 foot six, walked behind them and closed the door. "Patrolman, I've gone over the footage from the dash cam. The stop looks good. You handled the driver in an acceptable manner. I'm a little vague on the passenger. Why don't you enlighten me?"

Langley learned in police training that the procedure was to answer only specific questions and to make answers as concise as possible. "The passenger was a female. She made a run for it as I was securing the driver."

"I get that from the tape. You had the driver secure. Why didn't you apprehend the female?"

"I elected to wait for backup, sir."

"Why?"

"I was unfamiliar with the terrain and chain of custody required that I not leave evidence unattended."

"That would be a judgment call. The evidence of drugs had not been established."

"Yes sir."

"Yes sir, what?"

"It was a judgment call, sir."

"So backup arrived, then what?"

"We established the violation and seized the evidence."

"Then what?"

"Sergeant Goodwin took custody and I pursued the female on foot."

"Did you make contact?"

"I thought I saw her at one point, but it was dark and I wasn't certain."

"The suspect has a different story. Are you certain you made no direct contact with the female."

"Yes sir."

"Then we have a problem."

"Sir?"

"She says you aided her escape. She says she was on her way

243

to surrender and you insisted she continue away from the scene, leaving her to the elements." The captain's eyes bored into him like surgical lasers.

Langley held his gaze. "I never made contact, sir."

"You never told her to go down the hill and follow the stream out of the woods?"

"I never spoke with her." Langley's collar was becoming damp.

"Very well, that's our story. Any questions?"

"Yes sir," Langley began. "The morning paper mistakenly reported the seizure of a half-pound of heroin along with the marijuana. I helped process the evidence. There was no heroin. Was that a misprint?"

Nopalito stood and opened his office door. "Sergeant, you're excused." Goodwin left. Langley remained seated in front of the massive mahogany desk. The door closed behind him. Nopalito returned to his desk but instead of sitting, he opened a manila folder and shoved it under Langley's nose. "Is this your signature?" His voice was harsher, less controlled. Langley looked at the evidence log. His signature was just above sergeant Goodwin's. In addition to the marijuana and van was 8.64 ounces of heroin.

"There was no heroin. This was added after I signed it."

"Here's the deal," Nopalito growled. "It was there, period.

Judges these days are wishy-washy on pot. I'm not letting this guy walk. We need the bust. He fucking forced his pregnant sister to help him, but you know that. Don't think for one fucking minute I don't have this whole kit and caboodle figured out. She's going to testify against him, heroin included, then we're deporting her, paying her way home. You're not going to fuck this up. Do you understand me, son? I can have your badge faster than you got it."

"Yes sir. I understand."

"You're a good cop, Scott. Get out there and do what good cops do. Remember who's side you're on."

"Yes sir." Langley's head throbbed as he left the office. So this is police work. He took a deep breath, straightened his uniform and went to dispatch for his assignments.

∾

Vengeance became addicted to the flavor of iron. She began treating her revolver as both a lollipop and a sex toy. "Time to kill," it had so many connotations in her sleep deprived, chemically twisted cerebral cortex. She was unrecognizable, both mentally and physically, to any semblance of a high school cheerleader. Something was wrong. The house, her final destination, was silent; no AC, no music, same two lights on every night. During the day; still nothing. She only drove by three or four times a day, trying to avoid attention. Once she saw a locksmith's van at the curb. Had they moved? Their vehicles remained in the driveway. The confusion seared her cranium. She needed to finish this, and soon.

It was a Friday night. A mist added a sliminess to the streets. Folks were saving up for the following weekend, Black Friday, so traffic was light. She parked the pickup in the alley. The gate was unlocked. The patio door had a security bar, a useless deterrent to anyone with a wire hanger or a long screwdriver. Certain the house was empty, she made no real effort at stealth. The privacy fence provided cover. Once inside she was overcome by the elegant comfort of the home but she didn't really have a plan or even a reason, other than boredom and curiosity, for entering. She found a bottle of expensive scotch as she rummaged through the cabinets. A well visited bottle of her target's favorite bourbon sat next to it. She wondered if Jaqui ever drank straight from the bottle, if those full pink lips had ever graced that opening. She unscrewed the lid of the Evan Williams and, wrapping her own emaciated lips around it, let the amber rapids gush down her gullet.

Grabbing her new best friend by the neck, she began a tour

of the premises. Everything was so incredibly feminine, so un-Jaqui like. There was one Spartan bedroom but it didn't appear to be lived in, like a guest room with jeans and jackets in the closet. This, this had to be Jaqui's room, but no sheets shrouded the bare mattress. *Bitch has gone full on lesbian. She must be sleeping with that Russian slut.* An odd pang of jealousy swept over her. She kissed the bottle deep.

Strange thing about not eating or sleeping for days, old Evan Williams will slap your ass down hard. She started tilting right and left, wobbling and bobbing. The visions were sliding into the shadows of her periphery. A beautiful woman in a slinky skirt. A dark jazz club with men in tuxedos drooling into their martinis.

The canopy bed in the master bedroom was an inviting cloud. It captured her. She managed to drag her purse in behind her. The black iron revolver found its home between her thighs. Her visions rippled as an orgasmic stone splashed into her liquefied mind. Somewhere on the cusp of light and darkness she quieted.

Sarge stood beside Brenda's truck. His wet feet sunk into the red mud. "You might as well stay. The weather is getting worse. It's supposed to ice up by morning."

Brenda had already iced up. "I can't stay here and watch you pretend there's nothing wrong. You're her dad for Christ sakes. Step up!"

"And what? Shut her out for good? She's been through a lot. It's not like it was when we were kids. I'm not losing her."

"She's already lost. Don't you care about her soul. Have you even been listening in church? You've got to save her from this lesbian shit, for her sake!"

"Don't you think that's a little harsh? They're happy together, so what?"

Brenda started the engine and put the truck in reverse, her face set in stone. "I'm not going to be a part of it. Girls don't sleep with each other, and this damn witch wedding in the woods that Langley's involved in---you're okay with that? I'm not sure I even know you. This has all gotten way to strange for me." She started to let out the clutch.

"Wait," Sarge said. "What about us?" I love you. I thought we had a good thing."

"Love? No. If you love Jaqui you'll do something about this---this abomination. I don't think you understand. Sometimes love is hard. It takes sacrifice." She backed out. When she pulled away the wheels slung mud across the yard. He watched. As tail-lights fishtailed down the lane the rain began to soak his shirt. He returned to the porch and leaned his forehead against a cedar post. The old hound nuzzled his fingers. He stroked the dog's head a few times and went inside.

The girls were clearing the table when he came in. "She left quick," Jaqui said, "Didn't even stay for dessert. What's got her panties in a wad?"

"She's a — 'traditional' woman I guess, but more so than I thought. Y'all's closeness puts her off."

"What's it to her? We're not inviting her to join in."

"You know how these church folks are, always wanting to make you go by their rules. You know, though, she's not the only one that's going to give you grief."

"Don't I know it. That evangelist asshole Adam is making a career out of saving us from our unholy deeds."

"I am thinking he would like to join with 'unholy deed'. We are she-devils to him, wanting for his eternal downfall," Katrine said. Jaqui sputtered. She'd forgotten about Katrine's lack of filters. "I'm glad Brenda wasn't here for that little tidbit. Her head might have exploded." The girls giggled. Sarge didn't even crack a smile. He pulled a bottle of bourbon down from the shelf.

"You're planning to share that, right?" Jaqui asked.

"What the hell," he mumbled and grabbed three plastic tumblers from another cabinet. They took places at the kitchen table.

"You play poker, Katrine?" Sarge asked.

"A little, I am good fast learner."

The Crystal Ship

- The Doors

Adam made his third pass of the day. He had to warn her, if it wasn't too late. Keegan convinced him of her innocence. But if she wasn't the killer she was likely the next victim. It was already dark, and the lighting was different inside the house. In the back alley he discovered the pickup, and the open gate. Curious, but he didn't want to seem unsavory. He'd started off on the wrong foot with Jaqui and he needed to make amends. He drove back around front and knocked on the door. No answer. Strange. Pulling behind the house again, he parked buy a dumpster a 1/2 block away. The random pickup and narrow alley left little choice. He closed the gate behind him. When he saw the patio door had been jimmied his first instinct was to call the cops. The cops seemed to have almost as addle pated of an idea of his motives as Jaqui. Why couldn't everyone just realize he wanted to set things straight.

The house was quiet. A cabinet was open, a bottle of scotch, a bottle of brandy, the girls needed help before the alcohol ruined their lives. *Maybe I can help,* he thought. Walking through the house he found little else out of place, a beautiful home decorated in elegant French Provincial. The first bedroom had a stripped bed and little decor. The elegance of the master bedroom surpassed the rest of the house. The girl he had once known as Jaqui's roommate lay on the bed, fully clothed with the bedspread partially covering her.

"I'm looking for Jaqui," he whispered. The girl twitched under the covers. There was a flash, an explosion --- blackness.

Vengeance lived in a trance between crystalline clarity and dancing dream state images, vague visions. When she saw the devil appear with his burning skin and flaming eyes she knew he was sentient, true flesh. A web restricted her actions. Her arms, leaded with sleep and unresponsive, needed the full force of her mind to respond. The creature hissed, "I'm looking for Jaqui." *Hell no, she's mine!* Vengeance thought. The creature turned on her. She felt her iron lover in her crotch. It was flexible, rubbery. It took both hands; one for the trigger, one to guide the flaccid barrel toward its mark. The flaming creature bore down, fangs flashing. *All mine, you bastard!* As she pulled the trigger the creature's face exploded. Its wasted body slumped into a puddle on the floor. Vengeance put the warm iron to her lips and sucked the delicious vapors from the barrel. She had prevailed. Cocooning herself in the aromatic folds of satin, she drifted back to the realm of magic.

Sara had the invitations neatly stacked on the dining table when Langley came home from work.

"Hi Babe," Sara said. "dinner's not quite ready. I had to study for a test. The invites are ready for your signature though."

Langley hung his hat and took his place at the kitchen table His face rested in tired hands. "I don't know if I can do this."

"You don't have to right now, but I need to get them in the mail tomorrow."

"Not that, I mean my job."

"All that fame? You're in all the papers, local TV and even the Houston stations, a regular local hero."

"You'd think?"

Sara came behind him and massaged his shoulders. "What happened?"

"That heroin, they planted it. They're going to railroad that guy. He'll get twenty to life for hauling some pot."

"Can't you say something?"

"Yeah, well, I'm getting railroaded too. I made a bad judgment call. I'm not golden either."

Sara sat down at the table across from him, arms folded across her chest. She leaned back in the chair and waited.

"They apprehended the other perp," he said

"The woman?"

"Yeah, the guy's sister. He made her go with him for cover."

"You're only one guy. You couldn't chase her too. Besides they caught her anyway, so what?"

"But I did go after her too. I had her. I let her go, even helped her try to escape."

"What? Why?"

"She was pregnant and she was the victim, at least that's the way she put it to me."

"Shit, babe." Sara leaned her forehead on her palms. "Did they find out?"

"Worse, she said I made her leave, that she was coming back to turn herself in."

"Holy crap! What are they going to do to you?"

"Nothing, as long as I'm quiet about the heroin. I'm good PR. Rookie makes good and all. They're going to ship her back to Mexico ASAP."

"So what's the problem?"

"The problem is the way the system works. I thought I was

working for the good guys but their just as corrupt as the criminals."

"Yeah, well, like you say, you're not golden either. I love you, though, tarnish and all. You'll do whatever you have to do but if it was me, I'd let it slide."

"Would you, really?"

"I don't know. Probably. It seems like your heart was in the right place. Why don't you put it behind you? Lesson learned. You have to work in their system. You made it this far. I'm going to finish making dinner. You can sign the invitations."

Langley watched as Sara wobbled back toward the kitchen. In addition to the now obvious pregnancy, her angular frame had developed some enticing curves. He looked at the stack of red and gold invitations then back at his future bride. A little help with the cooking might allow for some much-needed touch time.

"What can I do to help with dinner?" he asked, following her to the counter.

Jealousy

Bettye LaVette

"**D**amn girl, your breath could drop a buffalo** in its tracks." Jaqui's voice was enough to pry open one of Katrine's matted eyelids. The snoring stopped. Jaqui backed up a few inches and brushed strands of hair behind her girl's ear. She didn't bother with the stream of drool soaking Katrine's pillow. "What the hell were we thinking?"

Katrine closed the eye and rolled onto her back.

"Come on, sweetie, we've got places to go and people to see." Jaqui said. "Wake up."

"I am." Katrine's lips barely moved. "Make it stop."

"What?"

"The bed. It's moving. You and that damn cheap whiskey. I am thinking of my death, please."

"Come on. We've got 3 hours to get to Keegan's."

"You go, leave me here. Bury me."

Jaqui showered and shaved all the pertinent parts. She emerged sparkling to find what was left of Katrine slumped over a cup of black coffee. Sarge sat across from her.

"Your girl here don't hold her bourbon too good," he said.

Katrine raised an eyebrow at him as if it were a riding crop.

"She's into scotch and brandy." Jaqui said. "Your turn to hit the shower, sweetie. Get purtified for our lover boy."

"You suck," Katrine said as she oozed toward the bathroom. "Did you rouphy me?"

"No, baby. You did all that to yourself."

~

There were only a few invitations; family, Sara's coven of course, as they were putting it together, a few mutual friends from school. Langley began signing them.

"Honey, for the sake of family harmony, what do you think of sending my mom and dad separate invitations?" He asked.

"Your call. There are a few extras in the kitchen drawer. Do what you want." He noticed that there was no invitation for Jaqui. That was unacceptable. Not really wanting to get into an argument he made one, then realized he didn't have her address. Did Sara think this was an excuse not to invite her? Doubtful. It had to be intentional. Jaqui needed to be there. He dialed Jaqui's number but no one answered. Sarge would know.

"Yeah, I know it," Sarge said, "but you can ask her yourself. She's here with Katrine for the weekend."

"Great! I haven't talked to her in a while," Langley said." Can you put her on?"

"You've been located," Sarge said as he handed the phone to Jaqui.

Her skin chilled as she took the receiver. She felt her muscles knot up. "Hello?"

"Hey Jaqui, I can't believe I caught you."

Jaqui relaxed and gave her dad a playful growl. "How you been. I heard you're going to be a daddy."

"Yup, next summer, late June. We're getting married too. That's why I'm calling. Can you come?"

"Wild horses couldn't stop me. Can Katrine come too?"

"Your girlfriend?"

254

"Yeah. I can't wait for y'all to meet."

"Of course."

"I've got an idea. Would you like us to sing a song at your wedding? She plays guitar and has a beautiful voice."

"Sounds great. It's called a handfasting though, not a wedding. Same concept, different ceremony, but you'll have to go acoustic. There's no electricity where we're having it."

"No problem. What would you guys like for a present. Are you registered somewhere?"

"No, no presents, that's part of the deal. Bring us blessings or you can bring a dish for the potluck after."

"You got it."

"I'll send the details in the invitation. What's your address?" Langley only thought Sara wasn't listening, not that it mattered, they'd been over this. Sara stood quietly in the doorway until the call ended.

"I'm not doing it," she said. "I'm not having all that negative energy around my ceremony."

"What! You've never even met her. She doesn't have a negative bone in her body."

"Do you live in a vacuum? People drop fucking dead around her! Besides, this is a private ceremony, secret even, and for good reason. We don't need a bunch of paparazzi plastering this in the tabloids."

"Oh please. She's not that famous. She's my best friend. She's coming. She's even offered to sing for us. Isn't that sweet? Give her a chance."

"Sing? Are you shitting me? You seriously think the press won't be all over that?"

"They won't know. I'll make sure she's discreet, okay? She's coming though."

"I don't think I can do it."

"You can. You're making too much out of this."

Sara ran to the bedroom, "You don't even care what I

want!" She slammed the door. Langley heard the latch engage. He continued to sign and address invitations.

Jaqui packed up while Katrine tried to pull herself together. "Dad, I need a favor. There's no way we can go by the house and get to Keegan's on time. Can you take us out there? It's west of Austin on the lake. You could even stay for the party if you want to, or we can catch a ride home later from Keegan."

"Sure, I'll drop you, but I've got to get back. I need to see what's up with Brenda."

"What's up is she's a prude, but a sweet one, so I hope you work it out."

"Me too, I think, but she's got to loosen up, stop making everything about her."

"You might try a different approach."

"No, she's got to take me like I am, Godless beast."

The bathroom door opened, Katrine shuffled past, swallowed by Sarge's bath robe. "Come," she murmured toward Jaqui. They went into the bedroom and closed the door. "Do you have a makeup mirror?" Katrine asked.

"Just the medicine cabinet in the bathroom."

Katrine looked around. She spied Jaqui's onyx jewelry box on the dresser. "This will be good." She dug through her purse until she came up with a small vial of white power. "I'll be better in a minute. You want?"

"I'm good for now. Maybe at Keegan's. Hurry up though, we've got to go soon."

Everyone was perky on the trip to town. They paused for breakfast. Katrine had only coffee.

Keegan's circle drive was full of cars. Not a single truck in the bunch, Sarge thought as he dropped the girls off. Is this even part of Texas? Truth be known, his daughter was one of the few native Texans in the crowd. Keegan and Bill met them at the door. Most of the band was there. A few had their partners on hand. Bill immediately grabbed Jaqui and took her to meet the Bluebirds. May and Chloe were sisters. They looked like they could be twin fashion models. Ruth was a tough looking redhead with a full sleeve tattoo and matching attitude.

"NYC high school for the performing arts, then Juilliard," Ruth mentioned. She shoved a prominent chin toward Jaqui. "Where'd you study?"

"Nowhere," Jaqui replied. "Nice ink by the way."

"Thanks. I suppose a pretty farm girl like you keeps pristine skin."

Jaqui turned her back on Ruth, dropped her jeans and bent over. The room went silent. Not to be outdone, Ruth swatted Jaqui's ass with her open palm, hard enough the noise carried to the next room. "Looks delicious," Ruth said. "I'd like to get a bite of that!" The room burst with laughter. Everyone knew the ice was broken. Everyone but Katrine, who froze up solid. Jaqui pulled up her jeans and gave the redhead a hug. Ruth's prominent chin fell tightly between Jaqui's breasts. "Nice to meet you, too," Jaqui said. As the room roared, Katrine slunk toward the bathroom, unnoticed, and locked the door behind her. She needed to keep the tears from smudging her makeup. She splashed water on her face and chopped a line of coke. *It is a bad girl for Jaqui*, she thought as she rolled up the bill. *This cannot happen.* There was a knock on the door. "Occupied," Katrine hollered.

"It's me, Baby." Jaqui said. "Come meet the Bluebirds. I want to show you off."

Katrine opened the door. Jaqui saw the line and the look on Katrine's face. She sat on the side of the tub, taking Katrine on her lap. "Are you okay? What's wrong?"

"That Ruth girl, she is wanting you. You just show her your secret."

"Aw, come on. We were just playing."

"What about when you are touring, I am home without you. Will you play then?"

Jaqui hugged Katrine. "No, I only play that way with you. I'm sorry. That must have been weird for you. I wasn't thinking. I love you. You know that, right?"

Katrine nuzzled Jaqui's neck. "I guess, yes, I know. I am getting scared sometime. You're being big star and everyone will be wanting some piece of you. Will there be some for me?"

Jaqui put her hand on Katrine's soft cheek and gave her a passionate kiss. "Please don't worry. I'm yours. Let's have some fun."

"Speaking of," Katrine said, "you would like a line?"

"Hell yeah! Give me a big ole bump." Katrine added more to the pile and railed out four long fat lines. By the time the girls returned to the party their grins were frozen in place.

Keegan was attempting to play his piano. Ruth leaned over the keyboard, exposing her ample cleavage and whispered in his ear. "Dude, you suck. Slide over and give me a whack at it."

Ruth began with Rachmaninoff to get everyone's attention. Then somehow slipped seamlessly into barrel house blues. When she began belting out Della Reese's "Love For Sale" it captured Jaqui's ear. She made her way over to the piano and threw down a spotless vocal harmony. At the end of the song Jaqui asked for some Bessie Smith and was rewarded with "Need a Little Sugar in My Bowl". This time she took the lead and Ruth packed in tight on harmony. They were reading each other's minds. The finish was over the top.

"Damn, you're a nasty girl" Ruth said when the applause finally died down.

"Yup, Texas best," Jaqui said.

"And here I thought you guys only whined tearjerkers."

While the celebration was going on, Katrine was standing on the sideline between Keegan and Bill.

"I hoped it would go like that," Bill said. "They're so much alike I knew they would hit it off or kill each other."

"I'm not surprised," Keegan said. "Jaqui's all about the music. She lives and breathes it ... and she knows talent."

The knot in Katrine's chest felt like it might break her ribs. Tears rose up in her eyes as she turned and slipped outside. She sat on the side of the pool dangling her feet in the water. The pool lights were off and the bottom looked like another dimension, a black hole she could escape through. She scooted her butt closer to the edge.

"I didn't think there were kids at this party. I don't think you're supposed to be out here. Kind of late in the year for swimming. Who are your parents?"

Katrine looked up when she realized someone was talking to her. The man's head was shaved, accentuating humongous ears. He had what appeared to be a studded black dog collar around his neck. "Fuck off, Fido," she said.

"Your mama know you talk like that?"

"My mama's dead, asshole."

"Whoa! Who are you here with?"

"The big star in there. Who is now on my shit page."

"Shit list?"

"Maybe you're right. I am not caring right now."

"You mean Jaqui? She doesn't look old enough to have a daughter?"

"I am 24, older than her, dog boy. Where is chain? You should be on chain."

The man smiled. "Twenty-four, right, and I'm a Polynesian princess."

"I am. I'm not caring for your belief. Who you are to matter anyway?"

"I'm Julian, the publicist for the Bluebirds. Jaqui's the catalyst that will blow us right through the top of the charts. She's got the voice and the bad girl rep. If she and Ruth don't kill each other we'll be riding high."

"Jaqui is not bad girl!" Katrine stiffened.

"Yeah sure. How many guys has she killed now? Two? Three? And gotten away with it?"

"She is not killer! Katrine was screaming now. Her fists were white with rage. "You don't talk about what you not know! Shut up, you stupid dog!" Heat was radiating from her face. She stood and faced him, coiled to attack.

"Hey easy, I'm just going by what I've heard. You probably know her better than I do"

Katrine eased off. "You should not say what you don't know."

"So how do you know Jaqui?" Julian asked.

"I'm her lover."

"You better get in there then. Ruth is a heartbreaker and she swings both ways."

"Jaqui is big girl. I trust her. You should take off collar if you not know meaning."

"Oh I know. It's like advertising."

"Well here is advertising for you. I am in entertainment business. Not cheap but good, if you are needing some training. I might work deal if you keep Ruth from making problem for me and Jaqui."

"How expensive?"

"Very. Four digits minimum, but must like child play. You help with Jaqui, I will help you."

"Hey, what if I help you make her jealous?"

"It probably not work. We trust."

"We could try."

"No, you just watch Ruth."

"You're the boss."

"I am, and that is good for you."

"It's time to break out the champagne," Bill said after several increasingly sensual duets had the air in the room reeking with hormonal excretions.

Julian sidled up to Ruth. "So what do you think? Are you going to be able to work with Jaqui?"

"My God she's hot. Work? Sure, but I'm going to have to get some of that for me!"

"No!" Julian said, "Bad idea!"

"You're not the boss of me."

"Use your brain, Ruth. Think career here. You know what will happen. It's a pattern with you, a couple of months of hot lust, then you start throwing things. This time when you explode, though, you sink your career. My advice? Keep it professional."

"You have no idea. This isn't a fucking manufacturing gig.

How am my supposed to handle that, I mean, just look at her."

"Big picture, Ruth. You fuck this up and John Q Public runs off with her, leaves you holding your crotch, playing covers at the Holiday Inn. Think about it."

"Damn it, Julian. You suck when you're right."

"That's why I make the big bucks."

The party wound down after 2:00 AM. "We haven't been home in days," Jaqui told Keegan. "I'd really like to sleep in my own bed tonight. Could you give us a ride?"

Bill coaxed the tipsy girls into the back seat of his Mercedes. Keegan rode shotgun. The night engulfed them as it pulled away from the house, precious silence accented by a hint of tinnitus in their aural membranes. The car lumbered gracefully around the curves. Katrine plastered her tiny body against the door; staring into the darkness, willing herself to disappear. Jaqui stretched out on the leather and watched. "Are you alright, baby?" She asked. "We haven't had a chance to talk much tonight."

"No," Katrine said and continued to stare into the night. Jaqui watched for awhile as exhaustion pressed on her brain. She had to put this off for now. Maybe tomorrow they would talk.

∽

As consciousness gurgles into the vapid squalor of her brain, Vengeance pulls the covers over her head, inhaling the femininity that her life has long forgotten. Her blood is jelling in her capillaries. A wanton ache oozes from her pores; for an earlier simpler time, for a lost semblance of morality, but most of all, for more of the poison she has wed. *A big ole shot, then I'll figure it out.* She creaks from the mattress cloud and angles for the bathroom. Her foot hits something solid. She looks down, doubles over in disgust and grabs her stomach. A dream sequence rips through her, something about a devil with an exploding face. She checks the revolver and realizes maybe, just maybe it now controls her. If she could she would panic. Instead she steps around the specter and continues on.

She treats herself to a fresh syringe. *Only two left, I need to make this one last.* She accidentally dumps a huge amount of the powder in the spoon. Then considers putting some back. *What the hell, I'll either get one hell of a rush or die. Maybe both.* Either outcome is acceptable now. The syringe is completely full and the contents are amber. As she pierces the vein she sees blood darken it even more and knows she's in. Slowly, she depresses the plunger. It's halfway empty when the rush starts. She pushes a little more and stops, not really wanting to die. She's attempting to cap the needle when the trembling begins. Raw bile ejects from her gullet and the angels began singing in her head. The train is coming for her. She knows. She hears it in the distance as her heart tries to beat its way out of her chest. She drops to her knees, bending the needle on the porcelain tile. Her body begins uncontrollably twitching. She is outside of it laughing. *You've done it now, you stupid bitch!* Dead men's bodies explode in her peripheral vision. Long dark roads whizz by. Day and night swirl together in a confusing gray mist.

After a time the tremors stop. She is a mechanical being blessed with fresh batteries of a too high amperage. The interfaces short circuit. She can clean. She does, meticulously, but avoids the bedroom. No cleaning there. Jaqui must have done that. Jaqui needs to pay for that. Let her explain her way out of it.

Vengeance takes a quick shower and wipes down the bathroom. She wipes down the bottle of bourbon and places it back in the cabinet. She turns on the TV to figure out what day it is. Sunday, judging by the church services. She turns it off. No point in that here. The clock reads 2:30 pm when she high-tails it. The body she left in the bedroom looks familiar, but she isn't sure, doesn't matter really.

American Revolver

- Lori McKenna

"**W**e're home," **Katrine barked at Jaqui,** ripping her from somnambulistic repose.

"Cool," she mumbled and began gathering her things. Katrine was already out of the car heading for the door. "I'd invite y'all in," Jaqui said, "but I'm completely shot. A shower and sleep is all I have in me." The Mercedes parked in the middle of the street indicated no intention of more pause than a taxi.

"See you Tuesday," Keegan said, "bright and early. My band in the morning, Bluebirds in the afternoon. It's going to be a long day. Rest up."

"Yeah, good night." She caught up with Katrine at the door. "Look, baby. I love you. If I pissed you off, I'm sorry." She put her hand on Katrine shoulder.

Katrine yanked away. "Not now. I'm tired. I will need my bed for sleeping. You have a room." No tear fell. Not even eye contact was made.

Jaqui held the screen door open while Katrine unlocked the door. "Just know, okay? Just know I love you," Jaqui whispered.

Katrine entered and made a beeline for her bedroom. Jaqui locked the door. When she heard Katrine's high-pitched wail she froze. It sounded like pain. It sounded like fright. Jaqui ran for her.

He lay on the floor at the foot of the bed, half leaning against a dresser. Much of his face was missing. The blood had run down his chest and pooled in a circle around him. Jaqui stared. Katrine threw herself on the bed. "Damn, Jaqui, damn you. Why do I even know you. I never have this, even in Romania. People died, people disappeared, but not like this. Why?"

"I didn't kill him." She was empty. That was all she had. "I think it's Adam. I have to tell the police. If you have anything illegal here, get rid of it."

"They will think it is us."

"Probably. It wasn't. They'll figure it out."

Katrine removed the vial from her purse. It was almost empty. She finished it off. "No sleep for now."

The police arrived in 10 minutes. Detective Bess O'Daniel was another 20 minutes behind. The girls were sitting on the porch as the police taped off the crime scene. TV crews were setting up on both ends of the street. Detective O'Daniel had them disburse but not before a crowd formed. By the time O'Daniel had the scene under control her chubby partner had arrived.

"Okay, ladies, we'll get some basic info then we'll head downtown. You know the drill. "Did you know the victim." Bess's voice lacked any of its former compassion.

"I'm pretty sure it's Adam Wolf," Jaqui said.

"So you know him, how?"

"He's a musician, goes to an open mic we go to some time." That was enough info for now.

"Can you think of a reason he would be here?"

Katrine broke in. "He is stalking Jaqui. He leave note on car. Drive by house, even at her work."

"He's the guy we thought shot Keegan remember?" Jaqui said.

"Right, so why was he in the bedroom?"

"I don't know. We weren't here."

A uniformed officer came out and took Bess's partner aside. When Chubby approached his face was white. "The CSI's say the vic's been dead almost 24 hours."

"Okay, I was afraid of that." She turned to the girls. "I have more questions but we need to go downtown. It's possible you're both in danger." Katrine burst into a wail. She was cursing in her native tongue. The effect was surreal, and frightening.

By the time they reached the interrogation room, resignation, with a large side order of exhaustion, filled the space. Bess got everyone coffee and sat across the table. The chubby detective lounged in the corner with a notepad.

"Do either of you know a woman named Lila Snipes?" Bess asked.

"We were on the cheerleading squad together in high school. Remember, I mentioned her before?," Jaqui said. "Why?"

"She supposedly disappeared in mid-September but we have reason to believe she may have been in the area. We're still trying to put the pieces together. Tell me everything you know about her."

Jaqui relayed all the pertinent details, putting the best possible spin on Randy and the pageant fiasco. Bess listened. Juan took notes.

"Do you think she would want to harm you?" Bess asked.

"Well, she's probably not real happy with me and she lied about me to Bruce. But physical harm? That would be pushing it."

"A car we found abandoned out by Burnet is the one from the surveillance cameras where Bruce was murdered. There is evidence of methamphetamine use. Is that consistent with your knowledge of her?"

"I don't know. I wouldn't have thought so but then she planted pills on me at the pageant, so maybe."

"Extensive, long-term use of methamphetamine can lead to psychosis. I told y'all to stay in town last time we talked. Apparently you didn't. I don't have evidence to charge you, and frankly, I don't think you've done anything wrong but I'm going to put you in protective custody until we can find a safe house."

Detective Juan looked up. "We've got an APB out for Snipes but we don't know if she's even in the area.

Jaqui pleaded. "I can't stay locked up. I have rehearsal and a wedding to go to. I'm in two bands that are leaving on tour in two weeks. I front one of them."

"So I've heard," Bess said.

"It's only your life," Juan mumbled from the corner.

Bess cut her eyes toward him. "You can't go back home until we process the crime scene. Probably tomorrow. Let us fix you a cot here and we'll talk in the morning."

"What about Katrine?" Jaqui asked.

"Her too. Y'all can be roomies."

Katrine lay her head on the table. "I never thought I would be glad for jail."

Static. AM radio hate talk through blown out speakers. Brain drive --- sleep deprived, transient highway junkie. Eye sockets drilled and fixed in babble blood and zombie vision. Jerky tongue and chicken fried, magnetic origin sucks Vengeance to her hometown. Hours to kill. In at dusk, main street slingshots her into the hills like a rock orbiting too close to the sun. Keep moving. Buying gas and radio waves. She finally has a modicum of fame.

These two beautiful lovers that awaken in the iron cage are no longer pretty. Maybe they're no longer lovers. Can we will them enough hours of life to know?

Bill Billings rents a room at the Holiday Inn Express. He never enters but passes the key card to Jaqui. He picks up a couple of pairs of sweats, some rubber sandals and a bottle of body wash. When he gets back with it, the girls are scrubbed clean and sleeping again. He drops the loot inside the door with his business card and leaves.

Their house is still a crime scene. The body is gone but not the blood. A crew is still processing. The girls are in no hurry to return. They will pick up their vehicles, maybe tomorrow, maybe not. Public transportation will have to do. They sleep. They watch TV. They say very little. Still caged, they lounge in separate beds.

"Daddy? Daddy, I'm so scared. I think I'm losing her. It's all so horrible. I messed up her whole life, her home, us, everything. It hurts so bad."

"I know, sweetie, I heard. Why don't you come home? Bring her if she'll come."

"What about Brenda? I wouldn't do that to you."

"That's done."

"Done?"

"We had some fun but I'm too old and set to change. I'd be faking it anyway and what's the point, really?"

"Oh daddy, I'm so sorry. I messed that up too."

"No sweetie, it was just a matter of time. We had some fun for a while. So, you coming?"

"Probably not. I've got the tour and I really need Katrine if she'll have me. I can't blame her if not, but I've got to try. She's my life, or the best part of it."

" I hope it works for you."

"See you at the wedding ... I mean, handfasting?"

"Of course. I wouldn't miss it."

"I love you daddy."

"I love you too, Jaqui."

Having a uniformed officer posted at the entrance to the studio, checking IDs, took some of the spontaneity out of rehearsal. The tour looming in the immediate future held their noses to the grindstone. It was all business. All day. Katrine fidgeted in the sound room, only slightly less bored than if she had remained at the hotel room. At least the scenery was different. Jaqui was thrilled that she wanted to come but she had misinterpreted Katrine's motivation.

The tunes were tight, choreography spot on. The band lacked the element of funk, spunk, whatever the positive energy is called that draws artists to their calling. They were going through the motions. They were doing it flawlessly but a problem was obvious. Jaqui's problem had become everyone's problem. Some were sympathetic. Some were angry. Some were downright scared. Although Keegan's eye patch had earned him the nickname Captain, no one addressed him that way today.

When they took the midmorning break, the officer informed Jaqui and Katrine that the police had released their house and the cleanup was completed.

"Can I have a ride from someone? I need to go home," Katrine asked. No one volunteered.

"We only have 15 minutes," Keegan said. "Maybe when it's lunchtime someone can take you." No one even acknowledged her, much less volunteered to chauffeur. Not surprising, all things considered.

"Sweetheart, you probably shouldn't go there alone," Jaqui said. "Please."

"I am fine. I am not target here. You are one to watch out."

A collective restlessness passed through the band like a stadium wave as they all glanced toward the policeman and remembered why he was there. Jaqui felt the pressure. It pushed her out the door.

The sun was bright, but the air was brisk. The wind slapped her with a cold clarity, a foreboding realization that she was teetering on the edge of her life and the ground was giving way beneath her.

"It'll be over soon." The cop's words startled Jaqui, like every other motion, noise or ambient change did.

"I know," she said. "I just hope they get her, or whoever, soon. I'm about to lose it."

"You'll be okay." The guy was trying to be reassuring, a trifle difficult seeing that his eyes were searching every nook and cranny in a 360° radius.

"Maybe we should go back inside," Jaqui suggested. "I hate it, but I feel exposed out here. Hell of a way to live, right?" The cop held the door for her, glancing behind him once before following her in. He still missed noticing the skinny blond girl waiting in the nondescript blue pickup near the end of the strip of warehouses.

Keegan gathered everyone around him in the center of the room, everyone except Katrine who still waited in the sound booth. Jaqui missed the pep talk. When she entered most of the band smiled at her, some even came over and gave her a hug.

Old Keegan, not such a bad guy, she thought. It was time to work on the duets. Some of the energy had returned. After the first song Tiff walked over. She leaned in and whispered, "That was fucking awesome. I'm so glad you're a part of this band. You've even made Keegan decent to work with." She gave her a little squeeze and skipped back to her spot. The groove had returned.

Jaqui even displayed some of her sass. She had Adela and Tiff strutting through the dance moves.

They broke for lunch around noon when the Bluebirds arrived. The Bluebirds usually had some backup musicians, although Chloe played bass and May played multiple instruments, mostly harmonica. Ruth had always fronted the group with only a microphone but with Jaqui in the picture she handled the keyboards, in all honesty much better than the guy who had covered the keys before. The girls insisted they keep their guitarist. He was a third generation Chicago blues guy with amazing chops. Art hung around the rehearsal to pick up licks. The rest of Keegan's band called it a day except the drummer. He was doing double duty for now.

Katrine kept a close eye on Ruth but saw nothing but professionalism. When Julian showed up out of the blue she saw a chance to escape. She sidled up to him. "Look like you have short leash on Ruth. She is behaving with modesty."

"I explained the big picture to her," he said. "If she wants fame and fortune she needs to play by the rules. Believe me, the girl wants fame and fortune. She won't mess this up."

"I have much thanking to do for you. If you want training discount I have house now available." She led him into the sound booth and discreetly slipped a hand down the back of his pants. As her pinkie massaged the perimeter of his sphincter, she noticed he was not wearing underwear. "Bareback boy, you're hoping for attention today, yes?"

He felt his member begin to fill with anticipation. "Do you need a ride home, ma'am?" he asked.

"Why yes I do, kind sir. Would you take me?"

"I would love to take you," he said, and they slipped away unnoticed, at least by those inside the building.

"Park in back so we get no attention," she said, oblivious to the futility. The blue pickup was already parked beneath the grackle infested elm tree.

To be true and just, Vengeance requires patience, and a plan. Time is fluid when daylight and darkness are two sides of the same plane. Her life, her love, her very future is demolished, stolen by that bitch who uses misfortune to thrive. It's time to steal her future, her love, her life and leave the world as equals. Now that Vengeance knows for sure who Jaqui loves, well it's a place to start. But first, let the tiny lover compromise herself. Then use her for bait.

Vengeance waits. An hour should do it. Let them get good and sweaty, stewed in their juices, oblivious---then, surprise! She has her steel friend for comfort and company. They have been through a lot together. They have grown very close.

Katrine is pleasantly surprised at the condition of the house. There is a mild aroma of cleaning products but otherwise no trace of the melee recently visited there.

"Nice place, very elegant," Julian said.

"Thank you, I do well. I am very good at what I do. This game we play, it makes body happy, very happy, but happiness comes from inside head. For you, I know by how you walk, what you wear, the job even. You want to return to childhood, to be taught how to please me and be rewarded, yes?"

Julian knew she had him nailed. "Right, teach me things."

"I can do that, but I will also teach you about you. That is my talent. It is why you will put $1000 on my nightstand. It is for therapy. So put down money while I get ready. Also, take off all clothes except leather collar and socks."

"What about jewelry?" Julian asked.

"What jewelry?"

"I have rings in my nipples."

"Oh yes, leave in. You are making me wet already, see?"

Katrine reached inside her panties and pulled out a slick middle finger. She held it up to Julian. "You want taste?"

He bent to lick it but she yanked it back, putting it between her own lips. "When it is time I will tell you. Get ready."

The new redesigned Bluebirds started from square one. With one album in the can and a single just slipping onto the top 100, the band had only a cult following. Having played together for two years they were primed for their big break. Jaqui was supposed to be the answer. They performed classic blues standards and some sassy pop originals that the sisters co-wrote, girl power lyrics with thumping bass and ample guitar shredding. Jaqui leaned toward the classics but the pop tunes had harmonies that showcased the humid blend of her voice with Ruth. They were fun to sing. They weren't a problem. Most of the blues classics weren't either, but the Bluebirds had recorded one torch hit from the fifties, Ella Fitzgerald's "The Nearness of You". When Ruth and Jaqui worked out a tight harmony it was like chocolate melting with sugar. Not the pristine Smores experience but something with exotic fruits and jungle nuts. It affected their southern hemisphere. By the end of the first run through they we're sharing a mic. The heat was making even casual observers moist. Neither Katrine nor Julian were there to act as a damper. When Bill suggested they take a break, Jaqui went straight for the sound booth, Ruth trailing behind. No Katrine! She checked outside. Bill mentioned she had left with Julian. Jaqui was aware of that potential tryst. It wasn't a problem, just a job in and of itself. It was Katrine's desire to return home that disturbed her. First she called the hotel, hoping. When she got no answer she tried the house. It was busy. Katrine had taken the receiver off the hook, something she did to keep the ringing phone from wrecking the spell of her therapy session.

"I've got to get home," Jaqui said. She sprung into panic mode. "Somebody give me a ride. Who has a car? Ruth?"

"I came with Bill and the girls."

Bill stepped up. I'll take you by later. We still have some work to do here."

Jaqui spun on him. "I can't. I've got to go. Somebody take me, please? My car's there. I'll come right back as soon as I pick up Katrine."

Bill got his keys. *Fucking artists,* he thought. *I should have been a CPA.* "Come on, let's make this quick. The rest of you guys stay here and work on Chloe's new chart, see if you can come up with a bridge that doesn't suck."

Katrine patted Julian dry with a soft cotton towel. She had blind-folded him and given him a shower. "I will take care of you," she'd instructed. "Put hands flat against wall and put all trust in me. Use the rest of body to feel with." She used only her tiny hands and body to lather him with her perfumed body lotion. She spent extra time in certain erogenous regions, some of which he was unaware of having until she massaged him. Well primed, his heightened sense of touch and smell electrified him.

Once she rubbed in the lotion, she ran a string of latigo leather through his nipple rings. "A much better guide than chain on dog collar, don't you think?" She gave it a light tug and his erection danced for her. She couldn't suppress a giggle. "I see it is good for you."

"You're amazing," Julian said.

"Yes, I am," she replied, "but no talking. I will teach you new pleasure but you must trust. Just nod. Can you trust?"

Julian shrugged.

"What you want to know is of pain, yes?" Katrine asked.

Julian nodded.

"Maybe some pain. If too much we stop, but much more pleasure than pain. If you pass training, I am prize, anyway you want. You trust?"

Julian nodded. Katrine took the latigo strap and led him to the bedroom.

~

Vengeance ran her tongue down the black iron barrel of the revolver. "It's almost over, Baby," she said. "Then we can finally lie down together and rest." She laid the pistol on the console of the pickup. "Wait a minute while I get ready." She drew up a shot but found all the veins in her arms exhausted. She pulled off a shoe and sock. Using the sock for a tourniquet she found a vein on the top of her foot. The vein wanted to roll but she pierced it eventually. She injected very slowly to prevent damaging that little vein. It worked. Her mind cleared. She focused.

Katrine and Julian were an hour into their session. Vengeance wanted to surprise them at the peak of the encounter, hoping she could observe and assault them before they had a chance to react. She walked to the end of the block and came up the alley. A gray hoodie disguised her and concealed her weapon. She found the back gate open. When she peered in the window the curtains were drawn. She heard only Katrine's voice, teasing and taunting. Her luck held. They hadn't locked the patio door. She took her iron companion in hand.

When she looked through the partially open door to the bedroom it was all she could do to stifle a laugh. Julian was bent over the foot board face down, elbows on the mattress, naked except for a blindfold. Katrine had on a black leather bra, knee-high boots and a long, thin strap on penis. She was on her knees massaging his buttocks and occasionally flicking her tongue around his sphincter. She stopped and picked a bottle of oil from the dresser.

"You're going to learn a new feeling," she told him. "It might hurt, but not so much if you relax. I will stop if you say.

but then no prize. Deep breath will help." She pulled on a latex surgical glove and saturated it with oil.

Vengeance became so fascinated with the session she temporarily lost focus. The weight in her hand brought her around.

～

When Jaqui arrived home she wasn't sure Katrine was there. If she was, she wasn't alone. Just inside the front door she announced, "Katrine, sweetie, it's not safe here. Please come back with me."

Vengeance slipped her pistol in her pocket. She scanned for a place to hide.

"I am having session, please leave. I'm good, but busy," Katrine replied.

"Baby, there's a killer running loose. Please come. You don't have to do that anymore. I can take care of us."

"That is not what I want. I will make my way, now please leave."

Vengeance stepped into the other bedroom but she had to turn the doorknob.

"Jaqui, please do not come in."

"No, I'll wait in the living room, but hurry. We need to go."

Katrine began losing patience. "I will finish my session. Leave now!"

Jaqui had no intention of leaving Katrine unprotected. Her 9 mil was in her closet where she'd stashed it before visiting her dad. She'd just get it and wait in the living room. Rehearsal had vanished from her thoughts. She took the gun from the lock box on the top shelf of her closet, put it in her waist band and put a spare clip in the pocket of her jeans. When she turned around, the barrel of a revolver pointing between her eyes sucked away her ability to move.

"Isn't this just too fucking perfect," Lilah said. "You finally get to know what it feels like." Lilah had both hands on her weapon. Her feet were spread. She meant business. "Lay your gun on the bed, bitch. One finger."

Jaqui obeyed.

"Ammo too. No, on second thought, keep it. That's even better." Lilah picked up the weapon and put her pistol in her jacket pocket, using Jaqui's gun to run the show.

"What the fuck, Lilah?"

"Because you need to understand," Lilah hissed. "You killed Randy. He was the only person I ever loved. Then you ruined my chance at the pageant. You fucked up everything, ruined my life. You have to pay the piper. This is too lucky for me. Your gun will kill her. It's obvious. You came in, caught her cheating, killed them both then turned the gun on yourself."

"Lilah, come on. Think about the good times we had. You don't have to do this. Besides, they already know you killed Bruce. They'll figure this out. We were friends once, remember?"

"Shut up. I hate you. I've always hated you, Ms. Perfect fucking Goody Two Shoes. It's fucking payback time."

"Jesus, what's going on?" Katrine hollered. Lilah pulled back the hammer.

"Nothing, just talking to myself." She had to think of something quick. "Sorry, I'll be quiet."

When the bedroom door opened behind her, Katrine finally lost it. "Get out!" She screamed.

"I don't think so." It was not Jaqui's voice. Katrine pulled her finger out of Julian's ass and turned. An insignificant yelp was all she could muster.

Julian, still blindfolded, heard the voice of an additional woman and burst into a grin. *Hot damn*, he thought. *The more the merrier.* Then the explosion hit him in the back, forcing him into the mattress. "Stop! Too much pain. I'm done," were his last words.

Lilah forced the hot barrel of the gun back into its owner's ribs. "Take that off it looks ridiculous." she ordered. Katrine unbuckled the appendage while never taking her eyes from the spot where the gun barrel touched her lover. "Get in the bed and wrap your legs around that fool's dead-ass head."

"You twisted bitch," Katrine said. "You will kiss my ass, shoot me now. You are to do it anyway."

"Do it!" Lilah screamed.

"No!" Katrine screamed back and stomped her foot.

Lilah pushed Jaqui against the dresser, smashing her face into the mirror. She lunged at Katrine who slammed a foot into her crotch. Lilah doubled over.

"Works on girls too." Katrine scrambled to get her pistol from the nightstand. Lilah recovered enough to aim at Katrine just as Katrine pulled her pistol on Lilah. The weapons fired simultaneously, then silence.

Jaqui could tell by the bleeding orifice above Lilah's nose that she would no longer be an issue. She went to Katrine. "Baby, say something. Are you okay?"

"No!" Katrine said. "The bitch shot me!" Katrine moved a hand from her abdomen. Jaqui saw the blood and went white. She felt her head get wobbly. A sharp sting on her cheek brought her around.

Katrine slapped her again. "Get it together, call doctors. Damn, girl!"

"Yeah, okay, sorry," but she could already hear the sirens outside. She opened the door to several guns aimed at her.

"Won't you come in." She put her hands on her head. "People are hurt in here."

The Green Man

- Martin Donnely

"So, at least you're okay," Langley said.

"I wouldn't say that, but I'm not injured or in jail." Jaqui replied.

"You shouldn't be. You didn't do anything wrong."

"I didn't do anything illegal. It's not quite the same."

"No shit, how well I know. I guess this ends your music career though."

"You'd think so but it's just the opposite. I haven't even put out a single and I'm some kind of phenom. Bill wants us in the studio this week, but I'm here with Katrine until we know something."

"I didn't think she was critical."

"She's not, but she has a bullet lodged in her spine. We're waiting for the neurologist to decide whether to operate now or wait until some of the other damage heals. It's right against her spinal cord."

"So she might be paralyzed?"

"She is right now, but we're hoping for the best. It's not likely she'll walk again though."

"So what are you going to do?"

"About what?"

"About Katrine."

"I'm going to love her."

It had never occurred to Langley that someone else could have a love as strong as his love for Sara. The sudden realization made his world a better place to live. "Yeah, of course. Are you still going to make it to the handfasting Saturday?"

We'll see. I want to be there for y'all but I might need to be here."

There was a motion in the hospital bed. Jaqui stood to check on Katrine. She was smiling up at Jaqui. "You go," Katrine slurred. "I have friend here to help me." She held up the trigger to her morphine pump.

"We'll see." Jaqui said.

It's strange what makes the papers. They almost never get it right. The strap-on made headlines. Julian got a passing mention. Lilah was a cheerleading rival not a drug crazed serial killer. The previously thug branded Bluebirds were now a pristine group of college coeds who have taken on Jaqui as a rehab project. Keegan was a wise patriarchal guru that helped it all happen. The spin was dizzying to those with a handle on reality, but even they knew better than to assert the truth, at least not now. Jaqui wouldn't make the studio that week, so Bill picked out one of Jaqui's recent tracks from a rehearsal tape and put the rest of the Bluebirds behind it. It hit the R&B charts at number 19 when it dropped the following Friday. By the day of the handfasting Jaqui was a household word. The paparazzi followed her to the farm. When Sarge brought the 12-gauge shotgun out to lock the gate, they decided that would be a good spot to wait. Even the reporters with telephoto lenses paid no attention to the guy in overalls who hitched the old Case tractor to the hay fork and took off toward the back of the property. Later the paparazzi followed Sarge's truck to the bar where they realized they had been hoodwinked. The person on the tractor parked out by the irrigation pumps, climbed off the tractor and into the Lincoln with Marjorie.

"I love this car," Jaqui said. "I'm glad you ended up with it." She stepped out of the overalls and let her hair fall from under the gimme cap.

Marjorie just smiled. "Sarge's the one that planned this out, you know. He's brilliant. Not brilliant enough to beat me at poker though."

"So y'all play?"

"We've practiced a couple of nights at the VFW. We're going to Vegas after the first of the year."

"Holy shit! So y'all are what? Dating?"

"Nah, just friends." She gave Jaqui a wink. "--- he thinks."

Jaqui played with seat controls until she was stretched out and reclined. "I'm so happy for Langley. He really seems to have his life on track. I can't wait to meet Sara."

"Hmm," Marjorie paused. "Yeah, I think they're good together. She's kind of quick-tempered though and crazy jealous of you. The only fight I know of was when he insisted you be invited."

"Shit. I don't want to cause a problem. I should've stayed with Katrine."

"No, you need to be there. You're his best friend, always have been. When all this went down, the papers and rumors, he never doubted you, not once."

"He's a good guy, takes after his mom."

Sarge was into his third bourbon when the woman sat on the barstool next to him. He hadn't seen her before but recognized her by the flaming red hair and the full sleeve tattoo. She took the glass from in front of him and tossed the contents down her throat. "Come on," she said, "let's go see a witch get hitched."

"So you must be Ruth."

"Right, and I can see where your hot ass daughter gets her looks."

Julio raised his eyebrows as Sarge followed the woman outside.

It was a circular convergence of sorts, very fitting. The crowd gathered on the shore of the lake, the exact spot where their son was conceived, though only Langley and Sara shared this knowledge. When all the guests arrived a burgundy wine was served and the guests formed a circle, with Langley in the center and Sara on the outside. Alternating man, woman, man, woman, they held hands facing outward. Sara broke the circle between Bud and Artis, the priestess. Leading Bud, she danced the revelers in a slowly descending spiral until she was snugly ensconced in her circle of friends with Artis guarding the perimeter, arms folded over her breasts. Langley stepped forward and kissed the crone as passionately as he could muster. Her arms and legs unfolded like a flower until she was fully extended into a pentangle. She then took the hand of the outer-most man of the circle and proceeded to unwrap the human chain until Sara spun off the end into Langley's arms. Artis then took her scepter, dipped it into the wine, plunged it into the cake and held it between the faces of the couple. Sara and Langley put the tips of tongues to opposite sides at the hilt of the blade. Artis drew it down until the tip of the scepter fell away and their tongues entwined. The circle formed back around them as they kissed, this time facing inward. That was the ceremony; no vows, no promises. Only Jaqui's clear acappella voice blending with Ruth on the first verse of "The Green Man". The crowd joined the chorus, some cheating from previously pocketed lyric sheets.

One Voice

The Wailin' Jennys

When **Sarge came in from planting vetch** in next year's cantaloupe patch, he found Katrine on the couch playing her guitar. She had managed to extricate herself from the wheelchair.

"Looks like you're feeling better," Sarge said.

"Tired of inconvenient chair. No room for guitar."

"Good, good. I'm glad to see you doing something. You're going to beat this you know."

"Jaqui called, ask if I was still practicing guitar. I say why bother. No one to play for now, but she say she want to hear me play and maybe other people too. She has four-day break in town. She is coming for me, will take me on rest of tour, New York City and West coast.

"Are you up for that?"

"I guess we know soon. I know she will take good care of me."

"I'll miss you. You're getting pretty good at poker."

"Maybe I will win all money from Ruth."

"I imagine Ruth can hold her own."

"As long as she not hold my own." Katrine started picking out a melody then stopped. "Oh yes, I need to call Langley and

Sara so they know when Jaqui is here. We are having night out. The Sara girl is making dinner, wants to meet me."

It was too cold for the porch when Jaqui arrived so Katrine parked her chair near the window. Jaqui drove up in a nondescript rental car.

"She's here!" Katrine squealed.

Jaqui came in and grabbed Katrine, kissing her long and deep. "God, I've missed you. It's crazy not having you with me." They kissed again and Jaqui sat down with Katrine on her lap. "I've got something for you." She reached in her coat pocket. "Wait, I have to do this right." She sat Katrine beside her and knelt. She opened a box containing a platinum band with a magnificent solitaire diamond. "Will you marry me?"

Katrine's eyes brimmed with tears. "Yes, I would, but we are Texans. Our plumbing is not adequate."

Jaqui burst out in giggles. "No, silly, we can go anywhere now. Lots of states will marry us. Fuck Texas. Pick a place you want to be married."

"Okay, might take time, have to check out some."

"As long as we're together."

It was too cold for the porch when Jaqui arrived so Katrine

The Bitter End is the oldest music venue in New York City. Tonight the intimate space is packed with an unusual crowd. One rumor circulated that a new talent will debut here tonight. That rumor alone isn't enough to sell out this venue on a weeknight. Still, there isn't an empty seat to be had. The crowd buzzes with anticipation.

Katrine is fidgeting. She's taken two hefty swigs from the El Presidente but the butterflies are still taunting her stomach.

"Don't roll me out there in chair please. Carry me, drag me, anything but wheelchair, okay?"

"Sure," Jaqui says and slips into a black hoodie. She picks up Katrine while a stagehand carries her guitar. When the lights come back up Katrine is alone on the stage with the iconic red brick wall behind her. She sits on a Victorian divan with her guitar lying across her lap.

"Hi," she says. "I am Katrine. I'm very little girl, one name is big enough for me now. I get bigger, maybe add name, okay?"

The audience chuckles politely.

"I am Romany. Sing some Romany, sing some English, maybe even French if you are very nice to me."

A couple more chuckles. Katrine cradles her guitar and begins singing a native Romanian folk song in her intense tremulous voice . The crowd is hooked. The applause roars at the end of each successive song. After six back-to-back songs she takes a lace handkerchief and pats her forehead.

"I am breaking sweat here. I will stop for a minute and tell little story before singing again. Many decades ago, when this club was baby and I was lustful thought in parent's mind, another girl of Eastern European descent played here. Her last name was Safka but she also only used first name of Melanie. She is famous for silly little song about roller skates, or fucking, depending on perspective."

The audience roils with laughter. Katrine has to give them a second. "Anyway, this girl, Melanie, did many other beautiful and even haunting songs. I want to sing one of her songs tonight. I'm going to need much help. You will help with chorus. Most know it. I am going to have fiancé help with verses. It might be you know her, too. She is Jaqui B."

As Jaqui walks to the stage the applause is thunderous. Katrine raises her palm and when total quiet is established they begin:

We were so close there was no room.

We bled inside each other's womb.
We all had caught the same disease.
We all sang the songs of peace.
Some came to sing. Some came to pray.
Some came to keep the dark away.

When the audience joins in the chorus, it sounds like a spiritual.

Lay down, lay down, lay it all down.
Let the white bird smile up at the ones who stand and frown.

~

About the Author

Tony Burnett is a poet, songwriter, storyteller, and now novelist writing from the sunny climes of Central Texas, more recently considered the gates of Hell. His short fiction and essays have been published in numerous national journals. He is the former President of the Writers' League of Texas and currently serves as the Executive Director of Kallisto Gaia Press. His homes are in Temple, Texas and Guanacaste, Costa Rica where he resides with his trophy wife of 30+ years and his four canine companions.

Ingram Content Group UK Ltd.
Milton Keynes UK
UKHW011537290323
419359UK00005B/655